Dear Reader,

Welcome to *Someone To Love*. I hope you like the story as much as I enjoyed writing it. Over the past three years, I've gotten very close to the Daniels family.

I introduced readers to this family in my previous title *You Are Loved*. In that novel, Lisa Daniels's struggle with infertility and her love for Matthew James touched many hearts. The saga continued with Cynthia Williams and David Daniels. David's drive for professional success and Cynthia's determination to find the parents that abandoned her as a baby garnered *Circles of Love* a great deal of recognition and a lot of mail from readers. *Someone To Love* will toss Lisa and David's younger brother J.D. and Shae Weitherspoon into the limelight.

There are occasions when writing can be a lonely job. It warms my heart to hear from readers who have interesting comments about the stories and the characters that I create. Don't be a stranger, feel free to e-mail me at romwriterkwo@yahoo.com or drop a note at P.O. Box 40366, Redford, MI 48240. I love hearing from you.

Happy reading!

Karen White-Owens

# "How about a couple hands of spades?"

"Okay, but why not make it interesting," J.D. said. "How about a kiss for the winner of each hand?"

"I'm in," Shae said boldly.

Lines creased his forehead. "Are you sure you want to do this? I wouldn't want to take advantage of you."

"This was my idea, remember?"

"Then you better get ready for a beat down," J.D. answered in a superior tone. The note of sensual promise in his voice encouraged her, adding a forbidden element to the game.

Minutes later, J.D. leaned against the wall, counting his books. "How did you do?"

Peeved, Shae rolled her eyes. "You know exactly how I did."

Chuckling softly, he touched her arm. "Time to pay up...."

Her attitude evaporated instantly as a ripple of excitement surged through her. Shae leaned closer and her eyes fluttered shut as J.D. claimed her lips. A sensuous current spiraled through her, completely destroying her previous calm.

Slowly loosening his hold, J.D. relaxed against the wall, although his eyes still glowed with a savage inner fire. "Ready for another hand?"

## KAREN WHITE-OWENS

is the author of four successful romance novels and one novella. *Someone To Love* will be her fifth full-length release. In addition to writing and her work as a librarian at the Mount Clemens Public Library, she divides her free time between her husband, Gary, editing manuscripts for aspiring authors and teaching essay writing to freshmen at Wayne State University.

# KAREN
## WHITE-OWENS

# Someone to LOVE

KIMANI
ROMANCE

I would like to dedicate *Someone To Love*
to my family and reading audience. Without both
groups' unwavering encouragement and support,
I'd probably give in to my lazy side and sit
in the center of my bed watching soap operas and
eating popcorn instead of writing. Thank you.

 KIMANI PRESS™

ISBN-13: 978-1-58314-775-7
ISBN-10:    1-58314-775-6

SOMEONE TO LOVE

Copyright © 2006 by Karen White-Owens

www.kimanipress.com

**Printed in U.S.A.**

# Chapter 1

Shae Weitherspoon caught her bottom lip between her teeth while twisting a lock of her hair around her finger. This was her third attempt to reach her father.

The voice mail kicked in and she heard the computer-generated voice stating that she should leave a message. Seconds later the message was interrupted by a breathless, "Hello? Hello?"

Relieved, Shae said, "Hey, Mommie."

"Shae-Shae," her mother responded. "Where are you?"

She grinned at the use of her childhood nickname. "Airport."

From her seat, she studied the patrons hurrying up and down the hallway, dragging luggage behind them as they searched for their correct destination. Shae shifted in her seat and glanced out the ceiling-to-floor window, watching the Northwest Airlines employees prep the gray-and-red planes for their next trip. "I decided to try one more time to say good-bye before the plane took off. Pop didn't pick up his cell phone and he wasn't at the office, so I thought he might be at home. Is he there?"

"No, honey. He left soon after you did. I don't know when he'll get back."

Shae swallowed her disappointment, blinking rapidly while fighting the urge to cry. Why wasn't she surprised? As far back as she could remember, Prestige Computers had been her father's obsession—his family, his life and his mistress. Albert Weitherspoon had started Prestige Computers in the basement of his Compton home; the company manufactured computers for consumers. At first, it wasn't easy. Albert and Vivian Weitherspoon struggled for years, fighting to keep both their home and their business afloat. Then, the boom in personal computers hit. Computers became more affordable and Prestige rocketed into the major leagues and competed with the likes of Dell, IBM and Hewlett-Packard.

Not satisfied with conquering the personal computer market, Albert had added a business division. The new division flourished and soon after Prestige went global with servers and software security systems. Now, Pop was at the top of his game. The computer company that had begun in the basement of their small town house had become a Fortune 500 company.

In keeping with the Weitherspoon's new financial and social status, they moved to a more affluent neighborhood. Their modest Compton town house was replaced by a ten-bedroom mansion with an inground pool located in exclusive Malibu. Shae's parents concentrated on her future—enrolling her in the best schools and making sure she had the proper friends during her childhood and adolescence.

She gained a wonderful education and lived the best life that money could provide, but…Shae lost her father in the process.

As Prestige Computers grew, Albert Weitherspoon disconnected from his family. Board meetings, business trips and making money replaced birthdays, family outings and holidays.

The Pop that taught her how to ride her first bike, read her bedtime stories and chased monsters from under her bed had disappeared. He was replaced by a stranger who put in cursory twenty-minute visits at family functions.

Tired of the jaunt down memory lane, Shae returned to her present dilemma. "Mommie, I'm not dropping off the face of the earth. You know how to reach me. Chicago is just a phone call away."

"How long do you plan to stay there? When are you coming home? What about your father's sixtieth birthday? Will you be back in July for that?"

"Mommie, it's April," she sighed, crossing her legs. "There's plenty of time to work things into my schedule. I'll figure everything out once I'm settled."

"Shae, I don't understand."

That line had become her mother's latest buzz phrase. Sadly, Shae's parents had never understood what drove her to complete her bachelor's and master's degrees and then accept the nurse practitioner and manager position in Chicago. No matter how many times Shae tried to reassure her parents, they balked and attempted to convince her to remain in Malibu.

Dropping her free hand into her lap, Shae added, "Once the medical director and I have our first meeting,

I'll have a better idea of the timetable he's recommend-
ing for the opening of the clinic."

Her mother's long-suffering sigh reached Shae's ear.
She rolled her eyes toward the ceiling as a reaction to
her mom's dramatics.

"Why do you have to do this?"

"Because people need help, Mommie."

"But, Shae-Shae, why you? There are communities
near Malibu that could benefit from your skills and
knowledge."

"Why *not* me?" It was Shae's turn to sigh. She
needed to feel that her life meant more, that she had
something to offer those who were struggling.

Because Shae's parents wanted to hand her the
world, it came as a major shock to them to find that their
sweet baby refused to comply with their wishes for her
future. Shae had vetoed their plans to send her to an exclusive liberal arts college; instead, she opted to attend
a university with an excellent nursing program. Once
she completed her degree, her father offered Shae a
position in his company, but Shae had accepted a traveling nurse position at a small community hospital in
Montana.

Shae's parents continued their attempts to manipu-
late her life whenever she came home. The Weitherspoons, hinting it was time to think about marriage and
a family, invited every bachelor they knew to dinner.
Their daughter countered this blatant matchmaking
with the fact that she was only twenty-six years old and
far from an old maid; there was plenty of time for love
and romance. For now, making a difference in the world
burned brighter in her heart.

"Honey," Mommie's voice turned soft and persuasive, "the position with Prestige is still available. Your

dad has always tried to get you to come on board with him. This would be a wonderful opportunity for you both. You'd have your own department to run. Things would be done your way. The employees would love to have a good nurse on staff. Think about it. You could do so much good."

"That's not for me, Mommie. I want to help people who need me and don't have the same resources that the folks at Prestige have. Besides, if I worked for Pop, I would be his glorified office pet. I don't want that," she declared, glancing at the attendants manning the NWA station. "I've still got a little time before we board. If Pop comes home, have him call me."

"I will, baby. I will."

"Love you, Mommie. I'll call after I'm settled."

"Love you, too, Shae-Shae."

Close to tears, Shae disconnected the call and slipped the phone inside her Emilio Pucci bag. Despair and loneliness threatened to engulf her.

This decision had not been made lightly. Although Shae hadn't lived at home in years, she shared holidays and vacations with her parents—well, actually, her mother. After weeks of soul-searching and listening to her parents' insistence that she didn't need to leave California, Shae had chosen the position in Chicago. It was hard leaving her mother and her home. Striking out alone hadn't been easy. It frightened her. But this choice fulfilled the promises she made to herself.

Shae shut her eyes and reached for calm. *I need to get my mind off my family,* she thought, rummaging through her bag for her Stephen King novel. Determinedly, she opened the book. At first, the words danced on the page before her, making little sense.

Soon, however, the characters drew her in and Shae forgot everything except the unfolding story.

The insistent soft repetition of words pulled Shae away from chapter four. The low buzz grew in volume. Frowning, she closed her paperback. Concerned that someone needed medical assistance, the nurse in Shae searched the sparsely populated Los Angeles International Airport boarding area for the source of the sound.

Her gaze zeroed in on a tiny Asian lady approximately fifteen feet away. Less than five feet tall, the woman was dressed in a pair of coffee-brown polyester pants and a brown, rust-and-white striped short sleeve top. Black canvas shoes covered her feet. Head bowed, eyes shut and arms wrapped tightly around her body in a protective gesture, the woman rocked back and forth, rhythmically chanting unrecognizable words.

The air in the boarding lounge practically sizzled with tension as the mantra sped up. Silently, the airport patrons in the woman's vicinity began to fold their papers and close their laptops and books. Travelers near the woman frowned and edged away. Several passengers rose from their chairs, gazing back at the woman as they located new seats in what they hoped was a safe location.

Uneasy, Shae tucked her book away inside her bag and rose from her chair. She moved swiftly across the grey carpet and slipped into the chair next to the little woman.

"Excuse me," Shae began, speaking softly so that she didn't frighten the older woman.

Ignoring her, the woman continued to rock back and forth. Her voice rose an octave.

Uncertain what to do, Shae waited a moment more, hoping for a response. When none came, the nurse reached out and gently touched the woman's arm, stroking her fingertips across the bare skin. "Are you all right?"

Instantly, the chanting ceased. The woman turned and her eyes seemed to clear as she focused on Shae. "Huh?"

Smiling reassuringly, Shae gave the woman a clinical once over. She felt the warmth of the older woman's wrinkled skin under her fingertips. "Hi. I'm a nurse. Are you ok? Do you need help?"

Deep age lines etched her tea-colored face, extending up into the gray-and-white peppered hair. "Noooo," the woman answered, then returned to her chanting and rocking.

Shae muttered softly, "Well, I've been dismissed."

Now Shae knew the woman was not suffering from any physical ailment; as to the woman's mental state, Shae was uncertain. Standing, she straightened her form-fitting silk, coral-colored top and matching Capri pants. Ready to return to her Stephen King novel, the young woman's gaze landed on a man seated several rows behind the older woman.

He was playing a game of solitaire on the empty seat next to him. His long fingers lifted cards and moved them from one location to another. Every few seconds, his uneasy gaze returned to the chanting woman and his forehead crinkled into a frown. As the volume of her chanting increased, the man's hand grew still above the cards, as if he were fighting to stay focused.

The imprint on the deck of cards caught Shae's eye. The design was unique. The background was brown with tan highlights and the lettering was in a red calligraphy. She couldn't make out the letters, but the cards were very unusual-looking.

Glancing at the Asian woman, the man gathered his cards and slid them into a box. He rose and wove his way through the rows of chairs to the attendant's desk. Shae admired the slick line of his tall, muscular

frame as he stood at the counter. Dressed casually in a
navy sweatshirt embossed with gold University of
Michigan lettering and denims, she couldn't help but
appreciate the striking image of broad shoulders,
narrow hips and smooth, blemish-free, caramel skin.

Dismissing this tantalizing picture, Shae returned to
her seat, gathered her belongings and prepared for the
flight. Soon, she would be on her way to Chicago and
a new life. A smile as big as her birth state of California spread across Shae's face.

The overhead pager squawked and the pleasant voice
of the gate attendant filled the area. "Ladies and gentlemen, we are ready to begin boarding for Northwest
Airlines Flight 734 bound for Chicago. This is a nonstop flight. We will begin boarding with first-class passengers, World Perk members and anyone with small
children or physical restrictions. Please step to boarding
gate 10. Have your boarding pass ready."

Shae rose, picked up her bag and started for the gate,
clutching the envelope containing her boarding pass.
She pulled the thin slip of paper out and handed it to
the attendant, stepped through the door and then hesitated.

Her father hadn't called. Shae gazed out the window,
past the tower, toward Malibu. Sadness filled her heart.
She hadn't been important enough to say goodbye to.
Although she hadn't lived with them in years, she would
miss them and the luxurious lifestyle they'd given her.
But it was time for her to get on with her life. Chicago
offered a challenge, validation of her personal worth
and more. It gave her a significant way to help others.

Drawing in a deep breath, she started down the ramp.
This was the right decision, and she planned to make
the best of her choice.

# Chapter 2

James Darren Daniels handed his boarding pass to the Northwest Airlines attendant, then strolled through the door and down the connecting ramp. His steps slowed as his heart hammered against his chest. J.D. brushed away the single bead of perspiration traveling slowly down his neck as he neared the airplane entrance. Flying bugged him. Long or short flights—it didn't matter. It felt unnatural to J.D. to travel through the air in a sardine can with wings. It was an opinion he expressed to anyone who would listen.

J.D. hoped this would be his last trip for a very long time. Once he made it home, he'd start the hunt for an assistant, someone who was willing to take on most of the travel and keep him out of the "friendly" skies. Then J.D. would be free to handle the negotiation portion of the business, the part of the business he could do by phone. He would only have to fly out for the final review. J.D. nodded. The more he thought about it, the more he warmed to the idea.

The pilot and lead flight attendant stood outside the open door of the cockpit. Dressed in black uniforms trimmed in red, they greeted passengers as they entered the aircraft through first class. The flight attendant ran an appraising eye over J.D., and then flashed him a little sexy smile. *Interesting,* he thought.

After acknowledging the crew members with a slight dip of his head, J.D. inched his way down the narrow, center aisle. Every few moments the line halted as travelers found their seats or stored the luggage in an overhead compartment. J.D.'s lips turned down at the corners as he studied the cramped, noisy cabin and waited.

Expelling a hot puff of air, the young man wished that this flight was over and he was home. If he had his way, things would soon be very different. There were better ways to enjoy a few hours after clinching a big deal. Ways such as shooting hoops with his buddies followed by two or three rounds of drinks at his favorite sports bar offered a much more pleasing alternative.

Finally, to J.D.'s relief, the line began to move again. Slowly creeping along the aisle, he considered and rejected several alternative modes of transportation. The train, a bus or even a car were safer, but all were much too slow. Deals that he normally concluded in hours would turn into days, maybe even weeks. Although he loathed to admit it, flying remained the most efficient and quickest way to travel and do business.

J.D. had considered a train trip home. It would have been nice but his new client, Amir Jonson, kept stirring up all kinds of problems at home. Now he needed to get back as quickly as possible to perform damage control. So J.D. had to fly.

Glancing at his boarding pass, J.D. discovered the location of his seat. *Oh, man!* Obviously, he had had too much on his mind when he'd booked this trip. He was stuck in the middle seat, squeezed like a melon between two equally uncomfortable travelers.

J.D. found his seat and stored his laptop bag in the overhead compartment. "Excuse me." He pointed at the empty space between two occupied seats. "I'm right here."

Nodding, a rotund woman in a pink silk pantsuit rose and shifted her bulk into the aisle, blocking others who waited impatiently for J.D. to move out of the way. He stuffed his large frame into the tiny seat and fumbled for his seat belt. Conscious of their limited space and to prevent accidentally bumping into his seatmates, J.D. pulled his arms tight against his body after he snapped his seat belt in place. Uncomfortable, he shifted in his seat. An older man snored softly, open mouthed. J.D. shut one eye and grimaced, rubbing his nose in an attempt to dislodge the stale odor of beer.

Was it possible for him to switch his seat to something more comfortable? His eyes darted around the cabin. No. The plane was filling to capacity. Shutting his eyes, J.D. decided sleep represented the best form of escape.

A howl of outrage shattered the quiet murmurings of the plane's cabin. J.D.'s eyes flew open. Glancing behind him, J.D. focused on a baby several rows back.

In a fit of rage, the red-faced infant shrieked. Within seconds, his cries turned into screams. Frantic, the boy's mother tried to soothe him, rocking the little one back and forth, offering comforting words.

J.D. flinched away from the baby's demanding tones. The aircraft hadn't got off the ground and he was already in plane hell.

The infant's mother groped inside her bag, produced a bottle and shoved it into the baby's mouth. Blissful silence followed.

Across the aisle J.D. noticed a woman rocking back and forth. Her soft murmurings were almost musical as they increased in volume. His heart slammed against his chest. This was the Asian woman from the boarding area. The chanting became more insistent and demanding. Praying for a quick and quieter flight, he tried to tune the woman out.

A blond flight attendant walked past the woman several times. Each time, the attendant's gaze swept over the tiny Asian and then focused on J.D. with a question in her eyes. After her third trip, the flight attendant stopped and leaned near the woman. "Ma'am." She waited. "Ma'am," she said louder. "Are you all right?"

The chanter's head lifted slowly. She stared blankly through almond-shaped eyes at the blond woman dressed in a black-and-red uniform. The tiny woman blinked several times as if she were coming out of a fog and needed to clear her vision. "Yes."

"If you're fine, then I must ask you to stop. You're disturbing the other passengers," she explained in a quieter tone.

Blissful silence followed and J.D. let out a thankful sigh of relief. He laid his head against the headrest and closed his eyes. Suddenly, he felt a gentle touch on his hand.

"Excuse me, sir?"

He opened his eyes to find the flight attendant leaning over his seatmate, watching him with concerned blue eyes. "Yes?"

"Is something wrong?" her soothing voice probed.

"No. I'm fine," he answered, darting a quick gaze at the Asian lady.

She smiled reassuringly at him. "I couldn't help noticing how crowded it is. We have a seat available in first class. Would you like it?"

*Yes!* J.D. yelled silently. He quickly rose and climbed over the woman in the aisle seat. Grabbing his laptop, J.D. followed the attendant up the aisle and to the front of the plane. He glanced at her badge, noting her name.

"Here you are." Smiling, she waved a hand at a steel grey leather chair that looked twice the width of his seat in coach.

"Katie, I really appreciate this."

"I'm sure you'll be more comfortable here," she answered before returning to her work.

"Thank you." He sank into the plush seat, stretched his legs in front of him and sighed. This was so much better than being sandwiched between two people.

J.D. glanced at the person sitting next to the window. Surprise, surprise. The woman who'd tried to help the chanting woman sat next to him.

Her complexion was the color of caffe latte, with skin that looked so soft that he had to fight to keep from running a finger across her cheek. Auburn curls framed her features. High cheek bones and full, sensual lips brushed with plum lipstick were framed by a delicate oval-shaped face. Long, thick auburn lashes showcased her beautiful eyes. Slowly her eyes opened and focused on him. J.D. caught his breath.

Gray. Her eyes were the most delicate shade of gray he'd ever seen.

This woman made up one gorgeous package. Pleased with what he saw, he smiled back at her.

Shifting into a more upright sitting position, she ran a hand through her hair. "Hi."

"Hi," he replied.

She stretched out her right hand. "I'm Shae."

He took the hand that she offered. When he looked down at their linked hands, he found his nearly swallowed hers. "James. Everyone calls me J.D."

"Nice to meet you, J.D."

"Same here." Shae's skin felt warm and smooth.

She smiled, tugging gently at her hand. Embarrassed, J.D. let go; it dropped to her lap. Her delicate scent floated around him, filling his nostrils with the tantalizing fragrance of exotic fruits.

Yes, indeed. This was much better than his previous seat. He got to stretch out and enjoy complimentary champagne and had the added bonus of a beautiful woman at his side. This was a hundred times more pleasant, and he planned to enjoy every minute of it.


"Ladies and gentlemen, this is Captain Floyd speaking. We seemed to have hit a patch of rough weather. I'm going to ask you to stay in your seats with your belts buckled until further notice. We'll try to move above the turbulence as quickly as possible. Thank you."

J.D.'s hands gripped the armrests as the plane shook. The cards scattered in all directions on the tray. After several unsteady minutes the plane leveled off. He sighed.

Hiding her own nervousness over the rough flight, Shae watched his movements. His hands shook slightly while he gathered the deck of cards into a single pile and shoved them into the box. She'd noticed the cards earlier. They had a distinctive design. A mocha brown background was bordered in a thick black line. The letters *J.D.* were printed in red and stretched from the left bottom corner to the upper right.

Feeling a spark of sympathy for this man, she decided to try to distract him. Shae tapped the box.

"Those are unique. Where did you buy them?"

J.D. turned the box over, then handed it to Shae. "A couple of my college buddies had these made for me as a gift."

"Very nice."

"Yes, they are. I call them my lucky deck. Whenever I travel I need to have them with me. They're a great source of solitary entertainment when I'm stuck in an airport." He chuckled. "It's my variation on the lucky rabbit's foot."

"I understand." Shae handed the box to him. He lifted his hips off the seat, shoved the box into the pocket of his denims, then dropped back down and returned the tray to its proper position.

Without warning, the plane began to rock and J.D.'s empty hands clenched into tight fists. The skin around his knuckles was taut. It was silent for several minutes as the plane rode out the bumpy weather. When everything settled, he blew out a sigh of relief and ran his hand over his shaved head.

Shae's gaze swept his face. Perspiration beaded on his hairless dome and forehead. His right leg rocked from side to side. A twinge of sympathy tugged at Shae's heart.

*Poor baby, he's so nervous,* she thought. For several minutes she debated whether she should intrude. He seemed so uncomfortable that she had to do something.

"J.D.?" she whispered softly.

He turned to face her. "Mmm?"

"Are you okay?"

"No. I'm not a very good passenger," he admitted reluctantly.

"Any particular reason?"

J.D.'s face scrunched up. "I've never been very good at flying. It's a necessary evil that I've learned to live with, but never like."

"What's different today?" Shae asked.

Wincing, J.D. shook his head. "I don't want you to think that I act like a wimp all the time. Unfortunately, I lost a family member a few years ago when his plane went down."

"Oh, I'm sorry. That doesn't make it any easier, does it?"

"No. And turbulence doesn't make me feel any safer. I'd rather be on the ground."

Chuckling, Shae responded, "You're not alone. Don't fret, a lot of people have problems flying. There's no shame in that."

He seemed to consider her remark before answering. "Since 9/11, my anxiety has increased. I'm more nervous. I put off flying as long as possible." He ran his tongue across his lips. "There's this mental image in my head that won't go away. I see those planes crashing into the World Trade Center and I can barely make myself board."

She patted his hand, not surprised by the fact that he would reveal such personal information to a stranger. Many times people find it easy to confess things to someone they don't have a connection with. "Maybe I can help."

He studied her with a troubled expression in his eyes. "How?"

Offering J.D. an encouraging smile, Shae gently pried one of his hands away from the armrest and enfolded it between both of hers. "It's easy. I can hold your hand, talk to you, offer a distraction from thinking about being in the air."

The expression in his eyes warmed her heart. Shae knew she had made the correct choice. Gratitude flashed from his eyes.

"Right now I'll take any help I can get."

"Don't worry about anything." She intertwined her fingers with his. "I'll be right here. Just hold on to me."

Shae kept her word; she didn't let go. For the next hour she kept them both occupied with questions about Chicago. When the flight got bumpy, Shae smoothly shifted the conversation to her life. She entertained J.D. with her stories about Malibu, her family and friends—any topic that would keep J.D. engaged.

As they neared Illinois, the flight settled into a smooth pattern and the pilot turned off the seat-belt sign. All in all, things had turned out well. Best of all, Shae had discovered a new and exciting friend.

# Chapter 3

"Ladies and gentlemen, we'll be landing at Chicago O'Hare Airport in approximately 10 minutes. For your safety, please remain in your seats with your seat belt fastened until the plane comes to a complete stop. Thank you for flying Northwest Airlines and have a wonderful stay in Chicago. Flight staff, prepare for landing."

J.D. watched the flight crew hurry up and down the aisle, removing empty soda cans and pretzel bags. They checked passenger seat belts and returned trays to the upright position before returning to their seats.

Right on schedule, the plane touched down on the concrete, bouncing along for several seconds before rolling to a smooth stop. J.D. felt his body go slack with relief. He'd made it home in one piece. Still holding Shae's hand, he turned to her, offering a smile of gratitude for her gentle support.

He wiped his brow and tried to come up with a way to make himself look less like a wimp and more self-assured. Honestly, he didn't know what to do. Maybe some wonderful inspiration would strike him before they parted company.

"Shae, thanks for everything. You are an angel."

"You're more than welcome."

He offered her a weak smile. "I've definitely made up my mind to hire an assistant. That person can handle all the long-distance travel."

"It sounds like a plan," she answered.

"The best I can come up with." J.D. unbuckled his seat belt, stood and stepped into the aisle, making a path for Shae. She opened the overhead compartment and reached for her bag. "Here, let me help you." He wrapped his hands around her waist and shifted her out of the way. Something intense flared between them when he touched her.

Stunned, he stood like a statue, gazing at his hand. Shae's sweet voice snapped him back into the real world.

"You don't have to do that."

"I…it…it," he stammered. Inhaling a deep breath of calming air, J.D. forced out, "It's the least I can do." He felt lightheaded from the emotions swirling inside him. The hours they had spent together had made him realize that he wanted to get to know this woman better.

Shae smiled her thanks and shifted out of his way as he pulled the bag from the white shelf and handed it to her. "Thanks."

J.D. pulled his black laptop bag from the shelf and secured it on his shoulder. He cupped her elbow. "Let's get out of here."

"I'm ready." Shae accompanied him past the flight

crew. J.D. studied her profile as they made their way down the ramp. She was a beautiful woman and he didn't plan to let her walk away without getting her telephone number or address.

He steered her down the ramp and into the boarding area. They entered the airport side by side.

Inside the airport, J.D. halted, taking a minute to acclimate to his surroundings. Different city and airport, but the same routine. Commuters hurried up and down the walkway, pulling luggage after them, talking on cell phones while they searched for their boarding area. "Come on, let's get our luggage."

Several passengers from their flight rushed by J.D. and Shae as they strolled toward the baggage claim area. At the baggage carousel they stood together, silently waiting.

The Asian lady who had caused such a ruckus on the plane shuffled past J.D. and Shae, stopping a few feet beyond them. Seconds later a small group of Asians rushed up and greeted her.

"Mei-Mei," an auburn haired woman called, wrapping her arms around the older woman. "You made it."

Each person took a turn hugging Mei-Mei. The tall, male member of the group asked, "How was your flight?"

Mei-Mei's lips pursed and her forehead wrinkled into a frown. "They wouldn't let me alone."

"Why not?" he quizzed.

A serene, knowing expression spread across her face. "I said the blessing prayer over and over for a healthy boy and that Miho wouldn't have much pain. They wouldn't let me continue after I got on the plane. They said I was upsetting the other passengers."

One of the women patted the older woman's hand and said, "Don't worry about that. Those people do not understand our customs."

"You are right." Mei-Mei asked, "How is Miho?"

"Miho gave birth to a nine-pound boy. His name is Henry."

Overhearing this, J.D. felt heat burn a path up his neck and into his cheeks. He really didn't intend to eavesdrop on their conversation, but the group was so close that he couldn't ignore them. He supposed he should step away, find a different spot to wait, but he was curious. So J.D. stood near the Asian family and acted as if he didn't hear them. Curiosity forced him to continue to listen.

The young man offered his arm sympathetically, "We received our blessing. Thank you, Mei-Mei, for all of your help."

Hugging the tiny Asian woman, the midnight-black-haired woman asked, "How long can you stay?"

"Until Miho is ready to return to her work."

"Wow! That long?" One of the young woman rubbed Mei-Mei's arm. "Great!"

J.D. turned to Shae and found her staring back at him with her mouth hanging open. She grabbed him by the arm and quickly drew him away from the family. "Good grief! I can't believe it. I thought she was in pain. Instead, she was praying for a healthy baby." Shaking her head, she giggled. "Amazing!"

Glancing back at the woman and her family, he smiled. "That it is."

Their conversation was interrupted by an orange light flashing and an intermittent *beep, beep, beep* coming from one end of the baggage carousel. Bags shot from the opening onto the rotating carousel. Within minutes, J.D. had retrieved their luggage.

"Is someone coming to pick you up?" J.D. asked.

"No. But don't worry. I'm going to take a cab."

"There's no need for that. I'll give you a lift."

Shae's gray eyes widened in alarm. Biting her bottom lip, she took a step away from him and pulled her purse snugly against her side. "Thank you for the offer, but I'm fine," her voice shook as she spoke.

*She's apprehensive,* he thought. A dart of anxiety shot straight into his heart. That was the last emotion he wanted her to feel for him. *Shae doesn't trust me. Why should she?*

Running a hand over his face, J.D. softened his voice. "Look, I'm not some mad rapist or killer. Other than my problem with flying, I'm an average guy." *Maybe if I show her that I am a decent man it will alleviate her fears.* All he wanted to do was spend some additional time with her.

Removing his wallet from his back pocket, J.D. flipped to his driver's license. "See, that's me. All I'm offering is a ride to whatever location you choose."

Her eyes shifted between the picture, then his face. "Why?"

He raised his hands in an act of surrender. "Because you've been so compassionate. I want to return the favor. The least I can do is make sure that you get where you're going. I mean, it's my turn to do something nice for you."

Her brow wrinkled as Shae evaluated the truth of his words. She caught her bottom lip between her teeth, studying him.

J.D. held his breath, silently praying she'd accept his offer, which might possibly open the door to a future meeting, maybe even a date. After what seemed like hours, but was in fact no more than a few tense seconds, Shae spoke. With the air of someone who had just thrown caution to the wind, she replied, "Thanks. I appreciate the help."

"No, thank you." J.D. grinned broadly at her. Until Shae had said "yes" he hadn't realized how worried he was that she might reject him. Sure, he found her beautiful, but there was so much more that he wanted to learn about her.

Now that they were going to be spending a bit more time together, J.D. was concerned Shae not believe he was a coward. "I want to thank you for helping me during the flight." He let out a sigh of relief, then turned to her with an expression of embarrassment on his face. "I kind of acted like a big sissy earlier. I'm sorry. That's not me in the normal scheme of things."

Placing a warm hand on his arm, Shae offered him an encouraging smile. J.D.'s skin tingled on the spot where her hand rested. "Don't be concerned, I understand. I'm glad I was able to help."

His embarrassment vanished. He felt his mood lighten. This woman was amazing.

Shae watched J.D. stroll toward long-term parking while she waited at the curb with their bags. She shook her head and giggled. Who would believe that after less than twenty-four hours away from home she'd be so frivolous? *What was happening to her?* she wondered. Why would she agree to get into a car with a complete stranger? *You know why,* a voice whispered in her head. She agreed—because she felt something special going on between them. Feelings that she wanted to explore.

Shae knew that her mother would be on her way up to God if she knew her only child was putting her life in jeopardy this way. But J.D.'s gentle face and expression pushed its way to the forefront; she believed J.D. when he said all he wanted to do was pay her back in some small way for all her kindness.

J.D. zoomed up to the curb in a black Chrysler Cross-fire. After he stored their luggage, the couple headed for the Downtown Marriott on Michigan Avenue. Forty minutes later he brought the vehicle to a halt in front of the hotel. Instantly, the valet and bellboy approached the car.

He popped the trunk, got out of the car and removed Shae's belongings. Immediately, the bellboy placed her bags on the cart and started for the entrance. J.D. tossed his car keys to the valet, helped Shae from the car and led her into the two-story lobby with a hand at her elbow. He waited while she completed the check-in process and followed her up the elevator to the pent-house, halting outside the suite's entrance.

"What do you have planned for dinner?" J.D. asked.

Shae shrugged, nervously turning her key card over and over in her hands. "I'll order from room service."

"Don't do that." He moved a step closer. The warmth of his body penetrated the layers of her clothes. "Let me take you out for dinner."

Her heart rate accelerated and a *rat-a-tat-tat* continued in her chest as she considered J.D.'s suggestion. Up to this point, everything had gone well. He had been a perfect gentleman. There were no accidental touches or intrusions into her personal space. Had he been setting her up for a major seduction? Was she pushing her luck by trusting him one more time?

Shae closely examined his handsome face. Albert and Vivian Weitherspoon's warnings came flying back. "You have to be careful," they always advised. "Remember," her mother would add in her special tone that always made Shae feel like the village idiot, "there are people that prey on wealthy young women as trusting as you are."

All her life Shae's parents had warned her about the pitfalls of allowing people to get too close to her. Mommie and Pop had continually reminded her of her social and financial status as the daughter of a wealthy man. Her father constantly harped about her girlfriends, boyfriends and the university she attended; he was especially harsh about her boyfriends. Albert Weitherspoon managed to find a problem with every male she'd ever brought home. The poor souls weren't serious, didn't show respect, were too silly or too old. Unless he hand chose the guy, no one was ever good enough for Albert Weitherspoon's daughter.

Yet, Shae had always fought for her own choices. Moving to Chicago was an example of that. This was her life. The life she chose. Now, a handsome young man was asking her out.

"Look, if you're still worried, we can leave a message at the front desk so that they know where we're going for dinner and what time to expect you back." J.D. added a disarming smile. "Please?"

It was time for her to take charge of her life. She needed to stop worrying about what her parents thought. "All right, I'll go."

A big grin slowly spread across his face. "What time would you like me to pick you up?"

"Why don't we get together at six? That'll give me a little time to relax," Shae suggested.

"It sounds great. I'll see you then." Hesitating for a moment, J.D. reached for her hand and squeezed it gently. "You won't regret it."

Shae shoved the key card into the door slit and turned the door knob when the green light flashed. She moved into the suite's hallway and took a quick glance over her shoulder. J.D. stood, waiting at the elevator.

She was going out with a person she had met on a plane less than four hours earlier. Smiling, Shae shut the door after her. She hadn't been in town for an hour, and already she had a date.

## Chapter 4

At 6:00 p.m. Shae opened the door to a freshly shaved and showered J.D. Casually dressed, he looked great in a camel-colored V-neck sweater, a coffee-brown crew-neck T-shirt and rust-colored trousers. White sneakers peeked from beneath the hem of J.D.'s pant legs.

Shae grabbed her bag and headed out the door, trying to push her concerns about the evening from her mind. She clutched the strap of her purse and studied her dinner date, hoping she wasn't making a major mistake. When J.D. turned away, she regarded him with somber curiosity. Who was J.D. really? After all, they had only known each other for a few hours.

They took the elevator to the lobby, detouring to the reception desk where Shae gave the clerk her door key card. Before leaving the hotel she instructed the woman behind the desk, "If I get any calls, you can tell them that I'm at dinner and to please try again in a couple of hours."

Flashing Shae a dazzling smile, J.D. cupped her elbow in his warm palm and they strolled out of the Marriott into the sixty-degree weather. Cars, SUVs and busses zoomed by as they made their way along Michigan Avenue.

He stopped in front of a mud-colored brick building sporting a cloth red-and-white striped awning; small, white tables with umbrellas lined the front of the building. J.D. opened the door and guided Shae inside. The mouthwatering aromas of oregano, tomatoes and garlic instantly greeted them.

A chubby man with midnight-black hair slowly waddled from behind a counter. The waiter shifted his large bulk between the tightly packed rows of tables, making his way to the door. "Table for two?"

J.D. nodded, then turned to Shae with a look of dismay spreading across his face.

Shae touched his arm. "What?"

"I just assumed that it was okay. That's not always true. You might have allergies or problems with milk. Who knows, you may not like Italian food," J.D. said. "It never occurred to me that you might not like pizza. I wanted to take you to someplace where you would feel comfortable and safe. I figured you'd be a little tired after the flight and wouldn't want to go someplace glitzy where we had to dress up and be on our best behavior." J.D. waved a hand around the restaurant. "This seemed a lot better."

Smiling, Shae patted his arm reassuringly. She wasn't the only person worried about their date. "Relax. Everything is fine. I love pizza."

They followed the waiter to a quiet section of the room. A white-and-red checked vinyl tablecloth covered the tiny square table. Two very shiny wood chairs faced each other from across the flat surface.

J.D. helped Shae get comfortable at the table, then slid into the opposite chair, flashing his companion a beguiling smile. "I know it doesn't look like much. Trust me, this place makes the best deep dish pizza that I've ever had."

"What do you like on your pizza?"

"Meat," he answered quickly. "I like pepperoni, sausage, chicken. Meat."

Frowning, the nurse asked, "What about vegetables?"

"That works for me," J.D. replied nonchalantly.

Together the pair studied the menu before finally selecting a Meat Lovers' Deep Dish Pizza. Shae added mushrooms, olives and green peppers and an antipasto salad. J.D. ordered a carafe of Lambrusco wine.

All of her adult life, her father's business associates and the men in her social circle had tried to impress her, hoping to get closer to Albert Weitherspoon. It was nice to be appreciated for herself. Here she was out on an ordinary date with a person who didn't know or care about her background or her connection to Prestige Computers.

Linking her fingers, Shae rested them on the tabletop; she intently studied the man across the table. "This is nice. I'm glad you convinced me to get out of the hotel. To be honest, I probably would have stayed in my room until the first day of work."

Grinning, he teased, "See, I'm having a positive effect on you already."

"Yes, you are."

The waiter returned with two long-stemmed glasses and a carafe of red wine. He filled each glass before strolling away on short, stubby legs.

J.D. lifted his glass and touched it to hers. "Here's to new beginnings."

Smiling, Shae repeated, "New beginnings."

Shae leaned back in her chair and sipped her wine, enjoying the sweet and fruity flavor. Watching her date closely, she decided to ask the question that had been on her mind since they'd met. "J.D., what do you do for a living that makes it necessary for you to fly all over the country?"

He smiled, swirling the wine in his glass. "I'm a sports agent."

Surprised, her eyebrows lifted. "Really? What does that mean exactly?"

"I represent new talent in the industry. Most of my clients are basketball players."

Impressed, Shae asked another question. "Are you allowed to name names?" She giggled, then admitted, "I probably wouldn't know who they are, anyway. I don't keep up with sports."

"The people I represent are new talent. You wouldn't recognize them. Most are on the college circuit and are seeking an opportunity to move to the pros. It's my job to help them make that transition. That's why I travel so much. Part of what I do is make sure there's a good match between player and team—then I coordinate things with the NBA draft. I have to see how they play, then talk to the teams that might be interested in making an acquisition."

Nodding, Shae queried, "Is that difficult? Do your clients have any idea where they want their careers to go?"

*Everything feels so awkward and stiff.* She smiled, thinking, *But that's how it normally is on a first date, until we settle down a bit.*

He leaned closer and grinned, "Most times, no."

Laughing, Shae said, "I imagine that makes things difficult for you."

"Very," J.D. agreed, taking a sip of his wine. "They all believe they belong on the top professional teams. Most times my clients have only played in high school and then for a short time in college. Very little pro ball. When I tell them they have to work at their careers, they give me plenty of grief. Kids don't understand that you have to build a career."

A smile lit up his face and made J.D. appear younger and more carefree. Shae tapped a finger across her lips. "Once you acquire new talent, how do you market them?"

J.D. reached for the carafe and carefully topped off both of their glasses. "The biggest problem I have is new clients who don't understand the building a career thing. No one becomes a superstar overnight. I try to explain that it's like being a movie star. Actors begin their careers with small roles. As they develop a reputation, they move to better, more ambitious roles."

"Does that work?"

"Sometimes. Unfortunately, I'm dealing with young guys straight out of high school or college who think they should be making what Kobe makes, because they're legends in their own minds."

Shae's shoulders shook as she laughed heartily.

"That's enough about me. Is this your first time in Chicago?"

Shae shook her head. "I was here about a month ago for a job interview."

"Did you get it?"

"Yes." She grinned proudly.

J.D. asked, "Doing what?"

"Nurse practitioner."

He tipped his head and his glass in her direction. "Very nice."

"Thank you."

"Are you going to work in one of the hospitals?" J.D. inquired.

"No. Actually, there's a new clinic opening on the south side that I'm heading up."

Nodding, J.D. folded his arms across his chest. "Good. There are some communities there that really need the help.

"What made you decide to become a nurse?" J.D. shifted the condiments on the table to make more room. The waiter wobbled the couple's way with a large bowl of antipasto salad and two plates.

Shae glanced covertly in J.D.'s direction. She hoped she hadn't sounded like a Goody Two-shoes. It wasn't her plan to destroy the pleasant mood of the evening, but he'd asked her a direct question about a topic that she felt passionate about. "When I was sixteen, my family took a vacation to Africa. It's a beautiful place, but, it's riddled with poverty and sickness."

J.D. nodded.

The waiter put the salad in the center of the table and distributed the plates. Shae took the salad tongs and scooped the lettuce, tomatoes, black olives and meat onto J.D.'s and then onto her own. She placed the tongs inside the bowl and shook out her napkin, spreading it across her lap.

Shae elaborated. "I remember thinking that there had to be something I could do—some way that I should be able to help. When we got home, I decided on a career in nursing. After graduation, I worked for Doctors Without Boundaries. We worked in El Salvador and several Africa countries. And you know what?"

Fork poised above his salad, J.D. said, "What?"

"I've never regretted it." Shae shrugged. "This isn't about money. So many people have so little and can benefit from my help. I can give back a little—maybe make life easier for people."

"You will," the young man answered emphatically.

Turning away shyly, she said, "Sorry. I didn't mean to pick up the bullhorn and preach to the choir."

Reaching for her hand, J.D. enclosed it between both of his. He began to stroke his thumb across the soft skin. "There's nothing wrong with being passionate about your work. It's important to care."

Before Shae could add a word, her cell phone rang. "Excuse me," she murmured, wondering who would be calling her. She checked the number, threw an apologetic glance in his direction and answered, "Hi, Mommie."

"Shae, you didn't call." Mrs. Weitherspoon accused in a worried tone. "I was concerned about you."

"I'm fine."

"I left a message at the hotel. I was surprised that you were out."

Shae rolled the edge of her napkin in her lap under the cover of the table. "I'm out for dinner with a friend. I'll call you when I get back to the hotel. Okay?"

"Friend? What friend? You just got to town." There was a note of hysteria in Vivian Weitherspoon's voice.

"Mommie, I'll call you later," she repeated firmly.

"But—"

"Bye, Mommie," Shae said before disconnecting the call. She shoved the phone into her purse and smiled apologetically at J.D. "Sorry."

"No problem. Your mother was worried that you hadn't arrived."

"Yeah. One of the hazards of being an only child. Parents are continually concerned about you."

J.D. grinned back at her. "I'm one of five and my mother always calls wanting to know when I'll be home. Will I be home for Sunday dinner? Or what I'm eating? Am I getting enough rest? Need I go on? I'm twenty-eight years old and I've been living on my own for at least ten years. I can take care of myself."

"I know exactly what you're talking about. I did a turn as a traveling nurse for two years. I thought my mother was going to worry herself into an early grave. The company sent me on some pretty interesting, uncomfortable assignments. I did fine. I can handle myself. Yet when I talk to my mother, I become five years old again."

He chuckled sympathetically. "You're not alone. I think that's how parents behave."

J.D. and Shae were so engrossed in their conversation that neither heard the server's approach. He cleared his throat before placing a metal pedestal on the table while balancing the pizza on a tin tray in his other hand. The waiter arranged the pizza on the pedestal and moved away.

Shae sniffed the air appreciatively. "This looks wonderful." Slicing into the pizza she reached out for J.D.'s plate. Placing a slice of the deep dish pizza on his plate, Shae handed it back to him before serving herself.

The pair fell into a comfortable conversation. J.D. talked about the city and Shae asked questions about the local sites.

"Mmm," she moaned, wiping her mouth with her napkin. "That was great."

"The pizza was exceptional and so was the company," J.D. complimented.

Shae tipped her head in J.D.'s direction. This evening had turned out much better than she'd hoped. "Ditto."

J.D. settled the bill and guided Shae out of the restaurant. The sun had set and the downtown area was quiet. They retraced their steps back down Michigan Avenue en route to the hotel.

As they strolled slowly back J.D. directed Shae's attention to local points of interest. He followed her into the Marriott and across the lobby to the front desk. Shae retrieved her door card and the pair took the elevator to her floor. All the while, Shae prayed that this wouldn't be the only time she had with him.

J.D. halted outside her door and put his hand on Shae's shoulder. "It's been awhile since I've had such a great time. I really enjoyed tonight."

"So did I." Shae smiled shyly.

His hand slid down her arm and he intertwined their fingers. "Would you like to go out again? Maybe we could see a different part of the city. Get you more comfortable with Chicago before you start your new job."

She squeezed his hand, then smiled before answering, "That sounds wonderful."

"How about tomorrow evening? Say around eight?" He took a step closer. Shae's heart pounded as she felt the heat of his body. His subtle scent wafted under her nose, making her tingle all over with anticipation.

"All right," Shae said after a moment of hesitation.

J.D. dropped her hand and leaned in, gently nibbled on her bottom lip. His lips were soft and encouraging as they touched Shae's tentatively. A delighted shiver coursed through her at this slight caress. Wanting more, she moved closer, parting her lips to offer him entry. J.D. framed her face with his hands as his tongue darted inside.

A low moan escaped from her as his tongue met hers. At first the kiss was gentle and soft, exploring. It grew more passionate as she stroked his tongue with her own. His hands trailed along the column of her neck, over her shoulders and wrapped her in his embrace, pulling her against the hard planes of his heated body.

Slowly, they separated. He leaned down a second

time and kissed her lips lightly, stroking her cheek tenderly with his fingertips.

Dazed, she gazed up at him.

"I'll call you tomorrow," he promised in a husky whisper.

"Okay. Good night."

"Good night, Shae," he said softly, softly kissing her lips a final time before releasing her and heading to the elevators.

Shae stepped inside the suite and shut the door, leaning against the wood surface. She'd never felt anything like this before in her life. Making this change in her life might turn out to be the best decision she'd ever made.

# Chapter 5

Although Shae had the credentials and work experience to run a clinic, she felt nervous about starting her
new job. First days were tricky. Information overload
added additional stress to an already stressful day.

J.D. had been wonderful. He'd offered his services
as her personal chauffeur until she bought a car. In
return, they had shared an intimate breakfast at one of
her hotel's restaurants.

Now she sat in the passenger seat of J.D.'s Chrysler
Crossfire as they pulled away from the hotel. As Shae
watched him maneuver the car, she realized what a
pleasant start to the day it had been to have him pilot
their commute to the clinic.

The scenery swept by unnoticed as her thoughts
turned to the day ahead. As she smoothed the imaginary
wrinkles from the front of her mauve-colored suit, Shae

took control of her fears and focused on the positive aspects to her new home and life.

A warm male hand wrapped around hers possessively. "Don't worry," J.D. said in a soft, encouraging tone. "You'll do fine." He added a reassuring squeeze with one hand while he navigated through the downtown Michigan Avenue morning traffic with the other. Within minutes they merged onto the freeway.

"I hope you're right. I'm so nervous that I'm tempted to get on a plane and return to Malibu." Trembling fingers pushed her hair from her face. "How am I supposed to direct a staff, make decisions on patient care and run the facility? That's a lot of responsibility."

He laughed, then stroked his chin with a finger. "Yes, it is. Let me think a minute. Didn't you tell me that you were part of a Doctors Without Boundaries program in El Salvador and Africa?"

"Yes."

"And if I remember correctly, you handled everything from mosquito bites to surgery. Correct?"

"Yes."

"If you can handle those situations then I'm sure you have enough experience to run a small, inner-city clinic." His fingers caressed the skin of her hand, sending her pulse into a gallop. "Here's my suggestion. Take a mental step away from your uncertainties and let the day happen. I'm positive things will gel just the way you want them to."

Taking J.D.'s advice, Shae shut her eyes, inhaled through her nose and exhaled out her mouth. After several minutes she felt calm and a sense of peace settle over her. "Thank you." She smiled at her driver. J.D. soothed her. He instinctively understood her unease and knew the right thing to say to alleviate her fears.

"It's part of the Daniels full-service treatment, pro-vided exclusively to you. First days are always difficult. You wouldn't be human if you didn't feel the pressure." He took his eyes off the road for a moment to gaze at her. Something special sizzled between them, causing her heart to flutter in her chest. "I know you can rise to the occasion. Make things work. Right?"

"Correct."

"Good. That's what I want to hear."

"I'm nervous," she admitted, then added, "I want to do the best job I can. What if I'm not ready? Or I don't know enough to help my patients?"

He turned to her with a frown on his handsome features. "Where is all of this coming from? You know your job and it won't take long for you to become familiar with the people in the area."

"I know," Shae admitted, patting his arm. "I've wanted to do this for so long that it doesn't seem right that everything is falling into place without some major drama. Ignore me, I'll be fine."

J.D. gave her an "Are you sure?" glance.

"Honest. Thanks for tolerating me through this little panic attack."

"No problem." His voice dropped an octave. "I want to help in any way that you'll let me."

Warmed by his gentle but moving declaration, Shae reached over and stroked his cheek. "Thank you. You are wonderful."

"And don't you forget it."

"Yes, sir." Shae saluted him.

They both laughed.

Shae concentrated on the scenery and recognized several landmarks. As they moved deeper into the city there was a distinct shift in the condition of the buildings and houses. Most of the properties were well maintained, some older, some not. Some needed repair. Within minutes, J.D. pulled in front of a white three-story brick building. "Urban Health Center" was printed above the front door in black letters.

"Your door-to-door limo service has delivered you safely to your destination," he declared, pushing the transmission gear into Park, but letting the engine run.

She glanced at the round clock on the dashboard. "And in good time, too. I have time to grab an extra cup of coffee."

"Before I forget, my mother wants you to come to Sunday dinner."

Butterflies danced in her stomach. "Dinner?" she echoed softly. His mother knew about her?

"Yeah. We do this family dinner thing most Sundays. My brothers and sisters and their families always show up."

Shae shifted in her bucket seat to face him. "J.D., we've only known each other a few days. How does your mother know about me?"

J.D. blushed a delicate shade of red and intently studied the dashboard as his hands tightened around the steering wheel. "I happened to mention you a couple of times while we were talking this week."

"Did you now?" she asked with a significant lifting of her brows.

He shrugged. "I talk about you because I like you. You are becoming an important part of my life."

Her heart danced with excitement. What could she say to that? *Tell him the truth.* "You're important to me, too."

Embarrassed, J.D. gazed out the window. "I talked to my mom last night because she was checking to see how my trip worked out. Mom wanted to know if I was coming to dinner. When I hesitated she shifted from mom to sleuth mode and kept digging until I confessed that I was seeing you and didn't want to leave you alone on the weekend. That's all it took. Mom insisted that you join us."

"I don't know." Shae nervously twisted a lock of hair around her finger. Was she ready to be introduced to the Daniels family? "We just met. Don't you think it's a bit early in our relationship for me to meet your family?"

J.D. grinned broadly at her.

The effect dazzled her and she found it nearly impossible to concentrate. "What?"

"I like the sound of that word. *Relationship.*"

Relaxing, she grinned back at him and admitted softly, "Me, too."

"Getting back to your question, Shae, my family is pretty laid back. It's dinner. No strings attached. I'd like you to come." His hand settled on top of hers and squeezed. "Please."

Shae grinned, shaking her head at the look on J.D.'s face. How could she resist that puppy-dog expression and endearing words? She had misgivings about meeting his family at such an early stage in their relationship, but she refused to let her concerns weigh down the time she spent with J.D. "Okay. I'll come."

"Thank you. You will love them," he declared. "Trust me."

Trust him. Of course she did. J.D. didn't know how much trust she'd placed in him. Worried for her safety and welfare of their only child, the Weitherspoons had cautioned Shae against letting people get to close to her. After years of watching every step, she had thrown caution to the wind and allowed J.D. into her life. It felt wonderful to enjoy this relationship and see it develop without her parents' watchful eyes and possible interference.

He glanced at his watch. "Ready to go to work?"

"I think so."

"Good luck," he whispered, leaning across to softly kiss her lips. He pulled one of her curls and stretched the lock straight before letting go. It snapped back into its original spiral shape.

"Thank you."

Caressing her cheek, J.D. added, "Go in there and save the world. I know you can do it."

"Will do, sir."

"You have my cell phone number, right?" he asked.

"Yes, it's programmed into the memory," Shae answered, touching the phone clipped to the waistband of her mauve skirt. "And you have mine."

J.D. watched a young man with his head wrapped in a do-rag and baggy wide-legged denims hung across his butt saunter past the clinic. "Watch yourself. I'll be here at five to pick you up."

"Are you sure you can do this? You have your clients to consider, and I don't want to interfere with your business. If you have things that you need to do, I can always get a cab home and rent a car tomorrow."

"Yes, you can. But I don't want you to. Don't worry about me, Shae. I make my own hours and, to be perfectly honest, I love seeing so much of you." He grinned. "Besides, we'll go car shopping real soon. I'm sure you'll have transportation in no time."

"If anything changes, call me."

"Will do." He brought her hand to his lips before dropping it. "I have one meeting this afternoon around three. Look for me out here."

"Okay. I'll look for you at five." Shae leaned closer and kissed him. "Bye."

Shae got out of the car and closed the door, moving up the sidewalk to the building. Before entering the building, she turned and waved. J.D. mimicked the gesture. She rang the doorbell and seconds later the custodian ushered her inside.

Halting in the lobby, Shae noted the changes to the room. Much had been accomplished since her last visit. The clean scent of freshly painted walls greeted her. A welcoming shade of violet covered the previous pink coating; plum carpeting hid the scarred wood floors and a brand new nursing station waited for the staff to take charge.

She strolled down the main hallway to the medical director's office. The door stood open and her boss sat at his desk with a headset pinned to his ears. The name plate on his desk read Kenyatta L. Reid, M.D.

"Good morning," Shae said from the entrance.

Dr. Reid glanced her way. "Good morning to you." He rose and made a quick move around his desk with an outstretched hand. As he drew closer, she was surprised by how quickly such a large man moved. Close to 6'4" and weighing in at nearly 280 pounds, Dr. Reid looked as if he should be on the football field instead of in an examining room. That impression wasn't far off. During their interview, Dr. Reid had revealed that he'd completed his undergraduate degree on a football scholarship.

"Want some coffee?" he offered, as he continued to hold her hand.

"Sounds good." She gave a sharp tug on her hand and he released her.

Dressed in a crisp white lab coat with *K. Reid, M.D.* in bold, black letters and blue-green scrubs, the medical director led her to his desk before grabbing a mug from a makeshift coffee station near the back of his office. "Black. One sugar, no cream. Correct?"

Surprised, she turned and watched him pour the rich brew into the mug. "Wow! That's some memory you have."

"It's not hard when you're the only staff I've hired."

She chuckled. "I see your point."

Dr. Reid returned to the desk and offered Shae the mug.

"Thanks." She placed her mug on the edge of the desk, then opened her briefcase and removed her portfolio and pen.

He rubbed his earlobe as he spoke. A diamond stud adorned his right ear. "Since I brought up the topic of staffing, I need to tell you that that is our top priority."

"Is everything else in place? The exam rooms, offices, nursing station? Have we ordered medications?"

"Most of them. It's time to get our staff in place. Here are some of the things you'll need to get started. This is your annual operating budget, keys for the building and your office." He laid each item on the desk as he identified them. "The security code to the front and back doors and your gate card for the parking lot."

"Thanks." She slipped the keys inside her jacket pocket and placed the code and gate card in her briefcase.

"Where did you park?" He leaned back in his chair to glance out the window. "Do you want to move your car?"

She shrugged. "No. I got a ride."

"Taxis can get pretty expensive." He removed a pencil from behind his left ear. "I hope you can find less expensive transportation."

"Not a taxi. A ride," she corrected. "And I do plan to buy a car very soon. Probably tonight or tomorrow."

"Are you going alone?"

"No. I have a friend."

"Friend?" His eyebrows shot towards his hairline. "I thought you didn't know anyone here."

"I didn't. But I do now."

He muttered something too low for her to hear clearly.

"What was that?" she asked.

The medical director shook his head, answering, "Nothing."

"Dr. Reid, how much time do we have before we open?"

"Grand opening will be the first of next month." He turned the desk calendar in her direction and pointed at the first Monday in May. "That gives you exactly three and a half weeks to hire six nurses, two LPNs, two nursing assistants and the front office people, including billers."

Surprised, her eyes widened. "Unless you've already placed ads in the newspapers, that's going to be difficult to do."

Dr. Reid pulled a white plastic mail bin from under his desk. "Done. You'll have to go through them, but this is a start."

"It looks like I have work to do." Standing, Shae placed her pad and pen in her briefcase and shut it. "It's time for me to get started. Where's my office?"

Grinning at her, he lifted the case in one hand, tucked it under his arm like a football and waved her towards the door with the other. "Let me show you. You're down the hall from me. If you need anything, holler."

"Will do," Shae responded, following him out the office.

# Chapter 6

Destiny's Child blasted through the Bose sound system. J.D. bopped to the lyrics while he poured orange juice into his black coffee mug emblazoned with "Number One Agent" in gold. Barefooted, he made his way through his loft to the living area and sank onto the steel-gray leather sofa. Sighing heavily, J.D. propped his feet on the edge of the rosewood coffee table and sipped his o.j.

Anger rose in J.D. as he twisted the face of his wrist-watch to check the time. His appointment with Amir had been scheduled for three p.m. It was half-past four, and the kid still hadn't put in an appearance, nor had he taken the time to call. J.D. had more important things to do besides wait for Amir Jonson to show up. *Man, I'm tired of this kid,* J.D. thought wearily. Why did he continue to take Amir's crap? J.D. wished fervently that Amir acted like a different kid with a better attitude.

J.D. knew the answer to his question: the plain and simple truth was Amir had talent and he had a good shot at transitioning to the NBA, if—and it was a big if— Amir got his act together and started taking his career more seriously, and if J.D. could steer the right people Amir's way. Talent represented only a part of the package. Nowadays, recruits needed to be team players. Plus, the NBA wanted mature and responsible players that didn't cause a lot of problems or require much maintenance.

Swallowing the last drops of liquid, the agent slowly returned to the kitchen. At the sink, J.D. rinsed the mug, placed it in the black dishwasher, and glanced out the window, watching the light downtown traffic.

While still a senior in high school, Amir Jonson had come to the sports agent's attention. Phil, J.D's buddy, had suggested they check out the team that his nephew played with. J.D. had agreed for two reasons: first—he never found time to hang out with his buddies the way he used to, and second—the opportunity to check out high school players intrigued him. Most of his clients were in college and transitioning to pro ball.

Loud, rowdy and fun described the game. One high school senior had dominated the court. With the skill of a seasoned pro, Amir had seemed to float across the court, scoring one basket after another. Once the game ended, J.D. had sought out the young man to talk to and to listen to his aspirations. Days later, J.D. met Amir's mother and had pitched a plan for Amir's future. Mother and son grinned happily, showing every tooth in their heads, pleased to receive J.D.'s support and help.

Although J.D. liked the kid, Amir was a royal pain in the ass. Before allowing him to sign the contract, J.D. had sat Amir and his mother down and explained the important aspects of the plan he intended to set in motion. Ms. Jonson had agreed. Amir had not. His mother had won. Amir had reluctantly agreed to the plan.

Problems started with Amir when he began to take the advice of his high school buddies over J.D.'s. His friends kept telling Amir that he should be able to step straight from the high school basketball court to the pros. Like most children, Amir refused to acknowledge how the system worked. Instead he wanted everything now and believed he could skip the hard work that led to a successful career.

As they began to work together, J.D. realized that although Amir possessed an abundance of talent, he lacked discipline. Most kids played college ball after graduation. They accepted college scholarships while waiting for the call of the NBA draft. Amir had balked at the idea of college. The young man fought J.D. on every issue. Amir believed that he didn't need to do the college thing because his future rested with the pros.

J.D. leaned into the soft leather as he rubbed his fingers across his forehead, trying to erase a headache. The kid hadn't showed his face and it was getting close to the time for J.D. to pick up Shae. Heading for his bedroom, he grabbed a pair of sneakers and white tube socks. Moving purposefully through the condominium, J.D. returned to the sofa, shoved his feet inside the socks and reached for a shoe.

Shae. He halted with a shoe in his hand, seeing her smiling face in his mind. She was a wonderful, exciting addition to his life.

J.D.'s pleasant reverie was rudely interrupted by the doorbell chimes. He dropped the shoe and padded across the wood floor to the intercom and video monitor located near the front door. Amir stood on his doorstep. "Damn!" J.D. shook his head, instantly deciding to make this the quickest meeting on record. He buzzed the young man into the building, opened the door and waited in the entrance for his guest to climb the two flights of stairs.

"Hey," Amir grunted. The lanky 6'5" basketball player's ebony face wore a permanent snarl. A red do-rag controlled his thick, shoulder-length braids. Baggy, wide-leg denims covered a pair of red silk drawers that hung outside his denims. His long, skinny legs poked out from white ankle socks trimmed in blue. His size fifteen feet looked like boats in his Michael Jordan sneakers.

Arms folded, J.D. demanded, "Where have you been?"

Amir strolled into the tiny hallway, a cell phone glued to his ear in one hand, while using the other hand to hold up his pants. "Got held up with some stuff."

"We had a three o'clock appointment."

The young man shrugged, then added belligerently, "Yeah and? I got held up. I'm here now, so let's get to it."

J.D.'s hands clinched into fists at his side. "Look. You have got to do better. How can I pitch you to anyone when I can't depend on you to be on time and make the best impression?"

"If it's important, I'll be there. You never have anything good to tell me, so why should I rush? All we're going to do is talk about what you plan to do. You still haven't done what I want you to do."

J.D. shut the door and started down the narrow passageway. "Let's go into the living room."

Amir followed without comment. When they entered the living area, the young man flopped down on the sofa and glared spitefully at J.D.

"Can I get you anything?"

"Beer."

"Nope." J.D. answered, snagging the chair near the sofa. He removed a sheet of paper from the file sitting on the coffee table. "I told you that you can't go pro yet. We have a lot of work to do before that happens."

"Talk. Talk. Talk." Amir flipped J.D. off with a wave of his hand. "That's all you give me. My boys think you're just trying to hold me back. You don't want me to go pro."

J.D. seethed angrily underneath, but maintained an outwardly composed demeanor. "Why wouldn't I? That puts more money in my pocket. Amir, you have talent and, if you can grow and learn, you'll have a fabulous professional career and the life that you crave. But not yet. There's still a lot of work ahead of you."

Amir scoffed and turned his attention to his cell phone.

"What happened to your mother?"

The young man's face scrunched into a snarling mask. "I don't know. What happened to her?"

"Why isn't she here with you?"

"I imagine she's where she lives," he quipped, crossing one bony leg over the opposite knee.

"I specifically asked to see both of you."

The young man glowered at the older man. "I'm grown. I don't need her up in my business."

J.D. gritted his teeth to keep from saying something that would set them both off. Amir's 'tude was getting old really fast. J.D. understood how important it was for Amir to handle himself like a tough guy in front of his friends, but his friends weren't here.

"That's not going to happen. You're only nineteen and there are concerns about your grades." He passed a copy of Amir's fall report card to the young man. "As you can see, and probably already know, you're on academic probation. Unless you bring up your grades and go to summer school to make up the classes you failed, you'll lose your free ride. If that happens, your chances for the NBA fly away with it."

Amir rolled his eyes and propped his feet on the edge of the coffee table. "Come on, man. This is all playtime. It don't matter what grades I get as long as I keep playing ball."

"That's where you're wrong. It all matters." J.D. roughly shoved Amir's feet off the table. "Young man," he started. "This isn't a game. If you want that career, get your crap together."

Sulking, Amir crossed his arms and studied the hardwood floor.

"Young man, look at me," J.D. voice rang out with authority.

Instantly, Amir focused on him. A flash of dislike flickered from his round owl's eyes.

"I'm going to drop you as a client if you don't get on track." This wasn't true. He'd understood that Amir was still in his teens and had come from a tough home life. His mother had worked hard to provide for him and to raise her son without a father's influence.

J.D. made allowances for Amir because J.D. grew up with the benefits of strong, supportive parents and he understood how his upbringing shaped his life. But discipline remained a key factor to Amir's path to becoming a pro.

J.D. laced his fingers together. He gave the younger man time to absorb what he'd said. The agent rose from his chair, moved around the coffee table, and sank onto the soft leather of the sofa next to Amir. "There's still time to finish out this year in the positive column. Just don't screw up. If you need help, I can get you a tutor or help you myself. But those grades must improve. Period. And as soon as possible. I suggest you go make appointments with your professors, talk with them about extra credit if you need to and find out if there's anything you can do to improve your grades. Do what needs to be done."

Rolling the edge of the jersey between his fingers, Amir thrust out his bottom lip and pouted. "College is supposed to be fun."

J.D. tapped a finger against his lips. "Not really. College involves learning and getting an education. If you plan to make it in pro ball, you need to understand how things work."

"What you're saying is that I can't have any fun."

"Not at all. Get your school work done first, then hang out with your friends. Until you get your grades on track, stop the carousing with your buddies and leave the ladies alone. Give it a rest until your grades are in order." J.D. waved a hand back and forth between them. "Have I made myself clear?"

Silence followed his question.

"Are we on the same page on this issue?" J.D. asked a second time.

Tension filtered into every corner of the room.

"I need an answer before you go."

Amir's lips pursed. "Yeah."

J.D. slapped his hand against the table. It sounded like an exploding bomb in the quiet of the room. He reached under the table and slipped his feet into his Air Force One sneakers. "Good." He rose and plucked his keys from the end table. "I've got to be going. Let me walk you out."

# Chapter 7

The constant bouncing of a ball drew Shae's attention from the stack of resumes to the basketball court next door. She stretched and glanced out the window, watching the rowdy bunch.

Her office had been painted in a soothing lilac and the floor covered with a rich lavender carpet. A used metal desk with a Formica surface sat in the center of the room. A gray cloth swivel chair and a black steel four-drawer file cabinet occupied much of the free space. The lack of space didn't matter because Shae suspected that most of her time would be spent in the exam rooms rather than in her office.

Glancing at the white wall clock, she noted the time. It was almost five and J.D. would be pulling up to the building any minute. Shae dropped the pile of typed pages, her yearly budget information and supply order into her briefcase before snapping it closed. Looking forward to seeing J.D., her heart rate accelerated. She retrieved her suit jacket from the back of her chair, slipped her arms into the sleeves and prepared to leave the office for the day. She shut and locked her office door and headed for the front of the building. On her way out, Shae halted at the entrance to the medical director's office. "Good night, Dr. Reid."

With a pencil stuck behind his left ear, the doctor was deeply focused on the information on his computer screen. She cleared her throat. He glanced her way with a distracted expression on his face, blinking several times before focusing on her. "Good night. See you tomorrow."

"Yes, you will." She turned toward the lobby.

"By the way," he said. "My name is Kenyatta. Please use it."

"And my name is Shae."

"Fair enough." Smiling back at her, he nodded. "I meant to come down to your office and see how things were going. I got caught up in work and everything flew out of my head. How did today go for you? Did you find all the things that you needed?"

"I made a great start today. Set up interviews for tomorrow and Friday." Shae placed her briefcase on the floor near her leg. "I'm going to decide on hiring over the weekend and then make offers Monday. That will give the applicants time to give their current employers two-week notices."

"Sounds good. By the way, where are you staying?" He removed the pencil from behind his ear and reached for a sheet of scratch paper.

"Downtown Marriott."

"Nice. You're not planning to stay there indefinitely, are you?"

Leaning against the doorframe, she answered, "No.

After we get the staffing issues resolved, I'm going to look for a permanent address. Why? Did you have any suggestions? Do you know of a place?"

"Sorry, no." Kenyatta's face lit up as an idea formulated in his mind. He lifted a finger. "But," he paused for emphasis before continuing, "there are some great real estate agents in this area that will do the leg work for you. While you're handling our business, they'll be handling yours."

"Sounds good. Do you have a name?" Shae asked.

"Not with me. My sister used one when she sold her house. I'll talk to her this evening and get back to you tomorrow."

"Fair enough."

"How are you getting home?" Kenyatta asked.

"My friend is picking me up." She glanced at her watch, then reached for her briefcase. "He's probably waiting. I better get going. See you Thursday morning."

"Good night."

There was an extra spring in her step as she hurried down the hall and out the front door. She halted outside the building. Instead of J.D.'s car idling at the curb, she found an empty space.

For a moment, Shae's confusion and disappointment overwhelmed her. Those feelings transported her back to her childhood and the times when her father promised to pick her up from school and then got so wrapped up in his work the he forgot all about her.

Shae shook her head, beating down the anxieties surging through her. Her feelings spiked before dropping back to a manageable level. *J.D. should be here,* she thought, glancing at the LCD screen on the cell phone. A small groan escaped from her lips. No messages. He was running a little late or traffic problems caused his delay. If he didn't show up in fifteen minutes, she'd go back into the building and order a taxi.

*It's rush hour and he probably got caught in traffic,* she thought nervously. No point in returning to the building. *I'll wait here for him.*

Deciding on a plan eased her anxiety and she felt more confident about waiting for J.D. Shae intended to embrace this opportunity and observe the community near the clinic. She shrugged and strolled to a wooden bench near a bus stop.

It was a typical inner-city neighborhood with lots of kids and music, and teenagers strolling up and down the streets. A variety of homes graced the area. Colonial, bungalows and two-family flats all shared space on the same block. Many of the structures were in need of repair, some major and some minor.

Placing her briefcase on the bench beside her, Shae decided to use her time wisely and tackle some of the work that needed her attention. If she must wait, she might as well make the best use of her time. Engrossed in resumes, she glanced up from her reading to find two children watching her. Dressed in a gray, red and black–striped long-sleeve T-shirt, denims and high-top sneakers, a small boy no older than five sat on the U-shaped handlebar of a bike. The older of the two children balanced the bike between his denim-clad legs. Their small round faces revealed the same facial structure and brown eyes. They had to be related.

"What you doin'?" the little one asked from his perch on the handlebars.

Smiling, she answered, "Reading. What are you doing?"

"Watchin' you," the older boy responded.

Giggling, Shae tossed the papers back into her briefcase and gave the boys her full attention. "Fair enough. Do you live around here?"

Twin heads bobbed up and down. The older boy pointed at a house down the block. "Yeah. We live down there. Near the corner."

"Where do you live?" the little one asked.

"Downtown, for now," Shae answered.

The younger boy slipped from the handlebars and moved closer. "What's your name?"

"Shae."

Pointing a finger at his chest, he volunteered, "I'm Desmond."

"Well, hello, Desmond." Shae dipped her head in silent acknowledgement, directing her attention to the other child. "And you are?"

"Sterling. Sterling Walls."

Shae rose from the bench and extended her hand. The young man hesitated for a moment, blushing profusely before slipping his small hand in hers.

Desmond walked over to her and touched her briefcase. "What are you readin'?"

"Work stuff. Do you like to read?"

"I'm too young to read," Desmond answered.

Turning to the older boy, Shae asked, "How about you, Sterling? Do you like to read?"

"Little bit. But I like video games and TV better."

Shae noticed Desmond kept wiping his runny nose with the sleeve of his striped T-shirt. The poor little thing looked miserable. *Germs,* Shae thought. Maybe she could help, mentally shifting through the items in her briefcase. She reached inside her briefcase, pulled out a personal size packet of tissue and crooked a finger, beckoning him closer. The younger kid cautiously moved to the bench and she took his small chocolate round face gently between her fingers and wiped his nose with a tissue. "There. Much better. Do you have a cold?" Shae tossed the used tissue in the wired trash basket near the bench.

He nodded.

"Keep these." She offered the tissues.

Cautiously, Desmond reached out his hand and took the white packet. His little forehead crinkled into a frown as he took her gift. "Thank you."

"You're welcome."

"Let me give you something to help." She rummaged through her briefcase and gave the boy a yellow vitamin C drop. Most children thought they were eating candy when in fact they were getting the daily requirement of vitamin C. "This will help you get rid of your cold quicker."

The older boy grabbed Desmond's shoulder and jerked him away. "Don't," he hissed softly. "What did Momma tell us? Don't take candy from strangers."

"She's nice. I like her. And I want it," Desmond whined.

"Momma will get us," the older kid cautioned.

Their mother had given them sound advice and Shae didn't want to contradict a parent's training and wishes. She cleared her throat and pointed at the building behind them. Both boys turned toward the clinic. "You don't have to be afraid of me. I work right here."

"Are you a doctor?" Sterling asked.

"No. I'm a nurse. If you get sick I can help you."

From the distance she heard their names being called. "It sounds like somebody is looking for you guys. You better get on home and see what it's about." Shae put the vitamin C drops in Sterling's hand. "Before you go, take these with you. Let your mother decide if you can have them."

"Come on, Desmond." Sterling shoved the drops in his pocket, then lifted the bike from the ground.

The little one hurried to the front of the bike and Sterling lifted him onto the handlebars. They sped down the street as J.D.'s black Crossfire zipped into the empty parking space in front of the clinic.

He climbed out of the car and hurried to the wood bench, watching the kids make their way down the street. "You okay?"

"Yeah." She glanced at the pair as they crossed the street. "I made a couple of new friends."

"Shae, I'm sorry. I'm so sorry."

"Is everything okay?" she asked, focusing on him. He looked as attractive as ever and she felt really happy to see him.

"The client I was expecting at three showed up at four-thirty with a lame excuse. Forgive me, please?"

"Sure. Things happen. I understand that." She smiled at J.D., patting his arm. "Don't worry about it. It gave me an opportunity to meet a couple of the kids from the neighborhood."

"I'm glad. Although I feel really bad about being late." The phone hooked to his belt began to vibrate. J.D. grimaced, glancing at the screen. "I've got to take this. Give me a minute." He unhooked the phone and answered the call. Seconds later he ended the call and returned the phone to his belt. "Sorry."

"No problem. Don't stress over it." Shae shut her briefcase and rose from the bench.

"Ready?" he asked, removing her leather briefcase from her hand.

"Yes."

"How about dinner?" J.D. asked, cupping her elbow as he guided her to the car and opened the passenger door.

"Dinner?" Shae didn't expect him to feed her every day, although she loved spending as much time with him as possible. "I don't expect you to entertain me."

"I know. But, I feel bad about being late. Plus, it's your first day on the job. I want to hear all about it."

# Chapter 8

J.D. and Shae decided to go directly to dinner. He'd said he knew the perfect place for them to have a good meal and privacy to talk. And he was right.

Riva's Restaurant was located on Navy Pier. It featured a breathtaking view of the Chicago skyline and Lake Michigan. As the hostess led them to their table, Shae got her first glimpse of the impressive 40-foot exhibition kitchen as the chef and crew worked diligently to prepare the Italian and seafood cuisine for their patrons.

"I love this place," J.D. admitted as he set his menu aside. "Can I help you order?"

"Sure. Everything looks so good, your recommendation would be helpful."

"No problem. I always have the Lobster Fra Diavolo," J.D. said, pointing to the item on the menu. "It's the best. It's a spicy dish with linguini topped with lobster."

Shae moaned. "That sounds heavenly."

"It is," J.D. assured her. "You won't go home hungry."

"I'm sold."

After the waitress took their order, J.D. turned his attention back to Shae.

"So tell me about your day. Was it everything you expected?"

Grinning, she answered, "It was good. I met Desmond and Sterling. My boss Kenyatta dumped on me. But I sort of expected that."

"Dumped on you how?"

"He had this large bin of resumes for me to go through. All the staff has to be hired by the end of next week."

He whistled.

"Yeah. Then I have to train everyone."

"You're going to be busy. When are you going to open?"

"The first Monday in May."

"Less than a month to get everything done." J.D. shook his head. "You're going to be very busy."

Laughing, Shae nodded. "Yes, I am. But I asked for it, right?"

"That you did."

"So how about you, J.D.? What kept you?"

J.D. scoffed. "Amir Jonson, the client from hell."

Frowning, Shae said, "Mmm. That sounds scary. Why is he the client from hell?"

"Because Amir stirs up more crap then all my clients put together." J.D. swallowed a sip of wine. "The young man has talent, but his friends know more than I do."

"That can be difficult."

"Yes, it can. I like Amir a lot. But he's beginning to get on my nerves," J.D. said.

"So what's his story?"

"No father in the home. Mother trying to be both parents and failing at both. He's got so much talent. I want him to have everything he's dreamed of. But he's so obstinate. Unless he changes his attitude we're not going to be able to work together much longer."

"Why are you putting up with him? I'm sure there are a lot of kids who'd like to have his opportunity," Shae pointed out.

"I grew up in a home with two parents. They loved us and were always available. They gave us what we needed, not what we wanted. There's a part of me that believes that Amir would be a different guy if he'd had the benefit of a father. Amir needed a male figure to care about him, give him guidance and spend time with him."

"J.D., that's not always true," Shae whispered softly, thinking back to her life in her parents' home. Having two parents in the home doesn't always mean that the child will turn out perfect. She remembered all the disappointments and pain that her father caused by his broken promises. "My pop lived with us, but he wasn't truly in the home. There's got to be more."

"I'm sorry, sweetheart." J.D. reached across the table and took her hand, holding it between both of his. "You're right. What I'm trying to say is that people have disappointed Amir so much in life that he's unwilling to trust anyone. I want to break through that and help him."

"I understand the need to help, J.D. I just don't want you to be disappointed," she squeezed his hand.

"It'll be okay. I'm going to do everything I can to help him," he promised. "Thank you."

She smiled at him, feeling warm and happy at the

closeness developing between them. Shae wanted to comfort him. J.D. seemed so concerned and sincere about the well-being of his clients. Somehow Amir had touched a chord in J.D.'s heart and he wanted to help the young man reach his dreams. "In the car you said you had something you wanted to talk to me about?"

"Yes. There's something I want to talk—" His cell phone rang and J.D. sighed, glancing at the LCD. "Excuse me," he turned away as he answered the call. "Hello? Yeah. Call me in the office tomorrow," he stated. "This is a bad time."

Shae blocked out the rest of his conversation, instead concentrating on trying to figure out what J.D. wanted to say to her. She hoped he didn't plan to stop seeing her. She really liked him and didn't want to lose his friendship or the budding romance they were establishing.

He seemed nervous. His hand constantly played with the silverware and he folded and refolded the napkin several times.

"Sorry about that," J.D. said, shoving the phone into his pocket. "Normally, I don't get a lot of calls after hours. Lately, it's been really busy."

"What do you want to say?" she asked, redirecting his thoughts back to their previous discussion.

"I know that we haven't known each other very long. And that you're used to a very different kind of life." He swallowed loudly, picking up her hand and linking their fingers. "You're new to town and there is a lot that you have to see and do before you get completely settled in, but I want to be part of your life. I want us to see each other and for you to know that I'll be available when you need me.

"I don't know how to say this. I'm embarrassed.

These feelings are new to me." J.D. held her gaze with his own. "I like you. Hopefully we've got time to get to know each other better. But I want to let you know how I feel."

Shae blew out a nervous breath of air. "J.D., I was worried that you wanted to end our relationship. To put some space and time between us. I like you, too, and I want to get to know you better."

Separating after a series of good-night kisses that had her weak in the knees and her head swimming, Shae said good night and closed the door after J.D. left. She danced through the suite on her way to her bedroom. Nothing could bring her down after the evening she enjoyed with J.D. She couldn't wait for their next date. Being with him just seemed so right. They had made plans to go car shopping tomorrow evening after work.

Shae sat on the bed and removed her diamond earrings, while she reached for the ringing telephone. "Hello."

"How's my princess?"

"Pop!"

"The one and only. Hi, sweetie."

"Hi, Pop. It's almost been a week, I was wondering when you would get around to me," she muttered.

"Princess, you know you're my number one girl. I'm sorry things got out of hand for a bit."

"Mmm. That's nothing new." She shook her head, putting her misgivings away. It was good to hear from her father and she craved news about her family. "So how are you? Or rather how is the business?"

"Everything is good. How was your first day of work?"

"How did you know today was my first day?"

"Just because I haven't talked with you doesn't mean I don't know what's going on," he reminded.

"So it seems." She twisted the telephone cord around her fingers.

"So how did it go?"

"Good. I think I'm going to be happy here. There's a lot of work ahead, but that's not a bad thing. I like to work." She chuckled. "I think I received that trait honestly."

"Mmmm. Are you trying to say that you picked that up from me?" her father asked playfully.

"Maybe."

"You're staying at the Marriott. How's that working out for you?"

"It's okay. But I want my own place. Next week I plan to do some apartment hunting."

"Don't feel you have to rush. We'll subsidize any place you want. I want you safe. That's more important than the money. You hear?"

"I hear. But, Pop, I'm fine. Remember, I'm an independently wealthy young woman. You made sure of that. I have the trust fund."

"I know. But it also worries me. You don't tell people about it, do you?"

"Of course not. That's my business."

"Good. How are you getting around?"

"I have a friend who took me to work today and we're going car shopping tomorrow."

"Friend?" He quizzed in a suspicious tone.

"Yes. We met on the flight to Chicago."

"What kind of friend?"

"A man that I met. He lives here."

Pop sneezed, then choked. It was a hard choking sound that sent shivers down her spine. Her father cleared his throat. "Excuse me. Tell me more about this guy."

Shae opened her mouth ready to discuss J.D., then halted. The last thing she wanted to do was get his suspicious nature going. At the last moment she changed topics. "How long have you had that cough? Do you have a cold?"

"No. I'm fine. What does this guy do for a living?"

"If that cough doesn't go away, you check with your doctor."

"If I get sick will you come home?"

"No. Chicago is my home now." She sat on the edge of the bed and silently waited for him to say more. He had tried this trick about two years ago. Calling her home because her mother had a heart attack. Fortunately, medication, diet and exercise solved her problems, then life went on. But Shae was very aware of her father's knack for finding reasons for her to return home.

"You know we're thinking of developing some software for a nursing program. Your expertise would be invaluable. If things don't work out with the job, you can come home and head up that division."

"Pop, don't."

"Think about it. Director of special projects."

Shae sighed. Pop was always trying to convince her to come home and work for Prestige Computers. This was not the first time that he had made her an offer like this. "Pop, I'm staying in Chicago. So stop."

Chuckling, he admitted, "Well, it was worth a shot. Whenever you decide to come home, there's a job here for you."

"I know you mean well. But this is what I want to do. Please respect my wishes, okay?"

"Okay."

"Good. So how's Mommie?

"She's good. Worried about you, of course."

"Can I say hi?"

"Sure. Let me get her."

The phone went silent as she waited for her mother to pick up the line. "Hey, Shae-Shae. How was your first day?"

"Hi, Mommie. It's good to talk with you. First day was good."

"Still at the Marriott, right?"

"Yes."

"I worry about you, baby. I don't want anything to happen to you."

"I just got through reassuring Pop that things are going fabulous. Now, what's going on with you?"

"I ran into Evan Drake. He asked about you. I told him that you had moved to Chicago and he mentioned that he might take a trip on business."

"Mommie, I'm not interested in Evan. That was over a lot of years ago. Stop matchmaking."

"I'm not. I'm not," Vivian Weitherspoon denied. "He just looked so good, I couldn't help wondering why you two broke up."

"We broke up because I wanted more out of life. My life needed to mean more than being a trophy wife to some man that doesn't value me. I'm going to say it again—stop matchmaking. I'm not moving back to Malibu. I like it here."

"Okay."

Hanging up the telephone, Shae laughed. It was good to talk to her parents. She missed their presence in her life. Maybe being in another city would help them get closer. Odd, it looked as if leaving home might be the thing that brought her family back together.

She shrugged and got off the bed, heading for the bathroom. Moving to Chicago may have been the best idea she ever had. A new boyfriend, hopefully a new apartment and a job that she suspected would fulfill her.

Things couldn't get better.

## Chapter 9

For a moment J.D. studied Shae intently, noticing how her fingers twisted the brown leather strap of her Coach handbag. Placing his hand over hers, he whispered, "Come on. Let's go in. Everything will go smooth."

Alarmed, Shae's heart jumped at the sound of his voice. Shielding her expression, she lowered her eyelids over her eyes and nodded, grabbing her purse and a brown paper bag from the backseat of the car before opening the door. Instantly, J.D. appeared at her side.

"It's going to be fine." The young man placed a protective hand at the base of her spine and guided Shae up the walkway. "My parents are really easygoing, friendly folks." Pride rang out loud and clear in J.D.'s voice. "They are going to love you."

Nervously, Shae ran a hand through her hair, thinking, *I hope so.* But her gut told her something different. It was far too early in the relationship to meet his family.

After all, Shae barely knew J.D. They had met only a little over a week ago. How would his parents react to that bit of information? Shae shuddered. Preoccupied with her troubling thoughts, Shae barely noticed the well-maintained lawn or the wonderful fragrance of azaleas that lined the walkway. Her normally keenly observant eye missed the potted plants decorating the porch.

He led her through the front door and down a foyer to the kitchen. "My mom loves to cook. Don't be surprised if there's a huge meal."

The appetizing aroma of chocolate filled the air and the young woman's belly responded, growling hungrily. Embarrassed, Shae's eyes widened and her cheeks flamed cherry-red as she gave the noisy organ a soothing pat.

The couple entered the kitchen and found a tall middle-aged woman with salt-and-pepper short hair standing behind an island. The black-and-gray speckled counter and chrome range sat in the center of the room.

"Mom," J.D. greeted.

Tearing her concentration from the recipe in front of her, Mrs. Daniels lifted her head and smiled at the pair. The older woman reached for a green, red and yellow floral printed towel and wiped her hands. "Welcome." She moved around the island toward Shae with an outstretched hand. Shyly smiling back at J.D.'s mother, Shae took Mrs. Daniels's hand in a firm handshake. The woman's kindly smile and welcoming manner loosened the tight knot in Shae's stomach. "Thank you."

"This is Shae Weitherspoon, Mom." J.D. piped in. "Shae, this is my mother, Helen Daniels."

"Thanks for having me over, Mrs. Daniels." Shae smiled.

The older woman rolled her eyes heavenward.

"Honey, my name is Helen. Only the students at my school call me Mrs. Daniels."

"Okay. Helen." Shae acknowledged the request with a tip of her head. She handed J.D.'s mother the brown paper bag. "Here's a little offering to add to your dinner table."

"You didn't have to do this, but thank you." Helen pulled a bottle of wine from the bag and glanced at the label before placing it inside the refrigerator. "I love this brand! It'll be great with dinner. Come on and meet the rest of the family. J.D., everyone is here except your father."

The trio started for the door when a buzzer went off. Helen did an about-face and headed to the shiny oven mounted in the kitchen wall. "J.D., take Shae into the family room and introduce her to everyone." Mrs. Daniels shoved her hands inside a pair of floral oven mittens that matched the dish towel and opened the oven door, quickly removing two nine-inch silver cake pans. The fragrant heat wafted through the kitchen.

J.D.'s hand slid down Shae's arm, cupped her elbow and gently guided her from the kitchen. He gave her hand a tiny tug, pulling her in the direction of the door. They left Helen to her work. The Supremes' "Baby Love" grew louder as they drew closer to the family room.

Shae stood in the doorway, taking a good look at J.D.'s family. Men and women of various ages and appearance filled the room. In many she noticed a marked resemblance to Helen Daniels.

Uncertainty made Shae hesitate. She felt like an interloper.

J.D. nudged her forward with a hand at the small of her back. "It's okay. They can be silly, but I promise they don't bite."

The couple entered a large room. In one section, two three-pillow sofas were separated by a coffee table. A marble fireplace dominated one ivory wall of the room. Photos of all sizes and shapes crammed the mantel-piece. Her gaze swung around the room and landed on a folding table blocking the patio door. Goodies of all kinds covered the top.

J.D. turned to her. "Are you hungry? Do you want something to eat?"

Shae shook her head. Even though she was hungry, her stomach was so full of butterflies, food wouldn't stay down.

A tall man dressed in denims and a gray long-sleeve T-shirt sauntered across the room. He slapped J.D. on the back. "Hey, brother man, how are you doing?"

"Good." J.D. hugged the other man. "David, this is my friend, Shae. Shae, this is my big brother, David. The pretty thing nibbling on a potato chip is his wife, Cynthia. Hey girl, come meet my friend."

Dressed in a raspberry scoop-neck top and a long, flowing denim skirt, Cynthia strolled up to the trio and kissed J.D. on the cheek. Instantly, her fingers dabbed at the lipstick on his cheek, wiping it away. "How are you doing?" She pushed her glasses up her nose, stretched out her hand and shook Shae's. "Hi, I'm Cynthia. Welcome to the Daniels's Sunday dinner." Cynthia's friendly disposition and approachable attitude made David's wife an instant hit with Shae.

She grinned back at Cynthia. "Thank you."

J.D. swept the room with his eyes. "Mom said Dad wasn't here, but where are Eddie and Jen?"

"Dad's on the golf course." David checked his wrist-watch. "He should be back any minute. Eddie and Jen are with her parents."

"Did you bring your cards, J.D.?" Cynthia asked, slipping her arm through her husband's.

David nodded. "I'm ready for a few hands of Bid Whisk."

Chuckling, J.D. removed the deck from his back pocket, displayed them for a minute, then returned the cards back to his pocket. "I'm on for after dinner. Right now let me introduce Shae to Lisa and Matthew."

Delighted by J.D.'s down-to-earth and friendly family, Shae allowed herself to be guided across the room. His mother and siblings were easy to talk to and welcomed her into their home as if she'd been part of their lives forever. Although she felt a little over-whelmed by the number of people she'd had to meet today, Shae didn't feel out of place. Relief began to replace those butterflies.

J.D. stopped in front of a couple sitting on the couch. "This is my big sister, Lisa, and her overprotective husband, Matthew," J.D. announced to Shae.

"Hey, watch what you're saying about me," Matthew warned good-naturedly as he rose from the sofa. Shae noticed that Lisa was in the final trimester of her pregnancy. She was huge.

David came up behind them. "Did you see that game last night?"

"I did," Matthew added. "It was bad, wasn't it? J.D., isn't Peters one of yours?"

Nodding sorrowfully, J.D. said, "It was an all-around bad game. I saw unprofessional sportsmanship and in-appropriate behavior. Believe me, when he gets in town Monday, we're going to talk. Actually, I've got a lecture planned for him."

"He needs it," David muttered grimly.

"Don't pay them any mind. The Daniels men are

sports addicts," Lisa explained, struggling to reach the edge of the sofa. Immediately, Matthew hurried to her side, helping her to her feet. Dressed in a fuchsia two-piece Capri set, Lisa stood next to her husband. She looked adorable, but very pregnant.

"You don't have to get up," Shae said quickly.

Lisa gave her the widest smile. "I know. But I get stiff if I sit too long."

"Is this your first?" Shae asked, pointing at Lisa's protruding belly.

Lisa nodded, then slipped her hand into the crook of Shae's arm and steered her toward the food table. "Let's get something to eat. I'm hungry."

"But I—I—I," Shae stuttered, pointing at J.D. "Shouldn't we wait for them?"

"Nah." Lisa waved a dismissive hand toward the men. "They won't miss us."

Shae observed the other woman for several quiet moments before asking, "How are you feeling?"

"Excited and nervous," Lisa admitted. "We wanted a baby and I can't wait for him to get here." Lisa glanced in the direction of the men, then lowered her voice to a soft whisper. "But at the same time I'm not looking forward to labor."

"I'm a nurse. Trust me. It'll be fine. First time mothers are always nervous."

"That's what my mom keeps saying."

"Well, Helen gave birth to five kids. I'm pretty sure she knows what she talking about." Shae touched Lisa's arm. "Things will work out just fine, but if you want to talk, give me a call."

"Thank you. That's so kind of you."

J.D. wrapped his arms around Shae's shoulders. "Sis, I'm going to whisk Shae away from you for a few minutes. I didn't finish the introductions. I have one more sister I want you to meet." He drew her along with him to the other end of the room. A young woman sat in a chair watching CNN. "This is Vanessa. We call her Vee."

Vee sat with her legs tucked under her. J.D.'s sister had beautiful brown skin and shoulder-length dread-locks. Shae hid a grin behind her hand. Vivian Weither-spoon would have had another baby if she caught anyone sitting on her precious, handcrafted furniture this way. Shae smiled at the other woman, feeling an instant connection with her. Shae really liked J.D.'s family.

With a slight nod, Vanessa said, "Hi. Have a seat."

"Thanks." Shae slid into the chair next to Vee's.

"J.D. said you're from California," Vee stated.

Nodding, Shae answered, "Malibu."

"Oh, nice."

Shrugging, the nurse added, "It's a pretty stretch of land."

"Ladies," J.D. interrupted the pair. "I'm going to talk with David and Matthew. I'll be right back."

Vee gave Shae a conspiratory grin. "Sports."

Laughing, Shae agreed, "You're the second person to tell me that."

Lisa ambled up to the two women and asked, "Can I join this conversation?"

Vee jumped to her feet. "Sure. Lisa, sit here. I'll get another chair."

For the next half hour, Shae sat with J.D.'s sisters quietly discussing everything from fashion to child rearing. The more she talked with the members of J.D.'s family, the more comfortable Shae felt among the Daniels clan.

"Dinner's on the table," Helen called from the doorway.

J.D. appeared at Shae's side and escorted her from the den. Matthew helped his wife from the sofa and strolled down the hallway to the dining room, his arm wrapped possessively around her. Cynthia and David sauntered into the room hand in hand. David took the chair at the far end of the table near his mother while Vee slipped into a seat near her dad.

A teal painted wall and silver vertical blinds framed the large bay window. A huge rosewood dining table with seating for sixteen dominated the room. J.D.'s father, Nick Daniels, sat at the head of the table. He reminded Shae of the football coaches she'd remembered from high school. Several tantalizing aromas filled Shae's nostrils. Broiled salmon, fried chicken, baked beef brisket, mashed potatoes and gravy and buttermilk cornbread were just a sample of the appetizing dishes covering the table's surface. Fresh steamed broccoli, candied carrots and green beans rounded out the meal. Everything looked heavenly. Ramsey Lewis's rendition of "Sun Goddess" filled the air as the family found their places and sat down. Everyone held hands as Mr. Daniels blessed the food. Soon platters of food made their way around the table.

"Where's the clinic that you're working at, Shae?" Helen inquired.

"South side of Chicago," Shae answered.

Worried, Helen's forehead wrinkled and she warned, "You be very careful around that area; it's not the safest."

"I will."

"Make sure you lock your car doors," Nick Daniels added, helping himself to a spoonful of mashed potatoes.

"I don't have a car yet."

Matthew asked, "How are you getting around town?"

"Don't worry. I'm Shae's taxi service until she buys a car," J.D. explained.

"Shae, do you have family here? Are you staying with them?" Vee passed the green beans to Cynthia.

"No. My family lives in Malibu. I'm staying at the Marriott."

David whistled. "Nice place. Expensive."

Cynthia popped her fingers. "Weitherspoon from Malibu. Does your family have anything to do with Prestige Computers?"

Shae nodded. J.D. had said that Cynthia and Lisa worked for a computer software company owned by Matthew. She should have known that one of them would connect the dots. "My family started it."

"Woo!" Lisa exclaimed, turning to her husband. "Matthew, don't you use Prestige's servers?"

"Yeah. They're great. Reasonably priced, energy efficient and durable."

David laughed out loud, pointing a finger in Matthew's direction. "Listen to our computer commercial."

Everyone laughed.

"Don't pay them any mind," Helen advised. "My children are quite insane."

The moment passed and Shae realized that they weren't intimidated by her background. J.D.'s big, boisterous family was fun to be around.

"How long do you plan to stay at the hotel?" Vee asked, stabbing a green bean with her fork.

"The hotel is my parents' idea." She chose a filet of catfish and passed the platter to Lisa. "They want me someplace that they believe is safe."

"You can't stay there indefinitely, can you?" Helen wondered.

"No. I've got to find my own place."

Cynthia leaned toward Shae. "What are you looking for? Anything in particular?"

Shae shrugged. "Town house…apartment…I'm not particular as long as I can call it home."

"Do you want to live downtown or in the suburbs?" David questioned, munching on a carrot.

"So far I've liked what I've seen of the downtown area. I wouldn't mind staying in the same general area," Shae answered, placing a scoop of fried corn on her plate.

Nick Daniels passed the cornbread to his right. "J.D. lives down there. He's got one of those lofts near the water. Have you seen his place?"

"Nick!" Helen admonished.

Puzzled, he asked, "What?"

An exasperated expression flashed across David's mother's face. "That's none of your business."

"What?" Mr. Daniels asked a second time, bewildered.

Helen reached out her hand to Shae, then sighed. "Excuse my husband. He's got issues."

"It's okay." Blushing, Shae studied the food on her plate. "No. I haven't seen it. David, do you know of a place?"

"Yes, I do. We just bought a house and we're looking for someone to sublet our apartment. The lease isn't up for another year."

Interested, Shae leaned closer. "Tell me more."

"It's a three-bedroom penthouse with a patio. Plus, dining room, kitchen, of course, two baths and an office, all on one floor. We're located on Lake Shore Drive. The penthouse overlooks the water."

"It sounds wonderful. But a little big for one person."

"A roommate would help." David shrugged. "That's your choice."

"Money is not my problem," Shae said softly. "When can I see it?"

David turned to his wife. "Honey?"

"Next week is fine with me. One day after work is best. Maybe Wednesday?" Cynthia suggested.

"That works for me. If I take the apartment, when would I be able to move in?"

"Within days. We've already moved into our house. Although there are some things left in the apartment because we haven't decided what to do with them. If you take the place, I promise they'll be gone when you get your keys."

"What do you do about parking? That seems to be a major problem in the downtown area." Shae took a slice of cornbread from the basket and passed it on.

"Underground parking. It's included as part of the lease."

She grinned broadly. "This makes my life so easy. If everything works out I'll have a place to live within a few days. Thank you."

"No. Thank you. We haven't started advertising because we weren't ready for the hassle." David grinned. "Maybe we won't have to deal with it."

"Maybe not," Shae agreed.

# Chapter 10

Excitement surged through Shae as she and J.D. strolled down Lake Shore Drive to David and Cynthia's apartment. "I like this block," she stated, examining the high-rises in the area. Leaning closer to J.D. she planted a soft kiss on his cheek. "Thank you for picking me up."

J.D. smiled down at Shae, stroking the soft skin of her bare arm. The familiar tingling that always accompanied his touch warmed her blood. "You're welcome, sweetheart. I don't get to see my brother very often. The bonus is I get to escort a beautiful woman at the same time."

Pleased, she blushed. The gentle breeze off Lake Michigan cooled her hot cheeks. "Thanks," she murmured in a soft voice.

A soft hum at his waist drew her attention. J.D. quickly tapped a button on his phone. "Sorry about that," he mumbled, checking the number.

"Maybe you should get it," Shae suggested.

J.D. shook his head before stopping in front of a high-rise building, pointing at the door. "This is it," he announced, cupping her elbow and leading Shae to a set of revolving doors. Seconds later Shae got her first glimpse of the lobby. A uniformed security guard waited as they approached his desk.

Mesmerized, Shae stood inside the door studying the striking image. The lobby walls were two stories high and painted a soft beige. A small visitor's area contained a plush, three-pillow couch decorated in brown, tan and cream, sitting opposite two tan-and-cream-striped chairs. A square-shaped glass-top table completed the sitting area, and a large floral arrangement added the final touch to the spot. Framed watercolor paintings hung over the sofa.

J.D. leaned close to Shae and whispered, "The lobby is bigger than my apartment."

Shae laughed, taking another glance at the surrounding area. "It's pretty impressive. What did you say your brother does for a living?"

"Attorney."

J.D. guided Shae to the security guard. She hid a smile. One point for her mother. Vivian Weitherspoon would love knowing that her daughter's apartment had twenty-four-hour paid security.

"How you doing, Clay?" J.D. asked.

"Not bad," the guard answered. "Here to see your brother?"

J.D. nodded.

"Hold on." Clay picked up a phone and punched in a number. Seconds later, the guard waved a hand at the bank of elevators. "Go on up. They're expecting you."

Silently, they waited at the elevator. Shae studied the

architectural structure of the building before asking, "How long have David and Cynthia lived here?"

"He rented this place before they got married." The hum of his cell phone interrupted and J.D glanced at the screen before continuing, "Maybe four years."

A bit annoyed by the constant ringing of his phone, Shae suggested, "You should really answer that. I don't think he's going to stop calling."

"Don't worry about it. It's Amir. There's always a crisis in that boy's life."

Nodding, Shae asked, "Are David and Cynthia newlyweds?"

"I guess so. Maybe. They've been married a little over a year. They've been together since high school."

"Wow! That's a long time." Shae compared the short period that she had known J.D. and wondered if they were moving too quickly. After all, the pair had known each other a sum total of two weeks and in that time J.D. had wined and dined her, brought Shae home to meet his family and played chauffeur until she purchased her Volvo. Disregarding these pesky doubts, Shae glanced at J.D. and felt the warm, happy feelings that she'd come to associate with him. Shae knew for certain that J.D. played a major role in how smoothly her life had gone since she moved to Chicago.

They entered the elevator and J.D. punched the button for the twenty-fifth floor. He took a step closer to Shae and rubbed her back. "Don't feel obligated to do anything that you don't feel comfortable with. If this place isn't right for you, we'll keep looking."

As she smiled at J.D. she realized how much she appreciated all the things he did for her. "Thanks. But I've liked everything that I've seen so far."

At the door to the penthouse, Shae glanced up and

down the hallway. This was a well-maintained building. Clean tan carpeting greeted them when they stepped from the elevator. The walls were painted in the shade of beige she'd seen in the lobby. The hallway and apartment entrances were free of handbills and noise from the other apartments.

J.D. rang the bell, then took a step away from the door. It swung open and David Daniels stood in the foyer. "Hey, brother man. Hi, Shae. Come on in."

Cynthia stood behind her husband. "Hey, you two. Welcome."

The Danielses moved aside, allowing Shae to precede them into the apartment. While she headed to the living room, she drew in a deep breath. A sense of peace and comfort enfolded her. Her fingers stroked the gold vertical blinds as she quickly acclimated herself to the room and her surroundings. Looking around, she realized that although this place was larger than what she needed or wanted, it felt right. It could easily become her home.

Shae moved through the living room and halted at a door that led to a patio. The balcony beckoned her to take a quick peek. She complied, moving through the doors and onto the patio. The view was spectacular. The air was brisk. It whipped across her cheeks, turning them red. She stood at the railings, watching the traffic below. If she agreed to take over the apartment, she would certainly sit out here, relax and enjoy the fresh air.

"Shae," Cynthia called from the doorway. "Are you ready to see the rest of the place?"

Smiling, Shae reentered the apartment. "Yes."

Cynthia led Shae through the apartment, stopping in the dining room, then continued down a hallway. She threw open the door to the master bedroom and moved aside so that Shae entered first. Fascinated, Shae moved around the room, admiring the mushroom-colored carpet and the king size bed. "This is lovely," Shae exclaimed.

"As you already know, there are three bedrooms and two baths. The master bedroom has its own bathroom and the other is down the hall." Cynthia leaned against the door and waited as Shae examined the room.

"Are the other bedrooms as large as this one?"

"Oh no. I use the smallest as my office and the third room is for guests. They're comfortable, but not huge. Let me show them to you, then we'll take a look at the kitchen."

Minutes later, Cynthia showed Shae a white-and-blue tiled kitchen. The room looked as if it had never been touched. White cabinets trimmed in blue wrapped around the walls of the kitchen. A granite island included a stainless steel range and grill that looked brand-new. Shae turned to Cynthia with a question in her eyes.

Cynthia shrugged, admitting shyly, "I don't cook much. David works late a lot and I don't like to cook for one. I can live with a sandwich and a lot of nights I do."

Nodding, Shae ran a hand over the spotless countertop. She would love spending an evening here trying her hand at new recipes.

"We have a lady that comes in once a week to clean. If you're interested, let me know and I'll put you in touch with her."

"That would be good. I suspect that I'll need someone." Shae leaned against the island. "The clinic will probably keep me pretty busy for the next few weeks and I can use the help."

David entered the kitchen and wrapped his arms

around his wife's waist and nuzzled her neck. Shae glanced beyond him. "Where's J.D.?"

"On the phone with a client. That Amir kid is going to drive my brother crazy," he said.

"Oh," Shae said, peeved that J.D. was more focused on Amir. It bugged her that this kid kept interfering whenever they were together. Sighing, Shae turned away. It wasn't Shae's place to say anything, but she truly wanted to. She took a deep, calming breath.

"So, Shae, what do you think?" David asked. "Are you interested?"

Cynthia elbowed her husband in the side. He faked a painful moan. "Ow!" She wagged a hand at David and stated confidently, "I didn't hurt you. Leave Shae alone. She needs time to decide what she wants to do."

"No. No. I'm fine. I like this place a lot." Shae turned toward the living room. "Let's talk money, then we can discuss when I can move in."

"All right!" David and Cynthia cheered in unison, giving each other a high five.

Back at her hotel, Shae stretched out on the comforter, counting the number of times the telephone rang before someone picked up the line. On the fifth ring her mother answered, "Hello?"

"Hi, Mommie."

"Shae-Shae!" Her mother's greeting was filled with pleasure. "I'm so glad you called. How are you, baby?"

"Good.

"We haven't talked for a bit. How's your job?"

"It's been really busy," Shae explained, wrapping the telephone cord around her finger. "We're opening the first of May. I had to hire all of the staff, plus train them and stay under budget."

"Budgets, yuck!"

Chuckling, Shae rolled onto the right side of the bed, cradling the phone between her chin and shoulder. "I have to adhere to them or I won't keep my job very long."

"I'm glad everything is going well. How about other things? Are you all right? Do you need anything?"

Shae took in a deep breath of air, then let it out slowly. "Actually, I wanted to let you know that I'll be moving next week."

"Really? You found a place? Where? Apartment or house?" Her mother's voice dropped as she added in a disapproving tone, "You're not moving near the clinic, are you?"

"No. It's an apartment in the downtown area. And I really like it."

"Good! Tell me more," Vivian Weitherspoon encouraged.

Shae slid her legs off the bed and dropped them on the floor. She rubbed her bare toes into the thick carpet. "It's a high-rise penthouse with three bedrooms on Lake Shore Drive."

"Excellent." Her mother's pleased tone oozed through the telephone lines. "It sounds very nice. How did you luck into a place like that? And so quickly. I expected it to take weeks, maybe even months."

"Did I tell you that the building has twenty-four-hour security? Plus it has a wonderful kitchen with all the gadgets." Nervous, she pushed forward, ignoring her mother's questions. "Can you image me whipping up a meal? I haven't had to cook for myself since my college days."

"That's nice," her mother said cautiously. "But you didn't answer my question. How did you find this apartment?"

This was what Shae was dreading, telling her mother about David and Cynthia. Her mother saw danger at every turn and she didn't approve of the bond developing between Shae and J.D. Vivian Weitherspoon felt that the relationship between her daughter and this unknown man was evolving much too quickly.

Shae didn't see her mother's attitude changing anytime soon, so giving Vivian this additional ammunition would probably make life more difficult. She hesitated for a minute, wanting to keep this part of her news to herself, but she knew that she owed her mother the truth.

Shae cleared her throat before answering, "My friend J.D. It's his brother's apartment."

A pregnant pause followed Shae's comment. After a moment, her mother replied, "Really?"

"Yeah. David, J.D.'s brother, and his wife just bought a house," she rushed on, hoping to avoid any additional questions. "They have another year on the lease. I'm going to sublet. It was a stroke of luck that I found out about it."

"Really?"

"Mmm-hmm."

"Shae," her mother began in a slow, ominous tone.

"I don't want to hear it, Mommie," Shae warned.

"Honey, stop. You have to hear it."

Shae sighed loudly.

"You have an excellent mind. Stop and use it. Honey, don't you feel that you're getting a tad too entangled with this young man's life and family? You've only know him a few weeks. Think about it. Why would he want to do all these things for you? This man wines and dines you. You have Sunday meals with his family. Now you're going to rent his brother's apartment. I can't help wondering why he's so accommodating."

"Because he likes me, Mommie. That's why. He's helping me get settled in Chicago."

"Mmm," Mommie muttered. "Shae, have you told J.D. anything about your father?"

"No." That wasn't true. "Actually when I had dinner with the Danielses, J.D.'s sister-in-law Cynthia put the name and the city together."

"Oh, honey. You know you need to be careful. Pop and I have always sheltered and watched over you. You're too far away for us to do that now. Remember, there are unsavory people who will take advantage of you or, even worse, hurt you."

"I know how to take care of myself, Mommie. I haven't lived at home in years and I've done fine so far. Don't worry. J.D. is a good guy. He won't hurt me. We're fine."

"Honey, everyone puts their best foot forward when they first meet. It takes a while for the truth to come out and you see the real person. Your new friends just seem too perfect. Everything you need, he provides. Why?"

"Mom, stop. I called to tell you about my new apartment. I'm not going to let you slander J.D. Or take shots at our relationship. He's been perfect."

"Oh, baby."

Shae felt as if she were back in grade school with her mother scolding her over a problem in class. When would they ever let her be an adult?

A change of topic was in order. "Mommie, is Pop home?"

Her mother stopped talking for a moment. "He's taking a nap."

"It's only six o'clock in Malibu. Are you sure he's okay?"

"Your father is fine."

"It's been awhile since I've talked to him," Shae reminded.

"He hears about you through me. Of course, I let him know how you're settling in."

"I'd like to talk with him. Hear for myself that he's okay. Would you tell him that a return call would be nice?"

"Of course."

"Thanks."

"I'll have him call you. Maybe he can talk some sense into you," Mommie promised.

"Good night, Mommie."

"Good night, Shae-Shae."

# Chapter 11

Fragrant steam rose from the spout of Shae's teapot as she moved down the empty clinic corridor on her way to the medical director's office. In the doorframe, she announced, "Tea time."

Dr. Reid gazed up at her from his computer screen, confusion spreading across his face. "What?"

She lifted the teapot decorated in blue and white so that Kenyatta recognized it. Two matching mugs hung from the fingers of her other hand. "Tea. Green tea to be exact."

Swiveling his chair so that it faced the door instead of the computer side bar, the doctor tossed his pen on the surface. "I could use a break. Come on in."

"Thank you." She crossed the floor and placed the mugs and pot on his desk, then returned to the door. "I'll be back in a moment. I've got shortbread cookies in my office."

Minutes later she reentered the room with a red-and-black box of cookies. Shae poured Kenyatta a cup of tea; she opened a cellophane-wrapped package and offered him a piece of shortbread. "This is a tradition I started at my last job. It gave the staff an opportunity to unwind at the end of the week and talk about any situation that needed resolving…a sort of cool down period. Once we're up and running, I plan to initiate tea time on Fridays for about thirty minutes before we close."

Kenyatta bit into a cookie. "It sounds like a good idea to me. Do whatever makes you and them feel like a team."

After pouring herself a cup of tea, Shae sank into the chair opposite him. "Here's an update. All of the staff has been hired. Everyone should be in-house by the end of next week."

"Good. I'm glad to hear that you've finished that project." The medical director leaned back in his chair, sipping his drink.

With a giggle Shae added, "Expect this place to be a zoo next week. Orientation will start next Monday for the nursing staff. The tech people, blood, machines and X-ray will begin the following week. I plan to work with the clerical and billing staff for two days before we open. We should be able to hit your target date for a May first opening."

"Excellent!" He offered her an approving smile. "I knew you could do it."

She chuckled. "Well, I'm glad you were so confident. I had my doubts. I didn't believe I could get everyone hired so quickly."

"It was a piece of cake for you," he said with confidence. "FYI, the last of the equipment will be delivered this week and assembled by the end of next week. Everything is shaping up pretty good."

"Yes, it is." Shae reached into the pocket of her lab coat and handed him a small card. "Beginning next week this will be my address."

"Wow! That didn't take long." The clinic director pursed his lips as he studied the card. "Nice address. It wasn't that long ago that you were asking me about places in this area."

"That's true." Shae acknowledged his comment with a nod of her head. "Things came together for me."

"How so?"

"I found this place by sheer accident. It's a beautiful apartment. It's got a balcony, three bedrooms and a home office. The penthouse has a large living and dining room. It's perfect," she explained.

"How did you stumble on this gem?"

She smiled. "Pure luck. My friend J.D.'s brother leased the apartment. They just bought a house and needed to sublet."

"They?"

"Yeah." Shae poured tea into both their mugs. "David and Cynthia. They still have a year on the lease. I'm taking it over."

He grimaced.

"What?"

"Shae, I'm going to say something you're not going to like. As well as being your boss, I hope you consider me a friend. Please don't take this the wrong way."

Instantly she stiffened against whatever Kenyatta plan to say. "Maybe you shouldn't say it."

"I think I should. For a man that you've just met, you're way too involved in J.D.'s life. You've only known the guy a month or so. Yet he's been your personal chauffeur from the first day you started here. Dinner every night. Now, he's helped you find the perfect apartment. Don't you think he's a little too good to be true? Could he have his own agenda?"

Silently sitting at the desk, she watched the doctor. What was going on? Kenyatta was the second person to warn her about J.D. Was it jealousy? Or true concern for her? She wasn't sure. Shae expected this from her parents. Villains lurked behind every door. They were always concerned that some man might take advantage of their little girl.

But Kenyatta was different. He didn't know her.

"What do you have against J.D.?"

"Nothing. My concern is for you." He reached across the wood surface to squeeze her hand.

Shae snatched her hand away, placing it in her lap. "I know enough about him, thank you."

He raised his hands in an act of surrender. "Sorry. I didn't mean to offend. I hired you and I feel obligated to warn you when I feel something isn't quite right. You're new to Chicago and you acquired a boyfriend before you set foot on Illinois soil. Plus, you've got that wealthy family connection. All I'm saying is, be careful. Take your time. Don't get so involved that you can't shake him."

Shae opened her mouth to counter his remarks. Kenyatta waved away her comment before a word left her lips. "I won't mention it again."

"Good."

Kenyatta lifted his mug to his lips. "Let's finish our tea. Okay?"

"It sounds good to me."

They sat for several awkward minutes before Shae glanced at her watch and rose. "It's late and I've got a few errands to run before I go home." She picked up the teapot and the cookies. "Do you want any more?"

He shook his head. "No thanks. I'm good. You take care and I'll see you tomorrow."

"I will."

The doctor turned to his computer and tapped the space bar.

Shae took the teapot and mug into the kitchen and rinsed them, placing the items inside the dishwasher before strolling to her office to retrieve her purse and briefcase. She slipped out the employee exit to the parking lot and found Desmond waiting near her car.

"Hi, Miss Shae."

"Hi, Desmond." She glanced beyond him, searching for his sibling. "Where's your brother?"

"At home."

"Honey, does your mother know you're down here?"

He shook his head. "I snuck out."

"Why?"

"I like that candy you gave me. Can I have some more?"

She retrieved a vitamin C drop from her purse and handed it to the child. "Here you go."

"Thank you."

"What if something happened to you when you snuck out? No one would know where you went. You can't do that, honey."

Shamefaced, Desmond promised, "I won't do it again. But can I have some more candy?"

She laughed and put a handful of vitamin C drops in his pocket. "Absolutely."

As usual, Desmond had a runny nose and his eyes were watery. The cold hadn't gone away. Shae checked his temperature by placing her hand on his forehead. "Do you still have your cold?"

"Little bit," he explained.

Shae dug inside her purse and removed a pack of tissue. Crooking her finger at the boy, she wiped Desmond's nose. Once she was done, Shae stuffed the package of tissues inside the pocket of his jeans. Withdrawing a second handful of vitamin drops from her purse, Shae handed them to Desmond.

"Thank you," Desmond said, unwrapping a vitamin drop and popping it into his mouth. He stuffed the remaining drops into his pocket.

"Make sure you share them with your brothers and sisters." She glared down at him. "I don't want you to come down here alone. You could get hurt. Understand?"

He nodded.

"Come on. I'm going to drive you home." She took his hand and led him through the parking lot to her sage-green Volvo coupe. After snapping him into his seatbelt, she hurried around the hood of the car and got in. "Okay, young man, we're going to your house."

They zoomed out of the parking lot and headed down the street to the opposite end of the block. "Desmond, do you like bananas or oranges?"

Nodding, he answered, "A little."

"How about grapes or pineapples?"

"What's a pineapple?"

"It's a juicy fruit from Hawaii."

His forehead wrinkled as he considered the question. "I like grapes. Momma says we don't have a lot of money for stuff."

"I'll tell you what. If you have your brother bring you to the clinic tomorrow, I'll have a surprise for you. But you have to promise to come with Sterling. I don't want you out and about by yourself."

"What kind of surprise?"

"Something to eat. Something special," Shae promised. "Come in the afternoon, okay?"

"Okay."

"Good. Which house is yours?"

He pointed at a two-family flat with broken front stairs. "That's my house."

Shae parked at the curb, unbuckled Desmond's seat belt and helped him from the car. Taking his hand, she said, "I'm coming in with you."

They went to the side door and Desmond let them in. Still holding her hand, he led her through the kitchen to the living room. Sterling and a young girl sat on the sofa, watching television. Oprah's voice boomed from the television in the living room.

Desmond hurried to the couch and grabbed the young girl's hand. He pulled her along behind him. "This is my sister, Kaon."

Smiling at the young girl, Shae shook hands and added, "Nice to meet you."

Kaon smiled shyly, then offered a soft "Hi" before returning to her spot on the sofa.

Shae did a quick examination of the house. The windows were covered with plastic. Although it was a spring day, the temperature tended to drop below fifty at night. The heat kicked in, blowing a lukewarm steam into the room. A rug was shoved against the door to keep out drafts. The heating systems and broken windows explained the runny noses.

At that moment a tall, brown-skinned woman in her midthirties entered the room through the dining area. She was carrying a basket of cleaned clothes. "Oh!" she exclaimed, surprised to find a strange woman in her living room.

"I'm sorry." Shae stretched out her hand. "Hi. I'm

Shae Weitherspoon. I work at the clinic down the street."

"I'm Anne Walls. Is something wrong?" She asked, studying her children for any signs of injury.

"No. I met Desmond and Sterling a couple of weeks ago outside the clinic." Smiling, she glanced at the youngest member of the family. "He told me that he snuck out of the house while you were busy. I decided to bring him home."

"Thank you." She turned to her son. "Desmond, what were you doing out of the house?"

He shrugged. "I wanted to see Miss Shae. I like her."

Shae laughed, drawing the child against her side. "I like him, too. He promised me that he wouldn't come alone again. Although he's welcome to come and see me anytime." Turning to the small boy, she reminded him, "Don't forget about tomorrow."

"I won't."

"Good bye." She smiled at Anne Walls. "It was nice meeting you. Bye, Desmond, Kaon and Sterling."

"Bye," they sang in unison.

Shae left through the side door and climbed into the car. Her thoughts lingered to Desmond's family. They could use a bit of assistance. There had to be companies or charities in the Chicago area that offered help to people in need. She stroked her chin as she considered canvassing the area for donations.

Maybe she could tap into the medical community for resources to help Mrs. Walls receive some much needed low-cost home repairs. New windows and doors would help the kids' runny noses.

Shae started the engine, then pulled away from the

curb, intent on getting to the grocery store. First, she needed to pick up some fruit and vitamin drops for the Walls family. Tomorrow, she'd check into ways to help them.

# Chapter 12

Yawning, Shae stretched her arms above her head, twisting from side to side as she tried to relieve the tension in her shoulders. With a short time to go before the clinic officially opened, everyone was overloaded with work. Behind her desk, Shae swiveled in her chair toward the window, admiring the late afternoon sky.

Delighted, she laughed out loud when she noticed a familiar pair. Desmond and Sterling had cut across the basketball court next door, heading down the street toward their home. In Desmond's hand she saw an orange. Strolling beside his brother, he munched on a banana while carrying a brown paper bag that Shae had stuffed with seedless grapes, peaches, plums, raisins and almonds. *Good,* she thought. Those items would help them get healthier.

Each afternoon for the past week the boys had dropped by the clinic after Sterling completed his school day. A bag of fruit and goodies waited for them at the front desk for them. The fruit would fight off colds and strengthen their immune systems.

Shae gnawed on her bottom lip while tapping her pen against the desk surface. There had to be another way to help families in the community without committing herself to grocery shopping and feeding them on a daily basis. Although Shae didn't mind buying fruit for the Walls family, as a long-term solution to their dietary problems, it didn't work. Besides, she sensed that Mrs. Walls felt uncomfortable with Shae's generosity. Anne Walls appeared to be a proud woman who struggled alone, doing the best she could with what she had, never asking for handouts or favors.

The solution lay in what Mrs. Walls fed her family. What and how much they ate of unhealthy foods or empty calories played a major role in their health. Desmond and his siblings needed more fruits and vegetables in their diet. Shae felt certain that Mrs. Walls bought the food items she could afford and prepared meals according to her financial situation.

An idea blossomed as Shae unearthed her yellow pad from the pile of work on her desk. What if she came up with a reasonably inexpensive diet plan which included healthful menus? A menu and recipes would be a big step to solving their problems, if the family would follow it.

*Soup,* she thought, writing it on her pad. A big hearty pot of soup with plenty of vegetables would boost their immune systems. Chicken soup topped her list. Soup could be stretched into several meals, as a side dish or the main course.

Doodling, in the left hand margin of the sheet, Shae frowned. Fresh vegetables were expensive. Daily re-

quirements could destroy a budget. A reasonable alternative choice would be canned goods or frozen veggies
that would be cheaper and last longer, plus go further.
Also, there were quite a few stores that sold dented
cans for less. Potatoes, rice or noodles would add bulk
to the one-pot meal.

Soup worked for dinner a couple of days a week, but
what about the other daily meals? Oatmeal with raisins
or canned fruit for breakfast would do just fine. A large
container of oatmeal would last for weeks. Forget those
empty carbs that came from sugarcoated cold cereal.
Oatmeal offered more nutritional value.

Additional ideas formed in her mind. There were
lots of ways to cut corners and still provide a family
with healthy and tasty meals. All Shae needed to do was
create a meal plan for two weeks. Once Mrs. Walls got
comfortable with the menus, she could adjust it to fit
the needs of her family.

Warming to the idea, Shae logged on to the Internet
and got busy. A knock on the door pulled her from her
work. Shae glanced at the clock and was surprised to
see that she'd been working from several hours. "Come
in," the young nurse called, returning to her computer.

Paula, the new office manager, poked her head inside
the office. "I didn't think you were still here. But if you're
busy, I can come back later." Although she'd only been
in the office for three days, Paula was a whiz at organizing everything from making coffee in the morning to negotiating the best deal for medical and office supplies.

At nearly six feet, the coffee-colored woman wore
thick African braids that brushed her shoulders. She
was an imposing figure who got the attention and
received the respect of her colleagues. Paula took her
job very seriously and made Kenyatta's and Shae's lives

easier. The resources available to her were numerous and she wasn't afraid to call on anyone who could help get this clinic up and running.

Leaning back in her chair, Shae waved Paula inside. "I'm not busy. Come on in."

"I'm sorry to disturb you, but Dr. Reid wanted me to confirm that you'll be available for the leadership meeting Thursday at seven a.m.?"

Shae turned the page on her calendar, and nodded. "I'll be there."

Paula looked around the office. "I love the color of the walls."

"So do I," Shae agreed.

"Did you decide how you wanted your office painted?" The tall woman moved across the room and stood in front of the desk.

"No. On my first day I walked into this room and it was perfect. I really like it. It's soothing."

"It sure is," Paula agreed. "I wanted to make certain I've got everything correct. Lunch for the staff. I've made the copies and confirmed Dr. Reid's appearance at the meeting. Is there anything else you want me to do before I leave for the day?"

"Maybe." Shae hesitated, considering a request that wasn't truly part of Paula's job. "You're local, right?"

"Born and raised in Chicago," the office manager answered. "What do you need?"

"I've met a family that can use some assistance. Mrs. Walls is a single mother with three children who could use a professional to look at her furnace, possibly find some firm that will help get replacement windows and front steps for her home."

Laughing out loud, Paula sank into the empty chair across from Shae. "You don't ask for much, do you?"

Shae tossed her hands into the air. "I'm sorry. I don't mean to add to your already busy day. But I truly believe that our jobs include helping the people in this community and that's what I plan to do. If we canvass some of the larger companies that offer charity work or financial resources to boost their visibility, we might be able to help Mrs. Walls and start a circle of resources that will support our patient base."

A knowing expression settled on Paula's stern face. "This doesn't have anything to do with those little boys that come by every day for that bag of goodies, does it?"

Shae shrugged, smiling sheepishly. "You got me. I met Desmond and Sterling my first day here. When I left the building, they were playing outside the door and we started talking. Since then, they show up here and there and little by little they've worked their way into my heart. I've been to their home and met the rest of the family. If we can find people or organizations willing to either do the work or make a donation, that would work."

"I'm right with you. Our role in the community goes beyond medical care. We must help the people in any way we can." Stroking her chin, Paula mused, "I can think of a few agencies that specialize in providing support to needy families. I'll get on this tomorrow."

"Thanks." Shae tore the page from her yellow pad and handed the menu to Paula. "By the way, I've been working on a nutritional plan for families similar to the Walls's. Please type it, make it look pretty, then copy and have this available at the front desk. That way our patients can pick up copies before leaving the clinic."

The secretary glanced at the yellow sheets. Her eyebrows rose. "Very interesting. You've worked pretty hard on this."

"Thanks. I want to help as much as I can. The proper foods will go a long way to supporting more healthy lifestyles."

The older woman studied the list for a beat. "Have you considered proteins like tuna or chicken salad? Add a few noodles or macaroni and you've got a decent meal that is fairly inexpensive to prepare. Plus, that'll be another meal that can stretch for a couple of days."

"Good idea," Shae agreed, taking the yellow sheet and adding Paula's suggestions.

"There's nothing like a pot of good hearty beans to stick to your ribs and fill you up. Trust me, I know."

Shae spread her hands wide. "This menu isn't written in stone. I'm open to any and all suggestions."

Paula rose from the chair and started across the room. "I'll get right on this."

"You don't have to do this ASAP. I know you have a lot of work to do. Just incorporate it into the stuff. But make certain it's ready for our opening day. Please."

"Will do."

"Thanks, Paula."

"You're welcome. Anything to help," Paula replied as she slipped out the door.

# Chapter 13

During J.D.'s college years, his group of buddies established a weekly ritual of meeting at their favorite sports bar. Almost ten years later, the Friday night tradition reminded intact. Normally, J.D. loved this interaction. Since meeting Shae, J.D. had foregone the weekly card games and sports discussions in favor of dinner and time spent with her. After a call from his best friend, Phil, J.D. had decided to put in an appearance before heading over to Shae's.

Downtown Michigan Avenue played host to a string of bars and lounges, and the Sports Extreme Bar was among them. When J.D. strolled into the darkened interior, all manner of memorabilia greeted him. Baseballs and bats, tennis rackets, and the uniforms of noted Chicago Bulls greats decorated the walls.

Brian, Marlon and Phil waved J.D. over to their table. His buddies sat before a fifty-inch flat panel television, watching a basketball game. A pitcher of beer passed from man to man as they refilled their glasses and munched on peanuts and pretzels.

The Chicago Bulls player jumped and shot, but missed the basket. Brian groaned, "Ah man! What is wrong with these guys tonight? They need to stop partying all night, get some rest so that they can play the game."

"Come on." Marlon swallowed a mouthful of beer. "Everybody is entitled to an off night."

J.D. slid into a chair at the table and grabbed a mug, filling it with the frothy brew. "What's going on?" he asked, bringing the mug to his lips.

"Who is that?" Marlon asked, shocked, putting a hand to his forehead. "The face seems somewhat familiar, but I'm not sure I remember him. Wait a minute—it's coming to me, David or Dennis. Something like that." He snapped his fingers. "I remember. It's Daniels."

"Ha ha. Very funny." J.D. reached for a pretzel.

Phil inserted himself between J.D. and Marlon, reaching for the beer pitcher. "Leave my buddy alone. He's in love." Phil slapped J.D. on the back. "And we all know what that'll do to a guy."

"Make him act crazy," Brian replied, scooping a handful of peanuts into his hands.

"Forget his friends," offered Marlon.

Ignoring Brian and Marlon, J.D. focused on his best friend. "Shut up, Phil. That's my business."

Marlon shook his head, then teased, "Wrong answer, my man. You've been holding this hand too close to your chest, J.D. What's going on? Who is this woman and why is she so special?"

Nervous, J.D. removed his deck of cards and began to shuffle the deck. He didn't want them dissecting

Shae the way they did most women, evaluating her at-
tributes and rating her performance in bed. Shae was
special and she deserved his respect and support.

"Are you afraid to let us know anything about this one?
After all, we're the ones that you've been ignoring. And
when everything falls apart, we're the ones that will have
to listen to you moan and piss."

J.D. dropped the complete deck of cards on the table
and shot back, "That's not going to happen."

Brian placed his hands over the cards and studied his
buddy. "This sounds serious, J.D. Is it?"

"Maybe. It's too early to tell." J.D. slipped off the chair,
leaned over Marlon and pointed a finger in his face. "You
don't know what you're talking about. What makes you
think you know anything about her or our relationship?"

Laughing, Marlon taunted, "Oh! Defensive, aren't
you?"

"Look, I don't appreciate the joke."

Everyone around the table grew quieter.

Marlon used his foot to push away from the table.
"I'm sorry, man. I didn't mean to cause you any drama.
Are we cool?"

Nodding, J.D. returned to his chair, picked up his
beer mug and said, "We're cool."

Brian slapped J.D. on the back and asked, "She's
special to you, so we want to know more about her."

They wouldn't let him out of the bar without giving
away some details. "Shae's a nurse practitioner working
at a clinic on the South Side. She just moved to Chicago
from California." J.D. wanted to be careful about how
much information she told his friends. He knew Shae
wanted a new life in Chicago and didn't want to be as-
sociated with her parents and the life she shared with
them before moving to Chicago.

"When do we meet this pillar?" Marlon asked with a note of spite in his tone.

"Never," J.D. answered promptly, nibbling on a pretzel.

Brian moved his chair closer to J.D. and asked, "Are you afraid we'll take her away from you?"

"No. I don't want your ugly faces to frighten her. It might send her back to California."

Silent until now, Phil added his questions to the group. "So, she's a California babe? Did she do the same kind of work?"

"Yeah. She worked as a nurse when she lived in Malibu."

Marlon folded his arms across his chest and asked, "You're not holding out on us, are you, buddy? California is an expensive place to live."

"No." J.D. grinned at his friends. "The bunch of you guys will scare her silly." His phone rang. "Excuse me." He stepped away from the table. "Hello?"

"Mr. Daniels?"

"Yes?"

"This is Susan Jonson. Amir's mother."

"What can I do for you Mrs. Jonson?"

She sighed sorrowfully. "I need some help with Amir. He came home drunk last night and I smelled marijuana on his clothes. The minute he came home, he fell right into bed."

J.D. groaned silently. They just had a serious discussion about his classes and career two weeks ago. What had he done in life to make this kid the client from hell? "Did he go to school today? Has he completed any of the assignments that his professors gave him?"

"I don't know," Mrs. Jonson answered helplessly. "Amir left home this morning like he was on his way to school. But I can't guarantee that he made it to class.

His friends picked him up. So there's no telling where they went today."

Shaking his head, he said, "I'm on my way. Give me about a half hour to get to your place."

"Thank you, Mr. Daniels."

"No problem. See you soon." J.D. slipped the phone into his pocket, returned to the table and dropped a twenty next to his glass. "I've got to go."

Phil studied his friend. "What was that all about? Is something wrong?"

"One of my clients needs an attitude adjustment." J.D. fished his keys from the pocket of his denims. "See you guys next week."

"Later." Phil slapped J.D. on the back.

When J.D. reached the door, he waved at the group before leaving the bar. He climbed into his car, then pulled out his cell phone. He sat for a minute collecting his thoughts.

He ran a hand over his shaved head. This was not the evening he planned. Mrs. Jonson's call had brought an issue into focus that had begun to trouble him. How do you balance your professional and personal lives so that everyone is happy? At this moment J.D. felt that Amir dominated his life.

Shae had been very understanding whenever his job took center stage. That wouldn't last forever. Shae was important to J.D. and he didn't want to screw this relationship up. There had to be a way to balance the areas of his life so that everyone was happy. The demands of his job were weighing heavily on J.D.'s mind as he tried to maintain his friendships, do his job and manage a developing romance. Amir's problems were difficult, but nothing beyond his reach. Timing was the issue bothering J.D.

"Hello?"

"Shae, it's me."

"Hi, J.D. Are you on your way?"

"Actually, I'm not going to make it tonight."

"Oh." That one word revealed her disappointment. "Is everything all right?"

"Yeah." He scratched the side of his neck. "That client of mine is in trouble again. You know, the one I told you about at dinner a couple of weeks ago."

"Amir."

"Right. His mother just called and she needs some help with him. I'm going over to their house and, if things go the way they've been going with Amir, it'll take a bit of convincing to get him back on the straight and narrow path."

"I understand. You be careful and I'll see you tomorrow."

"Shae?"

"Yes?"

"I'm sorry, honey. I was looking forward to spending the evening with you."

"Don't worry about it, J.D. I've got plenty of work to keep me occupied." Her voice dropped a level. "I'm sorry that I won't see you tonight. Be careful and I'll talk to you tomorrow."

# Chapter 14

"Where are we headed?" Shae asked, enjoying the warm spring sun kissing her skin as she strolled along Michigan Avenue with J.D.'s sister.

"We're going to Water Tower Place," Vee answered, brushing a handful of dreadlocks away from her face. "There are eight levels of shopping. You should be able to find everything you need for your apartment."

Nodding, Shae glanced around them. People, street vendors, taxis and buses zoomed up and down Michigan Avenue. She found it difficult to keep up and take in everything at the same time.

Vee grabbed Shae's upper arm. "Hold on." Vee stopped at a Good Humor Ice Cream truck and bought a Strawberry Crunch Bar. She unwrapped the ice cream bar on a stick, then looked at Shae and asked, "Want one?"

"Sure."

Seconds later they continued their stroll as they munched on their goodies. Shae studied the other woman from the top of her head to the fitted denim shorts. Why had Vee extended this invitation to shop?

J.D.'s family had been extremely nice to her. Although she enjoyed Vee's company, she didn't want to be a burden. "J.D. put you up to this, didn't he?"

"No," Vee vetoed with a wave of her free hand, sucking the last bite of ice cream into her mouth. As the women passed a trash bin, Vee tossed the wooden stick and paper wrapper in the wire basket. Shae repeated the gesture. "He's a man. Their brains aren't wired that way," Vee answered.

Laughing, Shae shook her head. "You are too funny."

"No, really. When I met you I thought you were a nice person. And you did pretty well considering the Daniels clan was gazing down your throat, checking your tonsils and counting your teeth."

Giggling softly, Shae felt she should object. "They weren't that bad."

"Right," Vee drawled, rolling her eyes. "Seriously, this was my idea. You're new in town and I thought you might appreciate a little girl time. I'm sure my brother is fascinating company, but things like buying clothes and cosmetics are meant for women to share. Since I don't think you know many people in town and I'm a bit of a loner myself, this is a great opportunity to get to know each other. I thought you might want a friend to talk with."

"Vee, it would be great to have a friend to share things with," Shae admitted, stopping at the traffic light as cars and trucks zipped by.

"Then I'll be that person for you. Fair enough?" Vee slipped her hand through the crook of Shae's arm.

Nodding, Shae grinned. "Fair enough."

Having a close friend would be wonderful. From childhood her parents had maintained a watchful eye over her friends and, later, dates, cautioning her against allowing strangers to get too close. Growing up, Shae had only managed to make a few close friends. She'd lost touch with them after college. They had scattered in different directions and established unique lives away from Malibu.

J.D.'s sister patted Shae's hand. "Good."

"Vee, what do you do?"

Shrugging, Vee answered, "I've followed in the family tradition of school teachers. I teach calculus at one of the high schools and do a few community college courses each year. Plus I help out in a literacy program teaching basic skills to adults."

"That's got to be fulfilling."

"Mmm." Vee shrugged, then replied, "Not really. Kids or adults, they act the same."

"Oh?" Shae muttered, surprised by this revelation. She assumed there would be a big difference between the groups.

"This is it," she announced, opening the door to the mall and ushering Shae inside. "Do you have a list of things you need?"

"Yes." Shae fished through her purse and removed a folded sheet. "Here it is. Let's see. I need bedding, kitchen stuff like dishes, silverware, towels for the bathroom… Actually, I need everything."

"No problem. I have all day." Vee headed down the corridor to the entrance for Marshall Field's. "Let's start here. You'll probably be able to find all of your bed and bathroom stuff."

Embarrassed, Shae hesitated at the door. "Um, Vee.

Maybe we should start with a mattress store. I don't have a bed."

Laughing, Vee hooked her arm through Shae's and led her through the doors of the department store. "This store carries them, too. I'm sure they have what you're looking for. What size bed do you want? That apartment is huge. I can put my whole apartment inside that place and still have additional space."

"It's pretty big. I'm not sure what I'm going to do with all that space." The women moved through the Marshall Field's fragrance department. Floral aromas filled Shae's nostrils as they strolled along the fringes of the cosmetic counters and headed to the escalator. Shae giggled, following Vee to the escalator.

"Well, you have room for an office, guest room and a bedroom. I've always loved the fact that the penthouse has a balcony. That way you can enjoy sitting outside during the summer months. Just for your future information, I'm always up for a meal at a friend's house. Can you cook?"

"Subtle." Laughing, Shae stepped off the moving stairs and stopped in front of a stack of towels. "Enough to get by. You won't starve or die from my cooking."

"Good. Whenever you invite me, I'll bring the wine." Vee grabbed Shae's arm and pulled her down the hall.

"I'll keep that in mind," Shae promised.

"How about furniture for the rest of the place? Do you plan on decorating or are you just going for the basics? This store has beautiful furniture. If you'd like, we can check it out before we leave."

They passed several rows of luggage before locating the mattress and bedding department. "Umm. I'm not certain that I want to buy furniture right away. So much in my life has changed. I'm not sure if I'm ready to make a decision on color palettes."

"No problem. We've got time. Besides, we can do this again." Vee sank onto a mattress. "This is nice. Come over and try it with me."

Shae complied, copying her new friend's action. "This feels really good."

Five hours later, completely exhausted and with aching feet, Shae sank into a chair behind a table at the food court. She had purchased a bed, linen, kitchen stuff and assorted items for the penthouse. She'd also bought a desk, file cabinet and laptop computer for her office, a wide-screen plasma television for her bedroom, and a Bose stereo system for music and CDs. Everything was scheduled to be delivered within the next week.

"I'm starved."

"If you stay with our bags, I'll go get lunch," Vee offered.

"Deal," Shae agreed, kicking off her sandals.

"What do you want to eat?" Vee asked, shifting her Lord and Taylor bag into the empty chair next to her.

Pushing her curly locks from her face, Shae took note of the local vendors and answered, "A sandwich would do just fine."

"Anything in particular?" Vee removed her wallet from her purse.

Shae spied a Panera Bread restaurant. "I'd like a chicken salad sandwich on nine grain."

"No problem. Anything to drink?"

"Lemonade."

"Got it." Vee pulled money from her wallet and returned it to her purse. She handed the purse to Shae. "Here, hold on to this. I'll be back in a minute."

Shae leaned back in her chair and placed her feet on the seat opposite hers. The mall had always been one of her favorite places to people watch. For the past couple of years she'd been out of the country with Doctors Without Boundaries and had little opportunity to engage in this pastime.

For the next few minutes Shae enjoyed the antics of a mother with a set of twins. The pair of boys were busy and mischievous. Tucked in a double stroller, they tried unsuccessfully to free themselves by climbing out of their open-air vehicle. Caught up in watching the crowd, Shae lost track of time until her stomach growled. Patting the loud organ, she scanned the area, searching for her shopping buddy.

Frowning, she checked her watch. Where in the heck had Vee gone? It had been more than fifteen minutes since she'd ventured into the throng to get their lunch.

Just as Shae contemplated gathering their bags and going in search of Vee, Shae saw the other woman move through the crowd toward their table. But there was a problem with this scenario. Vee didn't have a tray with her.

As Vee moved closer to the table, Shae noticed a tall man walking next to her with a tray in his hands. Shae took a good look at him. His smooth chocolate skin looked delicious and dark ringlets covered his head. He was way over six feet tall with the slick movements of a person who was comfortable in his skin.

He was one good-looking man and he had trouble printed in bold letters all over his body. He had that "bad boy, here for a good time" attitude about him.

Vee stopped next to the table. She was practically jumping with joy. "Sorry it took me so long." She took the tray from the guy and placed it on the table. "I ran into one of my students and we got to talking." Vee giggled nervously. "Before I realized it, we'd been talking for ten minutes."

"It's fine."

Vee placed a sandwich, potato chips and a cup of lemonade in front of Shae. "Jaden Brooks, this is Shae Weitherspoon."

He extended his hand and shook hers. "Nice to meet you."

Shae nodded back at him.

"Well, Jaden, I'll see you Tuesday night in class. Have a good weekend."

"You, too, Vee."

She slipped into the chair opposite Shae. Vee's face was bright with happiness. "What do you think?"

Shae shrugged. "He's cute."

Watching him move through the crowd, Vee agreed, "That he is."

Before biting into her sandwich, Shae questioned, "He's one of your students?"

"Yes. Literacy program. He's working on his GED," Vee explained, arranging her food on her black tray.

"Oh. So he hasn't finished high school?"

Vee shook her head.

"I went to high school with him," Vee explained. "We had one date. My dad did one of those Fred Sanford fake heart attack things. The next day my mom and dad ganged up on me. They told me that they didn't want me going out with Jaden anymore. They felt that he didn't have any promise. I went through the adolescent angst and cried for weeks. Mom and Dad ignored me and held firm to their decision. But I've always had the hots for him."

"That I can see." Shae took a swig of lemonade. "But you know that you can't get involved with a student, can you?"

"I know." She grinned wickedly. "But he won't be my student forever."

Laughing, Shae agreed, "True."

Vee picked up her sandwich and bit into it. After chewing silently for several minutes, she said, "Please don't mention this to my folks. Mom and Dad will have another baby if they find out about Jaden."

"I won't. It's not my place." Shae picked up a potato chip and popped it in her mouth. "But if you and Jaden start seeing each other, don't you think your family will find out?"

"Probably," Vee answered hesitantly. "I've got plenty of time before that happens."

Shae could see how important this was for her friend. She reached across the table and squeezed Vee's hand. "I won't say anything. Especially to your brother."

Vee sighed. "Thanks. I really appreciate this. I need time to decide what I really want to do. I need to decide if I want to be involved with him."

"My father always wants to control my relationships. So I understand how you feel. But your family seems so normal. Maybe you should talk with them and try to cushion the blow before it happens."

"I don't know," Vee answered slowly. "They don't always react the way I'd like them to. Dating Jaden might cause a rumble of madness throughout our house."

"Vee, you don't live with your parents, so it's not like they see who comes and goes inside your apartment. You're a grown woman and you can do what you want."

"I know. It's hard sometimes because I am so close to my folks."

Shae sipped her lemonade. "We're not going to resolve this today. Let it ride for a while. Why don't we finish our meal and do some more shopping. Let tomorrow take care of itself."

"I hear you." Vee lifted her plastic cup and touched it to Shae's. "Here's to shopping and leaving the rest of the mess to someone else."

# Chapter 15

The air felt crisp and the morning light shone bright with promise as Shae got out of J.D.'s car. She practically skipped toward the front door of the apartment building. Before entering, Shae took a quick glance toward the parking lot and found J.D. retrieving several of her bags from the backseat.

With a quick push of her hand on the metal handles, Shae set the revolving door in motion. The door groaned when she applied pressure, gaining momentum as it surged forward. Once she entered the lobby, a uniformed guard stood, waiting for her to reach the security desk. "Can I help you?"

Excited, she bounced on the balls of her feet. "I'm Shae Weitherspoon. David Daniels told me that he left the keys to his apartment with you and for me to pick them up here."

"Just a moment, let me check." The guard opened a

desk drawer and flipped through a series of brown en-
velopes before removing one and placing it on the wood
surface. "Yeah. Here it is. I need to see some identifi-
cation."

"Certainly." Shae handed her driver's license to the
guard and waited. J.D. moved next to her with her bags
in his hands. They waited together as the security man
checked her photo ID. After a moment, the guard
returned the ID and gave her the keys.

"Thank you." She ripped open the packet and
removed a ring of keys. Quite happy with herself, she
dangled them at J.D. "I have my own place now."

He set one bag on the floor, hugged her close, then
kissed her forehead. "Congratulations, sweetheart. You
are now officially a rent paying apartment dweller of
Chicago. Come on. We've got a lot to do today. Let's
get your stuff upstairs so that we can get you settled."

Nodding, Shae stuffed the keys in the pocket of her
denims and reached for one of the bags before crossing
the lobby on her way to the elevators. Minutes later they
were settled in the metal box on their way to the twenty-
fifth floor.

With a hand to his forehead, J.D. mumbled dramatically, "You have your own apartment and car. A job
that you love. I'm beginning to feel like a useless ap-
pendage. You won't need me anymore."

"Poor baby." Laughing, Shae wrapped her arms
around J.D.'s waist and hugged him tight while she ran
tiny kisses along his jaw line. "I'll always need you.
Plus, I do have a place for you."

Eyebrows raised, he asked, "Really? And what is that?"

"My willing love slave," she answered with a bold
stroke of her hand across his chest, feeling his flesh
quiver under her fingers and loving it.

"I can handle that." J.D. caressed her lips with his own, then deepened the kiss. He tasted of coffee, cream and the delectably unique essences of J.D. His tongue sent shivers of desire racing through Shae. Dazzled by the taste, the feel of his lips and tongue, Shae barely remembered where they were. They didn't come up for air until the bing from the elevator announced that they had reached the penthouse. J.D. broke off the kiss and stepped away, taking a minute to bring his ragged breathing under control.

Flustered, Shae smoothed her hair into place, adding in a husky whisper, "Yes, you can."

The elevator doors opened with a whoosh. Shae and J.D. gathered her belongings, vacated the metal box and strolled down the hallway to the penthouse. She placed her bag on the floor and fumbled with the keys until she found the correct one, and then turned it in the lock. The lyrics of Smokey Robinson and the Miracles greeted them.

Surprised, a soft gasp slipped from her lips and Shae turned to J.D. for an explanation.

Puzzled, he shrugged.

"They're here," a voice called from inside the apartment. Seconds later Helen and Nick Daniels rounded the corner from the living room and hurried down the hallway to the door. David, Cynthia, Matthew, Lisa and Vee were visible beyond J.D.'s parents. They all grinned back at her.

"Hi, honey." Helen wrapped an arm around Shae and drew her farther into the apartment.

"What is all this?" Shae moved slowly into the warmth of the house as Mr. Daniels removed the bag from her hands.

"Since you don't have any family in Chicago we wanted to help you get settled," Nick explained. "Come on in and check out what we've done so far."

"Yeah," David said. "I've been setting up your bed. You may want us to move things around a bit. J.D., can you give me a hand?"

"Sure." With her bags in his hands J.D. followed his brother.

"Wait." Mr. Daniels tucked the piece of luggage under his arm like a football and marched after his sons. "I'll help."

Smiling warmly, Cynthia moved forward and handed Shae a bouquet of yellow roses. "Welcome to your new home. I hope you enjoy living here as much as we did."

Touched by the Danielses' kindness and pleased by their thoughtfulness, Shae blinked several times, trying to keep tears from falling. "Thank you." She brought the roses to her nose, inhaling their delicate fragrance. This was indeed a wonderful beginning for her new life.

Cynthia linked her arm with Shae's and led her through the apartment with the rest of the Daniels family on their heels. "Vee organized your bathroom while Lisa and I put things away in the kitchen. Honestly, there's not much that girl can do. That baby is making it near impossible for her to do anything."

"Hey!" Lisa protested good-naturedly, waddling up to Shae. "Don't pay her any mind. I did my share."

Grinning at her sister-in-law, Cynthia continued, "As I was saying, if you don't like what we've done, tell us. We want to do things the way you'd like. After all this is your home."

Overwhelmed by their kindness, tears welled up in Shae's eyes, threatening to fall. This was the nicest thing anyone had done for her. The Daniels family was amazing. As she followed the ladies through the apartment, evidence of their hard work presented itself.

The silver vertical blinds that she bought when shopping with Vee three days earlier were up and anchored to the patio entrance. The high definition television, DVD player and music system were unpackaged and assembled. As they passed through the living room, Cynthia waved a hand at the setup and said, "We can change or move anything. Don't feel obligated to leave things the way they are because you don't want to hurt our feelings. This is your home. We're here to help you."

Shae never had people in her life like them. They welcomed her into their homes and lives unconditionally.

Vee brought up the rear of the group. "I worked on your bathroom. Everything has been disinfected and I arranged the stuff we bought last week. Once you've checked out the kitchen, come take a look."

"I'm sure I'll love everything. Thank you so much."

# Chapter 16

Her apartment was finally silent as the day reached for night and the purple hues of evening filled the sky. J.D.'s parents and siblings had returned to their own homes after consuming boxes of pizza and Greek salad, washing it down with plenty of soda.

Exhausted, but happy, Shae sat on the floor in her empty living room, her back pressed against the wall, listening to Kim Waters's "You Know That I Love You."

J.D. slipped into the spot next to her, then grimaced. He shifted to the left and pulled his lucky cards from the back pocket of his denims. The deck hit the carpeted floor with a muffled thump. "The kitchen's clean. I've bagged up all the trash and I'll take it out with me when I leave."

Linking her fingers with his, Shae sighed contentedly. "Thanks. This has been one special day. I really love your family for being here. They were wonderful."

"Yeah, that was nice," J.D. agreed proudly.

"Did you know they were coming?"

"Nope," he answered, playing with her fingers. "Mom asked me when you planned to move in. But I didn't think anything of it. I figured she wanted to cook you a hot meal or something like that."

"I felt as if I were part of the family."

"You are," J.D. agreed. "Sometimes they treat you better than they do me."

Giggling, she patted his leg. "Don't worry, I don't think I can replace you. But I would like to do something special for your family. Once I buy some furniture, I'd like to have everyone over for dinner. What do you think?"

"I'm sure they'd love it." J.D. rose.

Surprised, she glanced up at him. "What's wrong?"

"Nothing. I forgot to tie off one of the trash bag in the kitchen. I'll be right back." He hurried out of the room.

Shae picked up the cards, slid them from the box, and removed the jacks before shuffling the deck, all the while humming along with the CD. She leaned her head against the wall and shut her eyes as the mellow saxophone melody relaxed her.

J.D. returned and slid into his previous spot. Shae heard the soft clink of glass hitting glass. Slowly opening her eyes, she saw that he held a bottle of champagne and two wine goblets.

"What's all this?" she asked, pushing herself away from the wall.

"This is my personal housewarming gift to you. Welcome home, sweetheart."

She swallowed hard and held back tears, exclaiming, "Oh! Thank you." J.D. was wonderful and she felt truly blessed to have found him. How had she gotten so lucky and met a man that seemed to understand her so well? Sometimes he knew what she needed long before she knew.

"You're welcome," J.D. whispered, leaning close to steal a quick kiss. "Let me get this top off so that we can toast your new apartment." He handed the glasses to Shae, removed the wire cover and wrapped a dish-towel around the dark green bottle. The cap popped and flew across the room as the champagne spilled from the neck of the bottle.

"Watch it," Shae warned, lifting the glasses in time to catch the bubbly. She filled both glasses, then handed one to J.D.

He cleared his throat and turned to Shae, looking deeply into her eyes. "I wish only the best of things for you in your new home. May your life be filled with joy—" he softly touched his lips to hers "—happiness—" he muttered, deepening the previous kiss "—and love."

They touched glasses, then sipped their wine. For several minutes they kissed between sips while listen-ing to the CD.

Topping off their glasses, J.D. rose from the floor and headed for the kitchen. "You're not ready to go yet, are you?" Shae asked.

"No. I'm going to put the bottle in the refrigerator. Why?"

"I've got an idea," she answered, wiggling her eyebrows suggestively.

"Really?" His tone carried a hint of laughter. "What's that?"

Shae reached for the cards. "How about a couple hands of Spades?"

"You're kidding, right?"

Shae slowly shook her head. "Not at all."

"I'm an expert," J.D. stated.

"Talk, talk, talk," she teased. "Sounds like a chicken to me. Why don't you put your money where your mouth is?"

Grinning back at her, he said, "I can say the same about you. Okay. I'm in. But, let's stir things up a bit."

"How's that?" Shae asked with a suspicious lift.

"If we're going to do this, let's make it interesting." J.D. reached for the bottle and topped off both glasses again before adding in a voice that turned husky, "For each bid that you don't make, you have to kiss me. None of that kiss on the cheek stuff. A real kiss. Deep, slow and satisfying. Are you up for it?"

Maybe the champagne had shot to her brain or the fact that she'd just moved into her new apartment, where she could do what she wanted had given her a hearty sense of power. Whatever the reason, the idea sent her spirits soaring and a warm tingling started in the pit of her stomach and spread through her body. "I'm in."

A small part of Shae questioned the wisdom of the game they were playing. The calm analytical side of her brain had always maintained control. Today, Shae felt wild and frivolous, and wanted to test the boundaries of her relationship with J.D. Besides, although she'd never uttered the words out loud, Shae loved J.D. and had from the day they met. Yes, tonight was the beginning of many new things.

J.D. took the champagne into the kitchen while Shae rose and went into the bedroom for her purse. She returned minutes later with a small notepad and a pen.

Smiling at her opponent, Shae asked, "Ready?"

Lines creased his forehead. "Are you sure you want to do this? I don't want you to feel as if I've taken advantage of you in any way."

"This was my idea, remember? Are you getting cold feet?" she challenged, sitting on the floor opposite him, cross-legged.

"Not at all," J.D. answered in a superior tone. The note of sensual promise in his voice encouraged her, adding a forbidden element to the game. He placed the cards between them and tapped the top. Shae cut them. J.D. picked up the deck and began to deal. "Get ready for a beat-down."

Picking up her cards, she arranged them according to high, low and suit order. "Talk is so cheap."

"We'll see."

Shae studied her cards, then announced, "Three books."

"Conservative bid. I think I'll go five." J.D. tossed the ace of hearts on the carpet between them. She returned with her lowest heart. Snatching up the cards, he racked up book after book until Shae cut him with the three of spades.

"Yes!" she yelped triumphantly, tossing out the ace of diamonds. Immediately, her mouth dropped open when he cut her book with another spade. "Hey!"

"You should have seen that one coming, Shae. Sit back and enjoy the ride, because you're getting ready to feel the agony of defeat," he stated in his best Howard Cosell imitation before winning the hand. Minutes later, he leaned against the wall, counting his books. "How did you do?"

Peeved, she rolled her eyes, "You know exactly how I did."

Chuckling softly, he touched her arm. "Time to pay up."

Her attitude evaporated instantly as a ripple of excitement surged through her. Nodding, Shae leaned closer and her eyes fluttered shut. J.D. tenderly took her face between his large hands, claiming her lips. Slow and thorough described the kiss as J.D. explored the intimate recesses of her mouth. A sensuous current spiraled through her, completely destroying her previous calm.

Slowly loosening his hold, J.D. relaxed against the wall, although his eyes glowed with a savage inner fire. "Are you ready for another hand?"

"Huh?" Shae muttered stupidly, lost in the feel of his tongue and hands.

"Do you want to play again?"

Shae nodded, wondering how far they planned to take things. She couldn't deny the spark of excitement at the prospect of more kisses. This time she lost the hand but took pleasure in the reward of kissing J.D. Their caresses grew bolder, more heated and intense. It became difficult to decide where one kiss ended and another began. Each kiss made her ache for more.

"Maybe it's time to take our game to the bedroom?" Shae suggested in a hoarse whisper.

J.D.'s hot gaze settled on her face. A hopeful gleam flashed brightly from his eyes. "Are you sure?"

Smiling back at him, she nodded.

He swung her into his arms, stood and carried her through the apartment to her bedroom. Striding across the floor, J.D. gently laid her in the middle of the bed and followed her down.

A series of slow, drugging kisses followed as they explored each other. He traced his fingertips down her cheek to her shoulder and over the bare skin below the neck of her T-shirt.

Between kisses J.D.'s hands moved along the edge of her top. In a bold move, he drew the shirt off her body, over her head, and tossed it on the floor. In turn, Shae returned the favor, pulling his cotton shirt over his head. Shae eagerly admired his broad, chocolate shoulders and the muscles underneath. She unsnapped his jeans and pushed them off his slim hips, dragging them down his legs and over his feet, tossing the denims next to the T-shirt on the floor.

Only Shae's bra and panties and J.D.'s shorts separated them. Her heart pounded against her chest as J.D. gave her another drugging kiss.

"You are so beautiful," he whispered into the curve of her neck, licking her heated skin. His warm breath fanned the hair at her shoulder.

"So are you," she returned, brushing his cheek with the back of her hand.

His finger unclipped her bra, while he feathered kisses over the top of her breasts as he slid the garment off her shoulders and discarded it with the growing pile of clothing on the floor next to the bed. J.D. turned his attention to her breasts, weighing a chocolate globe in each hand.

He lowered his head and his tongue licked the sensitive swollen nipple while using his thumb to draw circles around the areola of her other breast. The sensation rocketed through her, creating a pulsating ache between her legs. He suckled one nipple as she cradled his head against her.

Curious and very eager to see the rest of him, Shae reached for the elastic band at his waist, pulled the shorts off his hips, and down his legs. J.D. sighed as his flesh sprang free. In awe, she reached for his flesh, fondling the combination of smooth skin over hard, hot shaft. J.D. kicked the briefs free and shifted away from her, grabbing his denims and removed an item from his wallet. Her gaze followed his movements and landed on the foil package he placed on her nightstand before returning his attention to her breasts. Slowly, he kissed and teased his way down her body. Sexual desire like she'd never felt before washed over her and she moaned.

His tongue seared a path down her abdomen, nibbling on the waistband of her panties. He drew the silk covering off her most precious parts, down her legs and off her feet, then returned to her apex, tasting her. The sensation was deliciously wicked and she wanted more. "Just a little appetizer before we get to the main course."

"Wait," she took the foil package from his hands. "My turn. I'd like to do this, if you don't mind."

Grinning, J.D. laid flat on his back. "Be my guest," he offered. His hard flesh stood proud and erect.

Shae tore open the packet and removed the latex protection, then kissed the head of his shaft before rolling the condom over his flesh. Satisfied that she had accomplished her task, she crawled up his body and captured his lips.

J.D. gently eased her onto her back as his body moved to cover hers. She writhed beneath him, eager to be joined with him, part of him. Posed at her entrance, he asked, "Ready."

Shae nodded and felt him enter her, filling her in a way no one had ever done before. J.D. moved slowly at first.

Moaning softly, she felt such overwhelming love for J.D. as he started to move inside her. She lifted her hips and wrapped her legs around his waist as J.D.'s hand cupped her bottom. Picking up his rhythm, she eagerly matched his movements as he pumped in and out of her. He moved quicker, deeper, filling and completing her beyond anything she'd ever felt before. Their bodies were in exquisite harmony. The pleasure was pure and explosive.

Groaning, Shae pulled J.D. tighter against her, absolutely loving how his shaft felt inside her. Her hips rose to meet each thrust in a moment filled with uncontrolled passion.

J.D.'s hands squeezed her bottom as he moved faster, taking them higher and higher, reaching for ecstasy. Her walls clenched and unclenched taking him deeper into her body.

Hovering on the brink of completeness, Shae clung to J.D. as she cried out her release. A split second later, Shae heard J.D.'s own harsh cry and felt his warm release. She held him close savoring this moment of closeness.

# Chapter 17

After almost a month of living out of a suitcase, Shae loved the idea of living in her own place. Eyes shut, Shae sighed contentedly, listening to the birds chirping happily outside her bedroom window. She snuggled closer to the large male furnace sleeping peacefully at her side. Last night had been fantastic! Making love with J.D. had capped a perfect day and evening. It had been a wonderful, enlightening experience that she hoped to repeat often in the near future. Lying among the rumpled sheets, she relived those glorious moments that filled her with a sense of coming home, of being loved and cherished.

A smile of pure delight crossed her face as she considered how her life had changed. *Had it really been only a month?* It seemed like a lifetime since she'd left California for Illinois.

"What are you smiling at?" J.D. asked, caressing her leg with his foot.

She flipped on her back, facing him. "I'm thinking about how my life has changed since I moved to Chicago and met you."

His expressive face grew almost somber. "For the better, I hope?"

A smile of satisfaction spread across her face. "It's all good," Shae answered, cuddling against his side.

He wiped an imaginary bead of sweat from his brow and blew out a worried breath of air. "You had me scared for a moment."

"Don't be. I've never been this happy." Shae stretched her arms above her head, then brushed her wild curls away from her face. J.D. lay quietly beside her, watching every move she made. His heated gaze met hers and she felt a tightening sensation in the pit of her stomach.

Shutting his eyes, J.D. nuzzled her neck. "I'm glad. And I'll have to say ditto on the happiness thing."

She tilted her head, enjoying the sensations he was creating. "I didn't wake you, did I? I tried to be really quiet."

"No, you didn't. I've been awake for a while."

"Really? What have you been doing while I've been sleeping?"

He leaned close, gently kissing her lips. "Enjoying you."

Surprised, she stared at him with a frown on her face. "Me? I don't understand."

"You looked so beautiful. I couldn't resist watching you." A husky note lingered in his voice.

"Aren't you sweet." Shae wrapped her arms around his neck and drew him to her for another sizzling kiss.

"Shae," J.D. breathed softly against her ear, pulling her more firmly into his embrace. "Thank you for last night. It was perfect."

"Yes, it was. No thanks needed. You were equally responsible for the good time we shared." She rested her cheek against his chest, listening to the solid, steady beat of his heart.

"What's on the agenda for today?" J.D. asked.

"I planned to get familiar with my new home," she answered, drawing small circles around his nipples.

He groaned. "Do you mind if I also get familiar with you and your new apartment?"

Smiling, she said, "I'd love that."

"Great. What do you say to breakfast downtown? We can go to one of those Sunday breakfast buffets."

Shae sat up and swung her legs over the side of the bed. "Considering the fact that I haven't been grocery shopping, your invitation sounds wonderful. Come on, let's get dressed." She rose from the bed, crossed the bedroom and entered the bathroom. She turned on the shower, letting the hot water warm the room and steam up the mirrors while she brushed her teeth. J.D. followed at a slower pace. Shae rummaged inside the medicine cabinet and retrieved a second toothbrush. "Here you go."

"My goodness, aren't you the perfect hostess." He unwrapped the brush and squeezed toothpaste on it before attacking his teeth.

"What can I say? I was a Girl Scout. I'm always prepared."

He pulled her against the hard planes of his body and added, "Yes, you are."

Giggling, she wiggled out of his arms, pushed the shower curtain back, added cold water until the temperature felt perfect, and stepped under the water spray. "You're more than welcome to join me." She grabbed the soap and lathered her body, before stepping under the shower head to rinse clean.

Seconds later, J.D. stepped into the stall behind her. He wrapped his arms around her waist and pulled her against him. Shae felt his erection pressing against her thigh.

His hand slid across her silken belly, up her slick wet flesh to cover her breast, fondling a round globe, its brown nipple turned marble hard. The other hand went south, gliding over her mound and dove inside her slit to rub the little button shielded by her pubic hair. Gently stroking back and forth across her nub, his touch stroked a gently flame into a roaring fire.

"Oh, my!" she moaned, wondering if her legs would keep her vertical.

Continuing his sensual torture, he whispered, "How's this working for you?"

"Good," she panted, spreading her legs to accommodate his questing fingers.

Breaking contact, Shae turned in his arms, wrapping her hands around his neck and drew his head down for another kiss. His tongue slid inside the waiting recesses of her mouth. The minty toothpaste and unique essences of J.D. made her want more. Instinctively, her body arched against his.

"Wrap your legs around my waist," J.D. ordered, lifting her.

She complied, locking her legs around his back and immediately felt the tip of his shaft probe her opening. He surged upward and filled her in one swift motion. Shae gasped, feeling her interior walls stretch to accommodate his size.

J.D. turned in the stall, pressed her back against the wall of the shower, and slid to the hilt inside her. She moaned softly into his neck. The combination of coolness against her back and heat between her legs brought her a hairbreadth away from climaxing. J.D. withdrew and surged into her second time. He repeated the action, pumping into her again and again, rotating his hips as he slid in and out of her tight sheath.

Aching for more, Shae enjoyed the ride, pulling him snuggly against her heated skin. Her interior walls started to quiver as he stroked her tight, hot sheath with his erection. Together they found the precise tempo that joined them physically and emotionally. Their bodies moved in exquisite harmony.

Shae cried out as the first wave hit her. J.D. surged into her for a final stroke and she flew over the edge. Seconds later he followed her. His harsh shout of completeness came seconds before his physical release.

Slowly regaining control, J.D. laid his head against her shoulder and began to kiss his way up her neck. "That was great," he breathed, lowering her feet to the tub floor.

"This is turning into one fabulous weekend," she muttered, leaning against the wall as she waited for her strength to return.

"I second that one." J.D. steered her under the water spray to finish their shower.

# Chapter 18

Urban Health Center officially opened its doors for the first time on May first. The UHC team had blanketed the surrounding areas with informational and welcoming flyers, encouraging the local residents to check out the clinic and meet the staff. To mark this special occasion, the board of directors had agreed with Kenyatta and Shae's recommendation to present their opening day as a healthy living fair. If the clinic's visitors had any health concerns, the staff stood ready to answer their questions.

With damp palms and hopeful thoughts, Shae unlocked the doors and greeted the tiny elderly woman waiting patiently on the building's door step. Shae helped the old lady into the building and led her to the reception desk.

Shae moved slowly down the corridor, escorting their first guest. "Paula, would you help Mrs. Grant? She needs to fill out our paperwork. After that's completed, please escort her to the blood pressure monitoring station and then to the conference room for the workshop on cooking healthy meals while living with diabetes."

Paula hurried around the edge of the desk with a clipboard in her hands and a broad warm smile on her face.

Shae patted Mrs. Grant on the shoulder and said, "I'll leave you in very good hands."

"Welcome. Why don't you get comfortable over here and let me help you?" Paula pointed to the empty waiting room. Mrs. Grant nodded and Paula helped the older woman into a chair.

Smiling at the pair, Shae turned when she heard the door open. Several individuals entered the building in a group. They headed to the front desk and were immediately greeted by UHC staff.

Health stations manned by UHC's nursing staff were set up to evaluate glucose levels for abnormalities, monitor blood pressure and offer advice on ways to reduce stress and make healthy food choices. The second floor auditorium and conference rooms had been converted into learning centers where specialists from the local hospital planned to conduct workshops, pass out brochures about living a healthy lifestyle, medication interaction and maintaining good health.

As the director and managing nurse practitioner in charge, Kenyatta and Shae planned to oversee the entire event. Dressed in white lab coats with their names and titles scripted in black letters on the upper right hand pocket, they spent the day circulating among the health stations and examination rooms, introducing themselves and offering advice to the patients.

To add a festive mood to the day, Paula had procured

the services of a clown to entertain the children while parents received free screening and testing. In addition, the kitchen was packed with tons of healthy snacks for the patients.

Emerging from one of the workshops, Shae checked the front desk and found a message from J.D. His friend Phil had called as J.D. was leaving his house. Phil's car had broken down on the freeway and he needed help. J.D. planned to head to the clinic as soon as he was done with his buddy. She shook her head, rubbing her hand across her face. Disappointment welled up inside her. Swallowing those feelings, Shae refocused on the day's festivities.

Three o'clock came and went without an appearance from J.D. Although he'd said that he'd be at the clinic to support her, so far he hadn't kept his word. Shae beat down a twinge of sadness. Lately, he'd developed this nasty habit of showing up late or opting out of an evening with her. Each time he disappointed Shae, she felt the wedge of distrust widen between them. The worst part was she didn't feel secure enough in their relationship to make any major demands on him. In some ways they were so close and yet…

*For goodness' sake,* she thought. *You're sleeping with the man—you have some clout with him. Yeah, but I don't know how he feels about me,* she reasoned. That was the reason she held back. She felt incredibly vulnerable about what she should or should not say or do. Who was she in his life? Where did she fit in? What rights did she really have?

By 3:00 the clinic had seen a steady stream of patients. Opening day had been a brilliant success. Between manning health stations and talking to the local residents, Shae kept J.D. from her thoughts. With her first real break, she stood near the front of the building, nibbling on her bottom lip. She searched the crowd for J.D.'s handsome face. *Where is he?* she wondered, glancing at the clock.

It was almost 3:30 p.m. and she hadn't heard from him since he'd left the message with Paula around noon. Last night, before he left for the evening, J.D. had promised to be at the clinic for her big day. They had made plans to have dinner after the clinic closed to celebrate all of the hard work Shae had put into making sure the clinic got off to a smooth start.

Shae grimaced, fighting her pain. She didn't want to feel this way, especially not today! These incidents transported her back to her childhood and the many times her father had failed to show up when there was an event she had either participated in or sponsored. Her father racked up major points in the disappointment area. He spent more time explaining his absences or apologizing for his late arrivals than he did attending many family functions. When his contrite act didn't work, he put plan B into action, sending a gift of some sort as a way to appease her. Generally, as Albert Weitherspoon's daughter, Shae came in a poor second to his business. His reasoning was always the same: "You understand, princess? Right? Your pop has to make the money so that you can have all those pretty things." Emotional guilt—Albert Weitherspoon was the king of dispensing it. Still, she expected and hoped for better from J.D.

"Why the long face?" Kenyatta strolled up to Shae and took a place at her side.

"Oh." Startled, Shae jumped. "I didn't see you there."

"I noticed." Silently, he stood beside her, observing the antics of the crowd. "Our open house went well."

Smiling with pride, Shae enthused, "It sure did! I was really worried that we'd have all this food and nobody to eat it."

Laughing out loud, Kenyatta added, "That'll never happen. Whenever you mention free food, that pretty much guarantees that you'll have people to eat it."

"True." Shae leaned close to him. "I was anxious, anyway."

Kenyatta did a quick sweep of the room with his eyes. "Where's the boyfriend?"

Frowning, she gazed at the doctor. "What?"

"J.D. Your friend. Where is he? I'd expected to see him in the middle of things, maybe taking a picture or two, or standing stoically beside you, offering support. I'm really surprised that he's not here."

"He had a problem that he needed to take care of. I imagine he'll be here when he settles whatever's going on."

Nodding, Kenyatta pursed his lips. "Really?"

"What's that supposed to mean?" Shae didn't like the tone of his voice. "Do you know something that I should know?"

"No. Not at all." Dr. Reid lifted his hands in a gesture of surrender. "I'm just surprised he hasn't made it here yet. That's all. I expected to see him."

Shae pushed her unruly hair from her forehead. "The day isn't over. We have another hour before closing."

"I'm sure he'll make it." Kenyatta touched her arm and walked away.

"Miss Shae," called a small male voice.

Smiling, Shae turned to find Desmond hurrying with another child following at a slower pace through the hordes of people toward her. Desmond halted in front of

Shae, grinning. His eyes were clear and for once he lacked the runny nose that seemed to be a constant part of him.

"Hey." Shae gave him a quick hug. "Where's your mom?"

"Over there." He pointed to where Mrs. Walls sat with the blood pressure cuff around her arm.

"Did you get to play with the clown?" Shae asked, running a hand over his thick hair.

Desmond nodded, munching on a handful of oatmeal raisin cookies. He pointed to the child next to him. "This is my cousin, Tyrin."

"Hi, Tyrin," she greeted, sticking her hand toward him.

The little boy shook her hand, then groaned.

Frowning, Shae dropped to her knees in front of the small child, running a clinical eye over the boy for injuries. "Honey, are you okay?"

"Tell her." Desmond nudged his Tyrin in the side. "She can fix anything."

Eyes shut tight, the little boy moaned. "Are you a doctor?"

"No. I'm a nurse practitioner," she answered, feeling his forehead for a fever. When she didn't find one, Shae checked his pulse. "But I can help you, if you let me. Tell me what's going on."

Desmond stepped in. "He got hit with a ball."

Shae studied Tyrin, searching for a bruise. "Where did it hit you?"

Embarrassed, he gazed at the floor and rolled the edge of his white T-shirt.

"Don't be shy. Tell me."

"It hit me here," he muttered so low that she didn't catch his words, but understood the gesture.

"Tyrin, where is your mother? Is she here with you?"

The young child shook his head.

Desmond piped in with an explanation. "He's staying with us for a while."

"Go get your mother, Desmond." Shae pointed in the direction she had last seen Mrs. Walls. "Tell your mom that I need to see her."

"Okay."

Minutes later Desmond returned with his mother. Shae shepherded the small group into examination room number three and briefly explained the situation.

Once the door closed behind the trio, she dropped to one knee and asked, "What happened?"

"We were playing baseball and a ball hit me down there," Tyrin explained.

Charting the information, Shae asked, "Can you go to the bathroom?"

Tyrin nodded.

"Good. Does it hurt when you go?"

"Little bit," he mumbled.

"Does it burn? What color is your urine when you go to the bathroom?"

"Little bit. For a minute. It burns for a minute, then it stops," Tyrin explained.

"Tyrin, I'm going to have to look at you. To see if everything is all right. Your aunt is in the room. She'll be here with you. Mrs. Walls, why don't you stand over here so that he can see you? Maybe you could hold his hand."

Nodding, he watched her with large, doe eyes.

Shae removed his pants and underwear, checked his pubic area, noting a small amount of bruising. Fifteen minutes later, Shae had completed her examination. "Okay, Tyrin, you can pull up your pants."

The two adults left the room. They stopped outside the exam room.

"Is he okay, Ms. Shae?"

Shae gave the aunt's shoulder a reassuring squeeze. "Mrs. Walls, he's fine. He's a little tender from the accident. We're going to apply a cold compress to reduce the swelling and then you can take him home."

Mrs. Walls hugged Shae. "Thank you. Thank you."

"You're welcome. That's what we're here for." Shae headed down the hall. "I'm going to my office for a moment and then I'll be right back to talk with Tyrin."

Nodding, Desmond's mother returned to the room.

Shae returned to the exam room and gave the boys hand video games to play with and a plate of treats. She offered Mrs. Walls a series of magazines, then turned to the young boy on the exam table. "Tyrin, you're going to have to take it easy for a little while. You and Desmond can stay in here and play. Stay put. I'll be right back."

As she shut the door after her, she heard Desmond tell Tyrin, "See, I told you. Miss Shae can fix anything."

Her heart filled with satisfaction. *That's one great testimonial,* she thought. On her way to the front desk to have Tyrin's medical file put way, she ran right into J.D. He grabbed her arms and steadied her. She glanced at the clock, noting the time. It was almost 4:30.

"Honey, I'm sorry I'm late. I was on my way out the door when Phil called. He had a flat tire and no spare. When I got to him, we had to go buy a tire and go back to the car and put it on. It took much longer than I thought it would. Please forgive me."

"It's fine. At least you made it," she said, grudgingly.

"Of course I made it. This is the clinic's opening day."

# Chapter 19

At dusk the Chrysler Crossfire rolled to a stop in front of a classic Victorian residence. "This is it," J.D. declared, checking the address against the black numbers painted on the curb near the driveway.

"Wow!" Shae muttered, loving what she saw. The turret's roof, wraparound veranda, and attached three-car garage took her back to her dreams as a child. "This place is beautiful. Now I understand why your brother and Cynthia were in a hurry to move."

Behind the wheel of the car, J.D. chuckled. "That's David. He's all into his family now."

"What do you mean?" Shae switched her attention from the home to the man in the car.

"Since he married Cynthia, he's changed. Before the wedding, it was all about winning, having the best of everything and making partner. Once he put that ring on his finger and said his vows, things changed.

Cynthia's wants and needs became his priority. What's best for their family matters most."

*That's the way it should be,* Shae thought, studying J.D.'s handsome face in the receding light. A spark of pain surged through her when she remembered the times her father constantly disappointed her by putting Prestige Computers ahead of his family. Hopefully, that wouldn't be an issue with J.D. Maybe David's attitude had rubbed off on his younger brother.

"I like that idea." She replied. "What's best for the family is more important than the individuals."

"It's a great approach to marriage and relationships." J.D. reached for Shae's hand and brought it to his lips.

"Yes, it is. We may not be married, but I like the idea of that kind of commitment to a relationship." She leaned across the transmission gear and kissed him gently on the lips.

He moaned softly. "Me, too."

Grinning back at him, she responded, hoping J.D. understood that she needed him to put their relationship before everyone else. "I'm glad we agree on this."

"Come on. Let's get this show on the road." J.D. switched off the engine, opened the car door, climbed out and moved to the passenger door. He helped her out of the car before removing their housewarming gift from the trunk. J.D. balanced the present in one hand while guiding Shae up the flower-lined walkway with the other hand at the small of her back.

"It was nice of your family to include me in the party."

J.D. laughed out loud. "You're family, whether you believe it or not. We are a couple in my parents' eyes. So when I'm invited to a family function, you are, too."

They stepped onto the veranda and halted. Shae

moved around the wooden area, admiring the structure. J.D. trailed along behind her. "I love this porch. It's so homey. If I were married, I'd like a house something like this."

"It is great." He took her arm and led her back to the front door and rang the doorbell.

David and Cynthia opened the door seconds later. "Hey, we're glad you made it. Come on in."

"Cynthia, I love what I've seen so far." Shae hugged the other woman.

Smiling at her husband, Cynthia said, "The minute we saw it, we knew this was the home we were looking for."

J.D. handed the brightly wrapped box to his brother. "It's sweet, brother man."

"Thanks." David placed the gift with the others on a table near the door.

"Want the nickel tour?" Cynthia offered, grinning with pride.

"Sure," Shae answered, turning to J.D.

David slapped his brother on the back, leading him away from the women. "Come on, man. Dad, Eddie and Matthew are in the den. Let Cynthia and Shae do the girlie thing." He leaned close to Cynthia and kissed her on the lips. "Have fun. We'll see you two in a little bit."

Cynthia began the tour in the large living area. Wood crackled in the fireplace and hardwood floors added to the comfortable room.

Shae perched on the edge of a chair. "Cynthia, I love this room. It's perfect."

Grinning broadly, Cynthia agreed, "It is, isn't it. The moment I saw this house, I knew this was where we belonged."

Vee entered the room. She jabbed her finger in the

direction of the front door. "Excuse me, Cyn. David's boss and his wife are at the door."

"Thanks, Vee." Cynthia rose from a chair and started out the room. "Excuse me, Shae. I've got to do the wife thing."

Shae waved her away. "Go ahead. I understand. Besides, Vee and I can catch up while you're gone."

J.D.'s sister gave Shae a quick hug. "Hey, girl. I didn't know you were here."

"We just got here. Cynthia was showing me around."

"Cynthia will be a while with his boss. I'll take over." Vee tugged on Shae's arm.

After peeking into the formal dining room that housed a large cherry wood table and twelve matching chairs, Vee led Shae into the country kitchen and breakfast nook. An office loaded with every home office gadget was tucked in a small corner behind the nook.

They climbed the stairs to the second floor. At the landing, they headed down the hall to Cynthia and David's bedroom that included a private bath with a Jacuzzi and balcony. Shae practically drooled when she entered the suite. As they took a look out the balcony door, Vee mentioned that the room next to David and Cynthia was being turned into a nursery and that they were working on expanding their family.

"Are you here by yourself?" Shae asked cautiously.

Grinning, Vee answered, "Of course. I'd never invite Jaden to a party with my parents. And besides, family parties aren't his thing."

"Really. Why not?" Shae perched on the edge of the leather sofa. She didn't like the sound of that.

"He doesn't do family functions—" Vee glanced around the room, then added "—or housewarming parties."

"Vee, he doesn't have to do anything. But if he cares for you, he'd be here regardless to how he feels about the occasion." Shae strolled around the room, admiring Cynthia and David's decorating skills. "Besides, Helen and Nick are great. They are not monsters from another planet. Your parents are good people. They've always treated me well and made me feel like I belong."

"That's because they like you."

Shae raised a skeptical eyebrow at Vee. "And they don't like Jaden? Honey, you haven't given your parents a chance to get to know him and vice versa."

As she twisted a lock of hair around her finger, Vee rolled her eyes. "I know. My dad doesn't get on well with people that are really different from us. For example, look at Matthew. He's a clean cut, all-American man. That's what my dad understands and appreciates."

Shae folded her arms across her chest and responded in a dubious tone, "I don't know about that. How do you know your dad can't adapt?"

"I don't."

"Exactly. Come on, Vee. Helen and Nick may be conservative but they are reasonable people. If you brought Jaden home, it might take a little time for him to open up and for everyone to get to know him, but they would respect your choice. Things might be awkward at first, but Jaden will do fine." Shae moved across the room to where Vee stood and placed a hand on her friend's shoulder. "The truth is you're afraid."

"You are so right," Vee admitted sheepishly, waving her hands in the air. "I don't want him to get scared off by my middle-class schoolteacher parents and siblings."

"I hear something more in your voice. What is it?"

Vee shook her head before saying, "That's enough about me. How are you and J.D. doing?"

"Doing," the nurse answered softly, sinking into the leather sofa facing the fireplace.

Vee slipped into the place next to Shae on the sofa and touched her arm. "Just doing? What about Amir? Is he still being a pain? Causing and getting into trouble?"

"Little bit," Shae admitted reluctantly, fidgeting with the handle of her handbag. "I know I should be more understanding, but I have to tell you that each time J.D. stands me up, for whatever reason, I feel abandoned and alone." She turned away and stared out the window. "A couple of days ago, we had the open house for the clinic. J.D. promised me that he would be there. He called, saying that he would be late. I could live with that, but he didn't show up until near four-thirty! The clinic was ready to close. I was so hurt. I felt like I truly didn't matter to him."

"I'm sorry, honey."

"It's not your fault. I know I have issues that go back to my parents. My father always let me down and I have a hard time dealing with anyone I believe I can't depend on. But at this point I feel like I come in a poor second to everything and everyone else in J.D.'s life and that's not the position I want in his life. Truthfully, I know I'm fussing about little things and I feel like a whiner baby talking about them. But they are important to me. I don't know if I can stay in a relationship where I can't depend on the man in my life. It's too painful."

Vee wrapped her arms around her friend and held her close. "Oh, Shae."

"Maybe I'm letting myself get too involved. Or I'm expecting too much from this relationship. I mean, it's still a new relationship." Shae shrugged. "It might be best to distance myself. That way I won't get my feelings hurt. One thing I'm certain of is, I don't want to feel disappointed or hurt all the time."

"And you shouldn't have to be. My brother is an idiot at times." Vee offered Shae a small apologetic smile while rubbing her arm. "But he is a good guy and I know that he cares very deeply for you. Hang in there. This situation will work itself out if you give it time to work out."

"We'll see."

"Have you talked to him about your feelings? Laid your cards on the table and let him know what you expect from him?"

Shae shook her head. "Not really."

"You can't expect him to understand. My recommendation, talk to him. Men are funny. Unless you tell them exactly how you feel, they think everything is perfect. Don't hold back—say what's on your mind. I think you two will be stronger for it."

"Maybe you're right." Shae said. "Even if it doesn't help our relationship, I'll feel a whole lot better."

"There you go." Vee rose from the sofa and pulled Shae to her feet. "Come on. My parents will want to see you and I'm sure they're wondering where we are."

Arms linked, Vee and Shae left the bedroom, took the stairs to the first floor and moved toward the den.

J.D. stepped into the room filled with his relatives. *First things first,* he thought, heading to where his mother sat on the sofa. He gave her a hug, then turned to his dad, extending his hand. After greeting and listening to the latest gossip about the rest of the crew, he took a seat.

"How've you been, son?" his father asked.

"Good. Busy." J.D. squirmed a little on the sofa, feeling as if his family had placed him on the hot seat.

With a soda in one hand, he glanced at the people surrounding him, he wondered what was really going on here.

David stood near the sofa, sipping on a glass of what J.D. suspected was scotch. "And Shae? How is she?"

"She's good. The clinic had its grand opening this week."

"Did you show up?" David asked.

"Yeah. What is this?" J.D. rose from sofa, glaring at his parents before focusing on his older brother. "I'm not on the witness stand."

"Just checking," David muttered, making his way to the bar setup and pouring a glass of scotch. "I ran into Phil the other day and he told me about his car and how you had to help him. He felt bad about keeping you from the open house."

"It was no biggie," J.D. explained, swallowing a mouthful of Coke. "I helped him get a tire, then hurried over to the open house."

David moved around the table with his glass and took the seat opposite his brother. "How do you think Shae felt about it?"

J.D.'s head snapped back as if he'd been slapped. This scenario felt like he'd been ambushed into the center of a massive family intervention and he didn't like it. "What's it got to do with you? This is between Shae and me."

"I'm trying to keep you from screwing up the best relationship you've had in a long while. How do you think she felt when you didn't turn up for her event?"

"Shae understands."

Chuckling, David leaned closer. "Does she now? She's a wonderful woman. The best. Don't take her for granted, because you'll end up alone."

"You don't know what you're talking about." J.D. retorted hastily. "Shae and I are fine."

Glancing steadily into his eyes, David whispered, "Are you?"

That steady gaze unnerved J.D. and for a moment he felt uncertain about his previous declaration. Were they really all right? he wondered. Had he been assuming too much? That's ridiculous. They were together practically every evening. He dropped by her place, or they shared dinner. *Yeah, but you always make excuses and leave early if something else comes up.*

J.D.'s cell phone went off. *Saved by the bell,* he thought, reaching for the phone before checking the number on the LCD. Great, it was Phil again. What could possibly be wrong now? J.D. rose from the sofa and found a little corner where he could talk.

The unique fragrance Shae wore filled the room and he turned to find her and his sister greeting the family. He studied Shae. She was graceful and elegant, and she mixed well with his family.

His brother was wrong. *Things are great between us,* he thought as he heard Phil's voice on the other end of the telephone. "Hey, man, what's going on?"

After several minutes of talk, J.D. replied, "Okay. I'm on it."

He rubbed his fingers across his forehead and sucked in a deep breath. As he moved across the room to Shae, J.D. studied his family. This was going to cause a whole lot of trouble. But he didn't have a choice. Phil was his friend and J.D. had to help him.

He took Shae's hand and pulled her to her feet. "Can I talk to you for a minute?"

"Sure," she answered, examining him with worried eyes.

They left the room and found a quiet spot in the kitchen. "I've got to go," J.D. said.

Confusion made Shae's forehead crinkle into a frown. "Go? Where?"

"Out to the airport. My friend Phil's car won't start and his girlfriend is coming in for the weekend. I'm going by his place to pick him up, then head to the airport. I should be back within the hour."

Shae's mouth opened and closed without a word being uttered. She sighed and waved her hand in the air before letting it drop helplessly to her side. "What about your brother's housewarming? This is their party."

David's remarks smacked him upside his head. J.D. felt like a jerk. But Phil had been his friend since the first grade.

Clearing his throat, J.D. said, "I know. David and Cynthia will understand. It'll be okay. I promise, I'll be right back." He leaned in and planted a soft kiss on her lips. "Honestly, I'll only be gone for a short while. Sit tight. Enjoy yourself. Eat, have a glass of wine and I'll be back before you know it. Okay?" He snatched a second kiss, fished his keys from his pockets and strode to the door. Shae was left in the middle of the kitchen floor, a stunned expression on her face.

# Chapter 20

The youngest member of the Daniels clan pulled up to the curb outside Shae's apartment and launched into her third attempt to redeem J.D. "I know you're upset. But don't do anything reckless until you've had a chance to calm down and think."

Shae got out of the car and glanced through the passenger side window and waved so long to Vee. "Thanks for the ride." Shae waved at the security guard as she crossed the lobby on her way to the elevator.

Riding the elevator to the penthouse, Shae let out a soft moan of pain. Tonight had been difficult. Actually it had been more than difficult. She'd barely been able to maintain a civil expression while spending most of the evening with the Daniels family without J.D.

Anger rose quickly and frighteningly when Shae thought of how he'd found a moment to call and tell her that he wouldn't be making it back to the party in time to take her home. She'd never been so embarrassed in her life. How could he have done that to her?

Concerned for her friend, Vee had volunteered to drive Shae. On the ride home, J.D.'s sister had talked nonstop, desperately trying to convince Shae to give herself some time to relax before making any decisions about her relationship that she might later regret.

What Vee didn't know was Shae had already made her decision. After entering the penthouse, she marched purposefully through the apartment to her bedroom. She removed her dress and heels, slipped into a worn pair of denims and a comfortable T-shirt, and headed into the bathroom to wash off her makeup.

J.D. would be here soon. Shae knew that. He'd step through her front door with his apologies and explanations, begging for her forgiveness.

As she waited, her thoughts drifted to her mother's remarks about her relationship. Vivian Weitherspoon had cautioned her daughter against opening her heart to a man that she barely knew, suggesting that she slow down the pace to give them time to learn more about each other. Ignoring her mother's advice, Shae had plowed ahead as her feelings blossomed into love. Heading into the living room, Shae dropped onto the sofa, reached for the remote and turned on the television, absently watching the ten o'clock news.

Could she do it? Would she be strong enough to break things off with him when she loved him so much? She didn't and wouldn't know until he walked through the door.

Thirty minutes later there was a knock on her door. Shae rose, ambled down the hall and let him in before returning to her spot on the sofa. J.D. rushed into the apartment and stood in the center of the room, hands shoved inside the back pockets of his Dockers.

"Sweetheart, I'm sorry," he began in a concilatory tone. "Everything went haywire once we got to the airport."

Silently watching the man she loved, Shae waited until he ran out of steam before saying, "We need to talk."

His eyes opened wide before he dropped onto the sofa. "Okay."

"J.D., I love you."

His face broke into a happy smile. "I love you, too," he responded.

Happiness swept through her like an avalanche. Her heart filled with joy before she took hold of her emotions. She had waited, hoping he would make that declaration. But she refused to let them sway her from what needed to be said. "I don't want you to say those words because you think it's what I want to hear and you believe they'll get you out of trouble. It's not going to happen."

"I'm not," J.D. denied, holding her gaze with his own. "I have loved you for a while, I just wasn't ready to say the words. I've felt that way since the first time we made love. But I didn't want to frighten you because we'd only been together a short while. I kept it to myself."

Determined to say what needed to be said, Shae focused on the multicolored pillow on the sofa. "Vee and I talked and she suggested that I tell you how I feel."

"My sister?"

Nodding, Shae added, "Yes. Actually, she defended you all the way home from David's house. So I'm going to take her advice." She shifted on the sofa, facing him. "We can't continue this way."

"I know, honey. Honestly this won't—"

She cut him off with a sweeping wave of her hand. "Stop. Please listen. An explanation is the last thing I want right now. I need you to seriously pay attention to what I'm saying and try to understand."

"Don't worry. I will," J.D. promised.

"I can't continue like this. I need a more stable relationship than what I've had so far with you."

"What do you want me to do?"

"When we first met you were great. You made sure I got to work on time and helped me get settled in my own place. Most of all, if I called you or needed anything you were right there willing to help." Shae stopped talking, searching for the proper words to express her feelings. "That's changed. I understand how important your job is to you. It's the same for me. Work is a central part of my life. But I don't allow my job to come between us, or before us the way you've let Amir and your friends take center stage whenever they call. I should be able to depend on you."

"Phil's my friend. I've known him since grade school," J.D. defended.

"I understand. But J.D., we were at a party for *your* family and you left me sitting there without a way home. Do you realize how bad that looked?"

"I was coming back."

"I understand that. And when you said the words, you actually meant them. Things wouldn't have been so bad if you had come back. J.D., your sister brought me home." She jabbed his head with her finger. "Think about that."

Red traces of embarrassment colored his cheeks.

"That should never have happened. I can't depend on you anymore. You're my boyfriend for lack of a better term. But there have been two incidents where you've either been incredibly late or left me alone like a snack you've put down until you got hungry."

Mortified, he studied the carpet.

"I deserve better, J.D."

"Yes, you do." He shut his eyes, then opened them. Surprised, she checked to make sure she'd seen the misery lurking in the depths of his brown orbs. "There are problems I need to work on. I don't know how to separate things. It might sound crazy, but it's true. These are my friends and whenever I need anything, they help me. I feel obligated to do the same."

Shae sat down on the sofa next to him. "That makes perfect sense to me. But you're going to have to figure it out. Because this is not my picture of the type of relationship I plan to stay in."

"I don't want to lose you, Shae."

"Then treat me better."

"I will do better," he said with strong conviction. "Please don't end us just yet. Give me a chance to make things up to you." He reached for her hand and intertwined their fingers. "Let me show you that I can do better."

Wrapping her free hand around theirs, Shae said, "For as far back as I can remember the most important man in my life has let me down. My father missed every milestone in my life because of Prestige Computers. His company came before my mother and me and anything that we might need." She faced him and held his gaze with her own. "I won't be involved with any man that expects me to come second to his career. Do you understand me?"

"Yes. Nothing like this will ever happen again. I—"

Shae placed a finger over his lips, hushing him. "Don't make promises you can't keep. All I want you to do is support me and let me depend on you a little."

"You've got it, sweetheart."

"Good. Thank you. Now we can put this discussion behind us, let's celebrate."

J.D. returned to the living room with a bottle of wine. He opened it, filled two glasses, then handed one to Shae. He slid into the spot next to her on the sofa, sipping the crisp, fruity white Zinfandel.

"Did you mean what you said earlier?" she asked.

Stroking her cheek, he answered, "I said a lot of things. Which one are you asking about?"

"Do you love me?"

He placed his glass on the end table, faced her, looking deeply into her gray eyes. "Yes."

Nibbling on her bottom lip, Shae wrung her hands together nervously. "What about you? Now that we have come to an understanding about our expectations for each other, do you want to take back your declaration?"

"No." He cupped her cheek, stroking the soft skin with his thumb. The caress made her flesh tingle. "I do love you." He leaned closer and placed a gentle kiss on her lips.

"There's another way we can celebrate," Shae suggested.

"Oh?"

Smiling, she stood and took his hand. J.D. rose, following her from the living room, down the hall and into the bedroom. Shae lifted her arms and drew his head down for a passionate kiss. His tongue slipped between her lips and met hers. "I love you, J.D."

"And I love you," J.D. replied, unbuttoning her blouse.

# *Chapter 21*

The hot noontime sun beat down on Shae's curly head as she exited her car. She strolled across the parking lot, singing the lyrics to a Kim Waters tune.

As Shae approached the employee entrance she switched to her game face, the calm and understanding expression she used when treating patients. Unfortunately, each time her thoughts turned to J.D., her lips curved into a smile that refused to disappear.

Shae couldn't help it. Her personal and professional lives were in harmony. She felt completely fulfilled at work and blissfully happy at home. Life had been extremely good for her and J.D. these past weeks. Revealing her concerns and fears had been the key to changing the direction of their relationship. It gave them both an opportunity to vent their frustrations and opened the door for a honest discussion.

Pleased with her little part of the world, Shae practically skipped down the quiet corridor to her office. After storing and locking her belongings inside the black file cabinet, she grabbed her lab coat from the hanger behind her door, slipped it over her tangerine Capri pantsuit and left the room. She stopped to greet several new patients in various stages of medical care as she headed to the front desk.

It had been a month since the open house and each week the number of new patients seeking treatment had grown.

Shae halted at the front desk, waiting patiently near the workstation until the receptionist finished helping a caller. "Hi, Paula."

Paula grinned at the nurse manager. "Hey! How you doin?"

"Good," Shae answered, leaning over the desk to retrieve her messages. "Any problems I should know about?"

"None that I'm aware of. Although—" Paula paused dramatically for effect. Her voice dropped an octave as she pointed toward the medical director's door "—Dr. Reid wants to see you."

Surprised, Shae stared wordlessly at the older woman, running through a quick mental list of disasters Kenyatta might want to discuss. Nothing stood out. What was up? The clinic had been running efficiently and smoothly. So she couldn't figure out what Kenyatta might need from her. Well, there was only one way to find out. She had to go to his office and talk with him. "Anything I need to know about?"

Paula shrugged, watching her with baffled brown eyes. "Don't know. He didn't mention anything in particular. Although I will say that he seemed very animated."

Her mind reeled with questions. That didn't make

any sense. Kenyatta was never animated. He was the most stoic, almost comatose, person she'd ever met.

With purposeful strides, Shae headed down the hallway. She knocked on the door before poking her head inside the room. "Paula said you wanted to see me?"

Kenyatta sat in his usual place, parked before the computer. He glanced in Shae's direction, then flashed a large grin, waving Shae into the room. "Hi. Come in." He rose in one fluid motion, stepped around the desk, and started for the makeshift coffee station location in his office with his mug. "Can I get you anything? A cup of coffee? Tea?"

"No. I'm fine."

Shae took the chair opposite his. "What's going on?"

"I got some exciting news this morning." He filled his cup with coffee, then added cream and sugar.

Turning to face him, she asked, "Really? About what?"

"The clinic and you."

Her heart skipped a beat. "Me! What about me? And the clinic, what going on here?"

Strolling across the room, the medical director returned to his seat behind the desk. "We got a call this morning from the mayor's office."

"And?" Shae prompted. Why was he dragging this out? Couldn't he just say what needed to be said and let her digest it?

"One of our patients sent a letter to Mayor Daley about you."

That got Shae's attention. Frowning, she folded her hands across her chest and leaned back in her chair. "About me? Was it a complaint?"

"No." He shook his head. "Not at all."

"Then what was it?"

Smiling proudly, Kenyatta explained, "Mayor Daley

has added your name to his annual list of 'Citizens Who Make A Difference' recognition dinner."

Stunned, Shae shared at the medical director. "Why?"

His eyebrows shot up to his hairline. "You're kidding, right?"

'No. You forget I'm not from here. I don't know anything about what goes on in the state of Illinois. Information would be a good thing right now."

"Sorry." Kenyatta sat forward and looked at her intently. "You took charge of your position so easily that I sometimes forget that you're still new to the staff and the city. So here's the deal. Each year the mayor selects six people that have significantly helped the residents of Chicago. This year you were one of the six."

"But why? I haven't done anything."

"The nutritional plan and menus you created for low-income families got a lot of press. You're our new local celebrity." Dr. Reid explained in a tone filled with awe and respect. He pulled a sheet from a manila folder and handed Shae a fax page with the mayor's seal on it.

The letter congratulated her for her contribution to the health and well-being of the city residents and detailed the process used to induct her into this elite group. The fax included an invitation for her to attend a banquet in recognition of her contribution to the city. She would share the limelight with five other local heroes who had donated their time and energy to the welfare of the city of Chicago.

"Woo!"

Dr. Reid smiled across the desk at her. "Good job. We're proud of you. You've put the clinic on the map."

"I hope this award thing will help convince the people in this area to come and see us."

"Me, too," Dr. Reid said.

Reading the fax a second time, pride flashed through her. She'd done something that had made a difference to the people she served. Shae stood. "It's time for me to get back to work."

He stood and extended his hand. Shae took his hand and shook it. "Congratulations. We're proud of you."

"Thank you."


Shae tucked her feet under her as she got comfortable on the steel-gray sofa. Luther Vandross cooed out the words to "There's Nothing Better Than Love" as she waited for J.D. to serve dinner.

"Okay, here's your drink," J.D. said, appearing in the living area with a blue-and-white oriental teapot on a tray. "It's jasmine tea."

She took a mug and sniffed the air appreciatively. "I love it when you cook."

"Thank you. I'm glad you appreciate my culinary skills."

"I do. Where did you get it?" She asked between sips of her tea.

"Jia's on Delaware," he answered, returning to the kitchen. "Maki rolls and kung pao chicken coming up."

"Yum. What did you get for yourself?" Shae hopped up from her place on the sofa, reached inside her purse and removed the fax. She placed the sheet on J.D.'s chair before returning to her previous position on the sofa.

From the kitchen, he answered, "Mongolian beef."

"Sounds good."

"I didn't ask earlier, how was your day?"

"It was interesting. We need to talk about it." She reached for the teapot, topped off her mug, then placed the fax on his chair.

"Hot food on its way in, we can talk when it gets here." Five minutes later J.D. served up the rolls and the chicken stir fry with diced vegetables and peanuts in spicy Szechuan sauce to Shae and placed the beef on the edge of the coffee table near his chair. Without looking, he sank into his chair and immediately got up. "What's this?" he asked, scanning the crumpled piece of paper.

Shae waited expectantly for his response.

"Congratulations!" He rushed to the couch, pulled her off the sofa, swung her around. He placed petite kisses all over her face. "I'm so proud of you."

"Thank you. Who do you think I should ask to be my date?"

Growling playfully, he laid Shae on the sofa and began to tickle her. "Who do you think?" he demanded as he made her squirm. "Who? Let me think. Maybe someone you're having dinner with."

"Stop. Stop," she cried, laughing so hard she could barely avoid J.D.'s touch. "Don't."

"Say J.D.," he demanded.

"No!" she shouted back.

"J.D."

Trying to sit up, Shae slipped off the edge of the couch and into a heap on the floor in front of the coffee table. She drew into a ball. "Okay. J.D."

"That's what I like to hear." He scooped her off the floor, deposited her on the sofa and sank into the spot next to her.

It took her a few minutes to regain her composure. Still giggling, she sat up, taking deep breaths as she recovered.

J.D. leaned closed and cupped her face in his large hand. He caressed her cheek with his thumb. "Seriously," he began in a soft, husky voice. "I'm really proud of you."

Tucking her bare feet under her, Shae admitted, "This is like a dream. I have you. My career is in high gear and now this award. I am where I want to be in life. And it feels great."

Pulling her close, he placed a gentle kiss on her lips. "Yes, it does." The love shining from his eyes made a corresponding surge of love fill her. Although they'd had a few rocky moments, it had been well worth it to get to this place in their relationship.

Another kiss followed the last and then another, and another. J.D. grunted, laying his forehead gently against her. "We better eat before the food gets cold."

"Always thinking with your stomach, aren't you?" Shae teased, looking at his face.

The fire in J.D.'s eyes made her breath catch in her throat. At that moment if he'd asked her, she would have forgotten everything to make love with him.

He lifted the tray with her food on it and handed it to her. "Come on, eat up."

"Thanks."

J.D. returned to his chair and picked up his plate. "So now that you're a local celebrity, will you still love me?"

"Every day," Shae answered quickly.

Smiling back at her, he muttered, "I'm glad to hear it."

She dipped her maki roll in the spicy sauce and bit into it. The cucumber and asparagus tasted heavenly. "The one good thing about all of this is the clinic will get some good, free publicity. UHC's patients have grown steadily, but I'd like to see us operate at full capacity."

"This event will end up in all the papers and on television. You'll get the coverage that you want." J.D. forked a mouthful of Mongolian beef into his mouth, chewed on it for a minute, then inquired, "Do you think your parents would like to come and see you receive the award?"

Her heart slammed against her chest as she thought of her parents. Shae placed her plate on the coffee table and picked up her mug of tea, taking her time to come up with an appropriate answer that would get her off the hook. "My father is probably busy. His company does a lot of business with schools and this might be a really tight time for him."

"Perhaps if your dad can't make it your mom would like to come. I'm sure she misses you and would love to spend some time with her only child."

Shae shook her head. "My mother won't come here without my father."

"Don't you want to at least ask them? I mean, they are your parents and I'm sure they're proud of the things that you've accomplished."

"No," she said. "J.D., my family is not like yours. We're not as supportive of one another, like you are."

"Shae, what's really going on here?"

She knew once he posed the question that she wouldn't be able to get out of this situation without the truth. What was the truth? Her father had always been disappointed because she was a girl and hadn't followed in his footsteps. God, that sounded so clichéd, but it was true. Albert Weitherspoon wanted a boy to groom into his personal Mini-Me and that was difficult to do with a girl.

Shae wanted to be honest with J.D. Their relationship was too important to her to have lies between them. "Sweetheart, I love my parents, don't doubt that. But my father hasn't made it to any function that I've been part of in years." Shae couldn't keep the edge of pain or the years of disappointment that followed every major event in her life from her voice.

Concerned, J.D. hopped off the chair and came to her, slipping his arms around her. He pulled her close, rocking her back and forth. "It's okay. Don't worry about a thing."

"I told you before that I can't live with that kind of uncertainty and disappointment in my life. I've had more than twenty years of it. Plus, my father was really upset with me when I rejected a job with Prestige in favor of the clinic. He's not the most forgiving man. I don't think he'll leave his business to spend time watching me win an award when he feels I should have stayed in Malibu."

"Honey, you should give him a chance. I think you should at least ask him to the event. My mom says regardless of how people react, you should always do the right thing. The right thing for this situation is to invite them to the ceremony. What they do with the invitation is their business, but your conscience will be clear."

Shaking her head, she disengaged herself from J.D.'s embrace. "I'm sorry, I can't do this. I can't take the disappointment. It hurts too much."

"Okay. I'll leave things alone." He kissed her forehead. "I love you. Remember that."

She wrapped her arms around him, holding him and his love close. "I will. And I love you."

# Chapter 22

J.D. entered his parents' home through the front door and called, "Mom, Dad."

"I'm in the den," his mother yelled from the back of the house.

He strolled down the hall, following the sound of Lionel Richie singing "Three Times a Lady." At the den's entrance he found his mother sitting on one of the sofas with a magazine on her lap.

"Hey, you." Helen Daniels patted the spot next to her on the sofa. She glanced beyond her son and asked, "Where's Shae?"

"Work." He crossed the room and flopped down next to his mother. "Where's Dad?"

"At David's," she answered, retrieving her glass of ice water from the coffee table. "They're working on plans for a patio for David's backyard."

J.D. nodded and settled into the soft cushions of the

sofa, nibbling on his bottom lip. He'd come to his parents' house for some much-needed advice. Now that he was here, he wasn't certain he was making the correct decision.

Helen and J.D. sat in a comfortable silence for several minutes. His mother flipped through the pages of her magazine and sipped on her water while J.D. hummed along with Lionel Richie, trying to figure out a way to ask his question.

After several minutes, she closed the magazine and tossed it on the coffee table. She turned to her son and asked, "What do you need, honey?"

Shocked, his mouth dropped open and then snapped shut without uttering a word. He turned his head to one side, staring at his mother. How did she know he needed her help? "How did you know I came here looking for advice?"

"You're sitting here chewing on your bottom lip the way you use to when you were a kid. Plus, you don't make pop-in visits. You're the one kid that I have who calls before you come over."

One thing about Helen Daniels, she knew her children. Smiling at her, J.D. nodded. "You got me."

"So what do you need?" she asked, placing her glass on a coaster.

"Help," her son answered quickly.

"Okay." Mom intertwined her fingers and rested them in her lap. "What's going on?"

"Shae's been selected as one of the mayor's 'Citizens Who Make A Difference.'"

Smiling brightly, Helen squeezed J.D.'s hand. "Great. Tell her I said congratulations. Don't bother, I'll call her myself."

"That would be nice, Mom."

"That's not the real reason you're here. There's more, isn't there?"

"Yeah." J.D. paused, collecting his thoughts. "I know our family is not the same as hers. There are more of us and we tend to band together and help one another when it's needed. But I don't think Shae's family works the same way."

"Honey, every family operates in its own special way. You can't judge people because they do things differently from what you're use to."

He looked at his mother. "I know. And I don't. I want to do something special for Shae without causing new problems for her."

"What do you want to do?"

"I want to call her parents and invite them to the banquet."

"Have you asked Shae if she wants them here?"

"Yes."

"And she said?"

J.D. shook his head. "She made this weak excuse for not inviting them. I don't believe her. I think she's afraid to ask them."

"Why?"

"I think she's afraid of being disappointed, that they'll say no. That would break her heart. I think she'd rather be alone than let them hurt her."

"That's too bad."

"Yeah, that's what I think, too."

"What's going on?"

"First of all, this is for Shae. I'm not doing this to score brownie points or anything like that."

"Okay. Keep going."

"When she told me about the recognition dinner I suggested that we call her parents and invite them to the banquet. I thought it would be a good opportunity for me to meet and get to know them. I guess I was a bit surprised by her reaction and I needed an impartial opinion on her response."

"Shae didn't want to call her parents. Am I right?"

He nodded.

"Honey," Helen wrapped her hands around her son's. "It's obvious to me that Shae and parents are not very close."

"Why would you say that, Mom?"

"Shae's parents live in Malibu. Your girl lives in Chicago. An only child doesn't normally leave their parents' home so easily. Shae has settled into her new life without a look back at her parents. Generally, there's a reason for that."

"Mom, maybe I want to change that."

"It may not be your choice to make."

He shook off his mother's hand and rose from the sofa, pacing the floor in front of her. "Of course it is. I love her and I want to see her happy."

"J.D., what are you really asking me?"

"I want to contact her parents and let them know about the recognition banquet. I'd like to invite them to attend."

"What does Shae say about this?"

"She doesn't want to bother them."

"Mmm."

"What does that mean?"

"Son, maybe you should leave well enough alone."

"I can't. Mom, she's hurting so much. I don't want that for her. If I can help, I've got to try. I'm thinking if they agree to come to Chicago, maybe Shae and her father can settle their differences and establish some kind of relationship. Everything she's ever worked for has come together and I want her to be happy."

Helen rose from the couch and stepped in her son's path, halting him. "J.D., listen carefully to what I'm saying. First of all, families are different. What we have may be and probably is totally different from what Shae is used to. Second, they have to want a different relationship, a better relationship, before the situation can change. Just because you want this for her doesn't mean it's going to happen. Third, maybe things are the best they are ever going to be for that family. You could be stepping in and creating a whole new set of problems that won't help the situation at all. You can cause Shae a lot of pain."

Chuckling humorlessly, J.D. admitted, "Believe me, I've thought of all of that. But she's hurting so much now."

"Then do your job as the man who loves her." Helen placed her hands on his shoulders and turned him to face her. "Be there for Shae and love her. That's really all she expects and wants from you."

Shaking his head, he said, "I don't know. I feel that I should do more."

His mother's arms dropped to her sides. "I can't stop you. I will say that you need to be very careful about what you're doing. You could be stirring up a hornet's nest far worse than the pain you think she's suffering now."

"I'm thinking about all of that, Mom."

Helen studied her son for a beat. "You're going to do this, aren't you?"

"Yeah."

She pulled him into her embrace and hugged her son tightly. "Good luck."

Stepping away, J.D. smiled at her. "Thanks, Mom."

J.D. dropped a scrap of paper with the Weitherspoons' telephone number on it next to the black cordless phone and nibbled on his bottom lip. His mother's advice swirled around in his head, weighing heavily on his shoulders. Torn, he rubbed his hand across his neck, trying to relieve some of the tension in his muscles. Should he be interfering in Shae's family problems? J.D. didn't know. Was he doing a good thing or causing new problems for the woman he loved? Although he still believed that he was doing the right thing, his mother's warning weighed heavily on his shoulders. What J.D. did know was that he couldn't stand to see Shae so miserable. She wanted her family to celebrate her good fortune.

Picking up the piece of paper with Shae's parents' number on it, J.D. turned the sheet over in his hands. Smiling, he remembered how easy it had been to get that number. All he had to do was go into her home office and open her address book. There on the front page was an "in case of emergency" page with the names, address and telephone number of her parents, waiting for him to come by and take it down.

*Oh, what the hell,* he thought, picking up the phone and dialing the number. If they couldn't make it, he'd keep that fact to himself. The phone rang four times before the line was answered.

"Hello?" came a woman's curious voice. Maybe it was Shae's mother. J.D. didn't know.

"Umm. Hi."

"Yes?" she inquired.

"May I speak to either Mr. or Mrs. Weitherspoon," J.D. asked.

"I'm sorry. We don't accept calls from solicitors."

"Oh no. That's not why I've called."

"Who is this?" the female voice demanded.

"I'm J. D. Daniels. I'm Shae's friend and I'd like to speak with her parents."

"I'm sorry. Who is this again?"

"James Daniels. Shae Weitherspoon's friend."

"Is something wrong with Shae?"

"No. She's doing really well. But something great has happened for her."

"This is Mrs. Weitherspoon. I'm Shae's mother."

J.D. took a deep breath, then said, "Mrs. Weitherspoon, Shae has been selected by the mayor to receive an award."

"That's my Shae-Shae," Mrs. Weitherspoon uttered with complete pride in her voice. "How did all of this come about?"

"The mayor received letters from patients at the clinic where Shae works, praising her and the things that she's done."

"That's my baby."

"Yeah. That's my Shae. I'm calling because I want to invite you and your husband to the event."

"Oh, I'd love to go. But I have to check with Albert. He may not be able to get away right now."

For the first time, J.D. understood Shae's frustration with her parents. If he was receiving an award, his parents and siblings would demand to be part of the festivities. They would plan celebrations and support him through the banquet. There wouldn't be any "let me check with my husband."

"Mrs. Weitherspoon, if you can make it, the banquet is next week. Shae and I can pick you up at the airport. Just let us know."

"Thank you for letting us know about the ceremony. I'll talk to my husband and we'll get back to you as soon as possible."

They exchanged information before hanging up. Silently, J.D. sat on the sofa, going over his telephone conversation with Mrs. Weitherspoon in his mind. He'd done what he believed to be right. The Weitherspoons should have the opportunity to attend the award banquet and support their daughter. If they declined the offer, J.D. planned to keep his mouth shut regarding the call. Shae did not need this form of rejection from her family. The Daniels clan would act as Shae's cheering section.

# Chapter 23

*It's all his fault,* Shae silently fumed as she paced the baggage claim area of Chicago O'Hare International Airport. Albert and Vivian Weitherspoon were due to arrive in Chicago within the next hour.

Speaking of J.D., the man in question sat in one of the black vinyl chairs, reading the *Chicago Tribune.* *Arrogant man,* she thought, folding her arms across her chest as she marched from the ceiling-to-floor windows to the black vinyl chairs and back again. Shae turned, narrowing her eyes at him and growled. Oblivious to Shae's mental tirade and evil eye, J.D. continued to scan the paper, ignoring her as she continued to pace, digging a trench in the gray industrial carpet.

After a discussion about the mayor's dinner and her parents, Shae had believed the issue had been settled and that J.D. understood her feelings and respected her decision to leave her parents out of the event. Things took an unexpected turn when her mother called with plane reservation information and arrival times. Shae turned to J.D., who shyly admitted that he had talked to Mrs. Weitherspoon about the dinner and award ceremony. Sure, Shae wanted to see her parents, but she didn't want to get her hopes up and have her feelings crushed. More than that, Shae didn't want to be disappointed. Albert Weitherspoon had a flawless record for skipping out on social functions at the last minute.

The attendant unlocked the door and announced the arrival of flight 7455 from Los Angeles International Airport. Biting her lip, Shae held her breath, hoping that both of her parents would step through the door.

Vivian Weitherspoon strolled through the door. A cheek-length bob framed her smooth, oval-shaped dark chocolate face. Dressed in a long-sleeve silk blouse with the collar turned up at the neck and long, black linen trousers that showed her petite waist and accentuated her narrow hips, Vivian looked as if she'd stepped from the pages of *Vogue*. At first glance, people would question the notion that this woman was the mother of a twentysomething daughter.

Moving at a slower pace, Albert Weitherspoon followed. His neatly trimmed reddish brown hair framed a round, fair-skinned face. Halting inside the terminal, he removed his Cartier sunglasses and shoved the outrageously expensive eyewear inside the pocket of his green Polo shirt. Intelligent gray eyes swept the room, observing the goings-on as he trailed his fashion-plate wife.

All of Shae's concerns and fears melted away the moment her parents emerged from the airplane ramp. Shae shook her head, laughing. At that moment, she forgave J.D. Maybe he knew her better than she thought.

Albert Weitherspoon never truly took a vacation. He refused to leave Prestige Computers in the hands of his competent staff. Instead, he ruled his computer empire by cell phone, PDA, fax and e-mail. Unaware of Shae's scrutiny, her father stepped through the door with his cell phone attached to his ear, barking out orders.

Her parents searched for a familiar face as they dodged the hordes of airline travelers. Love for her parents exploded to the surface and Shae found herself pushing past others to get to her mother and father. Excited beyond belief, Shae rushed up to them, practically flinging herself into their arms. "Mommie, Pop," she sang. "You came!"

Vivian Weitherspoon hugged her only child tightly, kissing her cheek. "Shae-Shae, I've missed you, babe."

"I missed you, too, Mommie."

Shae turned to her father. There was a moment of awkwardness before he opened his arms wide. She flew at him, hugging him close. "Pop, I'm glad you're here."

"Me, too, princess. Me, too!" he murmured into her hair, before slowly releasing her.

Grinning like a fool, Shae grabbed J.D.'s hand and pulled him forward. "First, I want to introduce you to my friend. Mommie, Pop, this is James Daniels. I call him J.D."

Always gracious, Vivian stretched out her hand and pulled J.D. into a loose hug, kissing his cheek. "It's nice to finally put a face to your voice. Thank you for letting us know about the award dinner."

Blushing, J.D. muttered, "You're welcome."

Shae grabbed her father's arm and pulled him to J.D. "Pop, this is J.D. J.D., my father, Albert Weitherspoon." Shae held her breath waiting for whatever fireworks might follow.

Her father stood before J.D., sizing the younger man up with a cold gleam in his gray eyes. The air crackled with tension as the two men in her life assessed one another. Her father's expression resembled a judge sitting on his bench, searching the accused defendant for the truth. After a minute, he held out his hand. J.D. took it. "Nice to meet you."

"Same here," J.D. replied, shaking Mr. Weitherspoon's hand. Shae examined one man and then the other. Albert Weitherspoon had never liked a single boyfriend that she brought home. He tended to be very reserved with new people. Although J.D. had brought the family together, that act of kindness wouldn't sway her father's opinion. "Let's get your luggage and get on the road," J.D. suggested, leading the Weitherspoon trio toward the baggage claim area.

"How long do you guys plan to stay?" Shae intercepted a sideways glance from her mother in her father's direction. She frowned. *What was that look about?* "It's not a secret, is it?"

"No. We figured at least a week, if that's not too long. We don't want to be a bother," her mother stated.

Shae squeezed her mother's hand. "Of course not! I'm looking forward to spending time with you, both of you. The longer your visit, the better."

At the baggage carousel the small group waited in silence. Shae took her first good look at her father. A sickly pallor lay below his uneven golden tan. She took a step closer, examining him with the critical eye of a health care professional. Dark circles marred the skin under his eyes. Closer scrutiny revealed the loss of a few pounds from Albert's tall frame. His expensive clothes hung loosely around his body.

Could this be due to overexertion or an illness? Shae

wondered. Was the company having problems that required his undivided attention to the detriment of his health? This wouldn't be the first time that the company had fought off a hostile takeover.

Her father had looked perfectly fine when she left Malibu. Shae had lived in their home for a few months following her return from Doctors Without Boundaries. She would certainly have noticed any problems.

Was he ill? That couldn't be. Her mother would have let her know, wouldn't she? The tiny voice in Shae's head whispered, not if Albert Weitherspoon didn't want her to know. Completely devoted to her husband, Vivian Weitherspoon would do whatever Albert asked.

Shae switched off the clinical portion of her brain and concentrated on the pleasure of having her parents in Chicago. She planned to get to the bottom of his gaunt appearance before they returned to Malibu, but she had a week to figure out what was going on.

J.D. stopped the car in front of the high-rise apartment building. "Shae, why don't you take your family up to your place? I'll park, then bring up the luggage."

Shae grabbed her purse off the floor of the car. "That's a good idea. Mommie, Pop, come on. We'll get out of here and J.D. can have security help with your bags." She pushed open the door of her Volvo, waiting at the curb for her parents to follow. They strolled up the well-maintained walkway and entered the lobby, halting near the security guard station. "Clay, this is my mother and father. They will be staying with me for a few days. I'm going to give them the spare keys, so don't be surprised if they're in and out of my apartment."

"I'll note that, Ms. Weitherspoon."

"Oh, Shae, I love this room. It's so elegant," Vivian cooed before her gaze landed on the guard, waiting at the desk. "You told me the building had security, but this is excellent!" Impressed, Mommie hurried over to the sitting area, running a hand over the soft fabric of the sofa, then turned a critical eye to the coffee table. "It's perfect if you don't want to take someone up to your apartment. You can meet them here and talk. I like it."

"Thanks, Mommie."

Albert Weitherspoon marched up to the security desk. He examined the uniformed employee for a silent and unnerving beat. A worried frown passed over Clay's face. "Can I help you, sir?"

"You provide twenty-four-hour security in this building?" Shae's father asked.

With a slight nod of his head the guard answered, "Yes, sir."

"This is a big building. Do you check on each floor? Doors and windows?"

"Sir, we do perimeter checks every hour. One guard stays at the desk while the other five patrol the building on foot."

Giggling, Shae turned away. The guard's stiff posture and tone of voice reminded Shae of the men she'd seen in those military movies where the enlisted man is questioned by a superior. She was half expecting the guard to salute.

"Good," her father said. "Thank you." He strolled across the marble floor and wrapped a loose arm around his wife as Shae searched through her purse for her keys.

"Found them." The keys jingled as she waved them in the air. "I'm ready." Shae headed to the elevator and held the doors while her parents entered, punching the button for the penthouse.

One finely arched eyebrow rose. "Penthouse. My, my."

"I like it. It's a nice apartment."

"We'll see," her father responded, folding his arms across his chest and resting his head against the elevator wall. Within minutes they arrived at Shae's floor and made their way to her front door.

Shae unlocked the door and stepped aside so that her parents entered before her, pointing a finger toward the living room. "If you go down this hallway, you'll find the living room." She followed after closing and locking the door behind them. "Let me show you the rest of the place."

Vivian Weitherspoon stood at the sliding door to the patio, admiring the view. "It's gorgeous." Albert sat on the sofa, checking his cell phone for messages.

Shae came up beside her mother and placed an arm around her shoulders. "It is nice, isn't it? Some nights I sit out here and watch the lights flicker on and off from the different office buildings. I love how the lights dance off the water."

"I'm sure it's quite stunning," Mommie agreed. From the sofa Shae heard a huge yawn.

"It sounds like somebody is tired. Let me show you to your room so that you can get comfortable."

She gave them the grand tour through the living and dining rooms, stopped at the kitchen, then down the hallway to the set of bedrooms. At the guest bedroom, she opened the door. "Make yourselves comfortable. J.D. should be here with your luggage any minute. This room has a bath. I think you have everything you need. If I've missed anything, let me know."

"I wouldn't mind a cup of coffee," her father said, testing the mattress.

"That sounds lovely." Her mother tossed her purse

on the bed and hurried after Shae. "Hold on. I'll come with you. I'd like to get a good look at your kitchen. Besides, you have to work. We'll have to fend for ourselves while you're away."

Her mother peered into every cupboard and the refrigerator, then took a seat at the small kitchen table, and watched her daughter scoop coffee grounds into the black coffee maker. After a minute, Shae asked, "Is something wrong with Pop, Mommie?"

"Wrong? Why do you ask?"

"He doesn't look his best." Shae snapped the top in place and added water to the machine. "There are dark circles under his eyes and he's lost a bit of weight. Is the company doing okay?"

"It's fine. But as usual, there are always groups trying to buy it."

"Mommie, you know that stress is not a good thing for someone his age. Is he taking his blood pressure medicine?"

"Of course. Stop worrying."

"I'm a nurse. It's my job to ask the questions."

"Shae, your father has been very busy the past few weeks. You know how much that company means to him. It's exhausting." Her hands fluttered around the collar of her blouse. "Albert doesn't believe in delegating. He has to oversee every aspect of the company. Sometimes he doesn't know when to let things go. It's the way he is."

"Are you sure he's all right?"

"He's fine."

There was a sharp rap on the door. "That's J.D. I'll be right back." Shae ran down the hallway to the front door. J.D. stood with one of the guards. The pair brought in the bags and dropped them in Shae's living room.

J.D. walked the guard to the door and handed the man a tip. "Thanks, man. I appreciate the help."

"My pleasure," the doorman said, shutting the door as he let himself out.

Returning to the living room, J.D. found Shae waiting for him. He sat on the sofa next to her. "Everything all right?"

"Yeah," she answered, running her hand up and down his thigh. "Thanks for going the extra mile for my folks."

He answered, "You're welcome. Does this mean you're not mad at me anymore?"

Grinning at him, she leaned close and kissed his lips. "No. I'm not."

"Shae-Shae, the coffee's ready. Do you want a cup?" her mother asked.

"No, Mommie. Enjoy!"

J.D. stood, linking his fingers with hers. "It's time for me to go. I'm going to take care of some business stuff and I'll talk to you later."

Standing next to him, Shae hugged J.D. close before admitting, "I know I wasn't very nice when you told me that you'd talked to my parents. I'm sorry. I took my frustrations out on you and that wasn't right. Honestly, I was afraid that Mommie and Pop would decline the invitation and hurt my feelings. I want you to know that I am grateful that you called them for me. Thank you."

"You're welcome."

## Chapter 24

The police precinct office hummed with activity. Phones rang continuously. The blues were everywhere, taking statements from witnesses, comforting victims and escorting handcuffed prisoners behind a thick steel door that J.D. suspected led to the cell block. He sat on a hard wooden bench with a cup of coffee as he took everything in. His thoughts turned to how an impressionable young man might easily get lost in the legal system.

J.D. shut his eyes against the bitter edge of frustration that gripped him. He'd had such big hopes and dreams for Amir. From the look of things, the kid may have thrown his future away for good with this latest stunt. *Why couldn't he stay out of trouble?*

After picking up the Weitherspoons from the airport and chauffeuring them to Shae's apartment, J.D. had volunteered to bring up their luggage. While parking the car, he had received a frantic telephone call from Mrs. Jonson. Her son had been involved in a car accident. A young mother and her three-year-old daughter had been injured during the incident. The police had mentioned charging Amir with driving under the influence and reckless endangerment.

Drunk driving! Did this kid have a death wish? During the arrest process the police had found empty beer bottles in the backseat of the car. At this moment, J.D. wanted to turn Amir over his knee and give him the beat down he deserved. What was going on in that kid's head? Were his brains completely scrambled?

J.D.'s first instinct had been to walk away from Amir and the whole sorry business. But Mrs. Jonson was a hardworking single parent and a caring soul who didn't deserve to be treated this way by her son. J.D. refused to leave her without help. Before meeting her at her house, he'd taken a moment to call David and get some legal advice on how to handle the situation.

Worried about the effects of jail on her son, Mrs. Jonson had put up her small home as collateral to get him out of jail. That house represented the only asset that the Jonson family had. Concerned that some un-scrupulous bail bondsman might take advantage of this nice lady, J.D. had tagged along to offer advice and moral support and to read the fine print on the contract. Truthfully, he felt Mrs. Jonson should leave Amir in jail for a few days. Maybe a little quality time in a small win-dowless room would teach her son a valuable lesson or two.

"Daniels?" called the desk sergeant. J.D. rose from his place on the hard, wood bench and made his way to the desk.

"I'm James Daniels," he answered.

The police officer glanced at a sheet of paper, then slid it across the desk with a pen. "Sign here," he ordered, pointing at a place at the bottom of the page. "Amir Jonson will be down in a minute."

Nodding, J.D. placed his paper cup on the desk and quickly read the sheet before adding his signature. He pushed the sheet back across the desk and picked up his cup.

The officer separated the triplicate copies and handed one to J.D. "You can wait here."

J.D. folded the sheet and stashed it in his back pocket. "When does he have to appear in court?" J.D. asked.

The officer referred to a spot on his copy of the official looking form. "Ten days from now. Bring his attorney with him. Are you his father?"

"No. I'm a family friend. His mother had to go to work. I told her that I'd make sure Amir made it home."

"We had a time with him. Mouthing off. Cursing. No remorse for what happened. This kid needs a good kick in the rear."

"I hear you." J.D. drew in a deep breath. "That's Amir. The 'tude is the worst part of him."

"He needs to grow up." The officer chuckled unpleasantly. The sound made J.D. cringed inwardly. "Actually, he's going to grow up. This situation will make a man or a punk out of him."

This didn't sound good. Swallowing the last of his coffee, J.D. tossed the empty cup in the trash, then strolled aimlessly around the small area, searching for the correct words to get this kid back on track. Behind him, he heard metal hit metal, then the turn of a lock. Seconds later, Amir ambled into the room, stopped at a desk and collected his personal belongings. The young man turned, searching for a familiar face. His expectant expression faded to a sneer when he noticed who was waiting for him.

In a flash, all of J.D.'s earlier anger returned. This kid was a major screw up, true, but nothing major had happened so far to change Amir's path. But J.D. suspected that this incident would cause gigantic problems in Amir's young life.

Blood oozed from an angry cut above the boy's right eye. A huge yellow stain covered much of the front of his white T-shirt and he smelled like an open can of beer. Amir glanced beyond where J.D. stood. "Where's my ma?"

"At work," J.D. answered curtly, taking Amir's arm and turning him toward the exit. "Come on. I'm going to take you home."

Amir shook off J.D.'s hand and started out the door without another word. J.D. followed. After climbing into the car, he sat for a moment. "Why?"

Amir grumbled, but gave no answer.

"Underage drinking is just one of the issues. You've put your mother's home in jeopardy. Your future is edging toward non-existence, plus you hurt two innocent people. And we haven't touched on the fact that you put your life in harm's way. Was a few beers and some laughs with your buddies worth all of this?"

Slouching in the bucket seat, Amir hunched his shoulders. "It was a game, man. We wanted to see how fast the car would go."

Pursing his lips, J.D. stated, "It's not a game anymore. This is going to cost you. You might end up in jail. Have you thought about that?"

"You're just trying to scare me. It's not happening. They ain't goin' put me in jail. We were only fooling around. You know, playing."

J.D. turned the key in the ignition, shifting the transmission into drive, but didn't move. "Don't bet on that. The mayor has been cracking down on crimes in the city. Drunk drivers don't get a lot of slack. Don't forget, it's an election year. He could make an example of you."

The change of expression on Amir's face almost made J.D. laugh. Unfortunately, this wasn't a funny situation. The young man had made a major mistake that could haunt him for all of his life.

"That ain't going to happen," Amir rolled the edge of his T-shirt, muttering in a tone far from the confidence he expressed seconds earlier.

Sighing heavily, J.D. pulled out of his parking space and headed for the freeway. "Let's hope not."

After a meal of roasted chicken, rosemary red skin potatoes, a garden salad, and stir-fried green beans, Shae and her parents relaxed in the living room while catching up on Malibu happenings.

It felt good to have her parents close. Shae watched her father drop onto the sofa and reach for the remote. He switched on the television and channel surfed until he found the business news, then turned down the volume so that all she heard was soft murmurings. Her mother sat next to him with a glass of lemonade in one hand while the other rested on her husband's thigh. She took several sips from her glass before placing it on a coaster on the coffee table.

"Shae-Shae, that was a wonderful meal," Vivian complimented. "When did you become so accomplished in the kitchen?"

Shae shrugged. "I've always enjoyed cooking. It calms my nerves after a busy day at the clinic." She gave her mother a pointed glare. "You never let me anywhere near a stove, so I never cooked."

"Well, you fixed that, didn't you?" Albert chimed in, "Yes indeed, princess. I enjoyed that dinner."

"Thank you. Roasted chicken is one of J.D.'s favorites."

During dinner, Shae had kept a close eye on her father. He had pushed most of his food around on his plate. She took a little comfort in the fact that he had enjoyed the meal, although he'd eaten very little of it. "Speaking of your friend, where is he?"

"J.D. is probably working."

"Hmm. Really. I expected him to join us." Shae's mother picked up her glass and offered it to her husband. Pop took a long swallow before handing it back.

Shae stood, crossed her arms, and gave her father the evil eye. It was time for the inquisition. "What are you implying, Pop?"

"Nothing, princess. All I'm saying is I would think that your friend would want to get to know your parents better and vice versa. After all, this is our first night in Chicago. Staying for dinner would have given us an opportunity to talk, unless—" he paused dramatically, "—he has something to hide."

"Well, knowing how considerate a man J.D. is, I suspect he wanted to give us some family time together alone. Let us talk freely without his presence. Don't worry, Pop. You'll get your chance to interrogate him."

Her father bristled, denying, "I—I—I don't want to cause problems."

"Sure you do. I know you better than that. If you could get J.D.'s elementary school transcript and use it against him, you would. Stop pretending. This is the way you think you're protecting me from the evils of the world." Shae stepped around the coffee table, sat on the opposite side of her father, and touched his arm. "Pop, I'm a grown woman and I care very deeply for J.D. I'm warning you, don't interfere."

Silence followed her statement. Her father frowned back at her and her mother looked as if she'd just sucked a lemon. Shae waited for a beat, then glared at her mother before turning to her father, adding, "Pop, you're here to see me get my award, add your support and spend some quality time with your only child. Don't make me choose between you and J.D. I don't want to. I plan to keep both of you in my life. Now, let's talk about something else."

"Are we allowed to ask a question or two about 'Mr. Wonderful'?" Mommie asked sarcastically.

Smiling, Shae returned to her chair across from her parents. "Certainly. What would you like to know?"

"What kind of work does he do?" Mommie asked.

"J.D. is a sports agent."

Her father tapped the mute button on the television and gave his daughter his full attention. "Is he any good?"

"I imagine so. He's been in this business for close to ten years. He seems to know what he's doing and has a good client base."

"Hmm," he grunted with a frown on his face.

Shae rubbed a finger back and forth across her chin. Her parents needed to see J.D. in action. Get to know him and find out that he didn't haven a hidden agenda. "I tell you what, the next time we're together you can ask him about his business, how's that?"

"Your mother and I are interested in your friend. We want to make sure that you're happy," he said, taking his wife's hand.

"I am happy. Everything at work is good. My *private* life," Shae stressed, "is going well and I'm pleased that you decided to come and visit."

"Princess, you're our only child and—"

Raising her hand to cut off her father, Shae said, "Stop! We've watched this video too many times in the past. Let's watch a different movie."

"Okay, we'll leave your life alone. How about this? I'd like to take you and J.D. to dinner. Think of it as your mother's and my way of repaying him for all of his help. The least we can do is buy the man a meal. What do you say?"

"I say that's an excellent idea. Then you can see that he's a great guy and not some gigolo after my money. And Pop, that will be your opportunity to ask J.D. all the questions you have on your mind."

"We're only looking out for you, Shae-Shae," her mother reminded.

"We only want the best for our girl," her father added.

Chuckling, Shae held her mother's gaze. "I've got the best. You'll see differently when we're together." She turned to her father. "Dinner tomorrow?"

He nodded.

"I'll call him later and let him know. Now that we've settled that, would you like to see where I work? I thought you might want to go to the clinic and meet some of my coworkers and friends."

"That would be wonderful, Shae-Shae," her mother said. "Are you sure it will be all right? I mean, we don't want to interfere in your work day."

"You won't. I took time off so that I can be with you guys. We'll just take a quick trip to the clinic, then do whatever you'd like to do."

Her father hit the mute button and the anchor's voice filled the air with international news. "Sounds good, princess."

# Chapter 25

Although they hadn't made a single comment, Shae could easily tell that her parents were appalled by the community that she worked in. Their tight, pinched-mouth expressions said it all.

Shae didn't care, because she knew she belonged at Urban Health Center and she felt needed. She parked in the employee lot and ushered the pair into the building. As they stepped through the employee entrance, her father stated, "You know, I've been thinking of adding a clinic to the daycare center. The place could be run by a nurse practitioner."

Vivian squeezed her husband's hand. "Honey, that sounds wonderful." She turned to her daughter. "What do you think?"

"I think it's a great idea," Shae said, patting her father's shoulder. "I went to school with a couple of nurse practitioners who would love the opportunity."

Her father glared hard at Shae. "That's not what I meant."

"I know." Chuckling, she stopped in the middle of the corridor, turned to her father and held his gaze. "I'm fine right where I am."

"But you can do so much more in Malibu," he suggested.

"I probably could. But this community needs me much more." Shaking her head, Shae wrapped an arm around each parent. "Come on, I need to check my messages, so let's go see Paula. She's the office manager and she's excellent at her job."

Shae led her parents through the clinic to the front of the building. As usual the Urban Health Center was a hive of activity. Patients were scattered in the waiting room and lobby, and moving from one examination room to another.

As Paula ended a telephone call, she glanced from the file in her hands and said, "Hey, Shae. How's our local celebrity?"

Blushing, Shae tried to play down the whole mayor's recognition award. "I'm no celebrity, Paula. I'm an employee of UHC just like you." Turning to her parents, she waved a hand in their direction. "Paula, I want you to meet my parents, Albert and Vivian Weitherspoon. Mommie, Pop, this is Paula Duncan."

The office manager took her father's hand in a firm handshake, then turned to her mother and repeated the gesture. "Nice to meet you both."

"Same here," her father answered.

Shae hooked an arm through her father's, and then her mother's, guiding them down the hallway. "Let me introduce you to my boss. He's the medical director."

At his door, she knocked before poking her head

inside. The doctor sat behind his desk, reviewing a patient's medical chart. "Kenyatta, hi. Are you busy?"

"No." He beckoned her into the room. "Nothing I can't stop for a few minutes. Come on in."

The trio entered the office. "I want you to meet my parents."

As Kenyatta moved around the edge of his desk, Shae noticed a corkboard with a blown-up copy of a newspaper article and a photograph of her. She pointed at her picture as she moved farther into the room. "What is all of this?"

The medical director grinned down at Shae, placing a hand on her shoulder. "You're a popular woman. The *Chicago Tribune* came by the clinic yesterday and interviewed the staff and a few of the patients about you. They wanted to do a profile of all the award recipients."

Grimacing, Shae did a quick glance at the article, skimming a couple of paragraphs. "Oh my goodness, this is so embarrassing. I didn't think they would go to these extremes."

"Sorry, Shae, this is a big deal around here," the medical director explained before turning to her parents. He flashed a charming smile and said, "I'm Kenyatta Reid."

Albert stepped forward and shook the younger man's hand. "Albert Weitherspoon." He placed a hand in the small of his wife's back and pushed her forward, before adding, "My wife, Vivian."

Shae took a step away from the group, watching her mother give Kenyatta the once-over as she talked with the young doctor. After a moment, Vivian caught her daughter's eye, then gave her a broad smile of approval.

"Mr. and Mrs. Weitherspoon, why don't you take a look at the article?" Kenyatta suggested as he steered them to the corkboard. "It's a great piece on the clinic and your daughter's accomplishments. We're really proud of Shae and love the work she does for us."

The couple complied, reading the pages.

"May I have a copy?" her mother asked.

"Absolutely," Kenyatta relied. He removed the push pins from the sheet, took it off the corkboard and headed for the door. "Wait here. I'll get you that copy."

Embarrassed, Shae brushed her curly hair from her face and asked her parents, "Are you sure you need a copy? I mean, it's only an article."

Shocked, Vivian stared at Shae. "You're my baby. Of course I want to show off to my friends."

Shae was surprised. She didn't know her mother talked about her and her life. After all, Shae hadn't got married or had babies. Shae chuckled. Who would believe that her mother talked about her to her friends?

The doctor returned minutes later with warm pages that he passed to her mother. "Here you are."

Mommie folded the sheets, put them in her purse and rose.

"Come on. I'm sure Dr. Reid has work he needs to get back to." Shae crossed the room and opened the door. Her parents followed. "I'm going to take them back to my office and then we'll probably do some shopping this afternoon. I'll see you in a few days."

"Shae?" Kenyatta called as she started out of the door. "Yeah?"

"Before you skip out for the day would you stop back by here? I need to see you for a minute."

"Sure. Let me get them settled and I'll be right back."

"Don't worry about us," her father said. "If this is business, we can wait out here for you."

"No. No," Shae vetoed. "You can wait in my office. It's more comfortable."

As the trio turned the corner, her mother hooked her arm through Shae's. "So tell me more about this medical director of yours."

"Nothing to tell," Shae sang back. "Don't be getting any ideas. He's my boss and we work together."

"Is he married?"

Shae crunched up her face. "I don't know. I don't think so. He's never mentioned a wife."

Exasperated, Vivian Weitherspoon stopped in the center of the room with her hands planted on her hips. The toe of her high-heeled shoe tapped rhythmically against the linoleum floor. "You are impossible. Here's this wonderful man practically sitting in your lap and you haven't looked his way. Where is your brain?"

Albert wrapped an arm around his wife and moved her along. "I'll tell you where her brain is. It's with J. D. Daniels. That's where."

"Okay, you two, that's enough." Their daughter unlocked her office door, announcing, "This is it. Make yourself comfortable. I'll be back in a few minutes."

Hurrying, she retraced her steps back to the medical director's office and tapped on the door. Kenyatta sat in his usual spot. "Come on in."

Shae crossed the room and took a seat in front of the desk. "What's up?"

"I just wanted to talk with you a minute about the recognition dinner. The mayor's office sent extra invitations and Paula and I decided we'd be there to support you."

Shae's heart swelled with thanks for these people. They were such a large part of her life, so giving. "Thank you."

"No thanks needed. We're all part of the team. I know your parents will be there. Anyone else?"

"J.D."

Kenyatta nodded. "Okay then, we'll see you there. Enjoy your days off and your family."

Feeling like she'd been dismissed, Shae rose from her chair and headed for the door. "Bye."

"Princess, this is a beautiful restaurant," Albert stated, studying the decor.

Vivian chimed in, "Yes, it is."

"I like it," Shae answered, looking around the Marriott hotel's elegant restaurant.

Appetizers of crab-stuffed mushrooms and lobster filled egg rolls, and a bottle of pinot noir wine had been served to the small group. Now they all were studying their menus to choose their entrees. "T-bone, medium-well," Pop stated as he handed his menu to their server. "Yes indeed, there's nothing like a good piece of beef."

"Hopefully, you consume beef in moderation," Shae stated with an upward lift of her eyebrow.

Her father gave her a pointed glare. "No nurses at this table tonight."

Shae glanced at J.D. and grinned. "Sorry."

Her mother sipped from her wine goblet and said, "Shae tells us that you are a sports agent. What exactly does that mean? What do you do?"

The inquisition had begun. Shae got comfortable in her chair and watched dinner patrons entering and leaving the restaurant. Worried, Shae had called J.D. to prepare him for the evening ahead. He'd laughed away her concerns, assuring her that he'd be able to handle her parents.

"I represent new pro basketball talent," J.D. answered as he sliced a mushroom in halves, stabbed a piece with his fork and brought it to his lips.

"Is that a good business to be in?" A skeptical note entered Albert's voice.

"It's been profitable for me. I was able to turn my love of sports into a career that's incredibly gratifying."

Pop asked, "Do you have clients that I would recognize?"

"Maybe," J.D. answered as the server refilled his wineglass. "But I work with young hopefuls who want to move from the college teams to the pros."

"Do you travel a great deal?" Vivian asked.

"Some." He scrunched up his face. "I'm not a good traveler. I've hired an assistant to do most of the leg work."

Vivian tapped a finger against her lips. "That's how you two met, isn't that so?"

Shae decided to give J.D. a break and answer this question. "Yes. We met on the flight from Malibu. J.D. sat next to me, offered to drive me to the Marriott and took me to dinner my first night in town."

"Hmm," her father muttered. "Do you have family here?"

J.D. chuckled. "Absolutely. My parents, brothers and sisters all live in Chicago."

"How many siblings?" her mother asked.

"What do your parents do?" her father quizzed.

J.D. decided to answer the last question first. "My parents are educators. My mom is a principal at a high school and my dad teaches kindergarten."

"That's different. I would think your mother would work with the young children," Vivian commented.

"Most people do. But you'd have to know my parents." Admiration rang from his words. "Mom is perfect with teens and adolescents. She's patient, but stern. I think she's in the best place for her skills. My dad can charm any child. The kids love him. Even when we were kids they divided us up the same way. Dad worked with us when we were younger and Mom took over when we moved into the dreaded teen years." J.D. touched his hand to his side. He checked the number on his cell phone. "Excuse me. I need to take this call."

Surprised, Shae blinked like an owl. J.D. hadn't let his cell phone interfere with their life in a while and it startled her to find that he even had the thing with him.

"Does he do that often?" Albert asked, watching J.D. move between the tables to a quiet corner.

"No. It must be important," Shae answered, concentrating on her lobster egg roll. She didn't want her parents to see her face and how surprised she'd been when J.D. left the table.

J.D. returned minutes later and slipped into his previously occupied chair. "Sorry about that. One of my clients got into a world of trouble and I needed to consult with my brother for legal advice."

Albert's head snapped up. "Your brother is an attorney?"

"Yes." J.D. picked up his water glass and sipped from it. "He's agreed to help this kid."

"What happened?" Vivian questioned.

J.D. grimaced. "He's been a trial since I discovered him. Amir is a tough kid that doesn't understand the business. He lets his friends lead him into some inappropriate situations and then he ends up taking the fall for them."

Concerned, Shae touched J.D.'s hand. "What did he do now?"

"Drunk driving."

"Oh my goodness," Shae moaned sorrowfully, shaking her head.

"Yeah. It's bad. He hit another car and injured a woman and small child. I convinced David to take his case because Amir is in real trouble. But I can't seem to get that idea into Amir's head."

"Honey, I'm sorry." Shae covered his hand with her own. "I know you wanted great things for this kid." She softened her voice a notch, stroking his hand as she spoke. "What I've learned is sometimes people don't know how to want more for themselves. Their fears get in the way of them making any progress in life."

"Thanks, sweetie. I really wanted to see Amir succeed. But he won't grow up and take responsibility for his life or career. I'm going to help him get out of the legal entanglement and after that I plan to cut my losses."

Under the cover of the tablecloth, she patted his thigh. As she drew away her hand accidentally brushed against a small box inside the pocket of his trousers. She smiled at him. Mr. Confidence had carried his lucky deck of cards with him. Shrugging, he remained silent, but grinned back at her before turning to her father. "Mr. Weitherspoon, I know you have some reservations about Shae and me and I understand. If I had a daughter, I'd probably have the same concerns. I don't know if I can reassure you. But I do want you to know that I love your daughter. Shae is the better part of me. There isn't a thing I wouldn't do for her and I want her to be happy with me and with the life she has chosen."

Her father drew in a deep breath and let it out slowly. "You're certain that you love her, even though you've only known each other for a few months?"

"Absolutely," J.D. answered. He turned to Shae, linked their fingers and grinned. "I knew within minutes of meeting her. I didn't want to crowd her so early in our relationship. But things are different now and we have a commitment to one another. Believe me when I say, I want what makes Shae happy."

Albert cleared his throat. "Those are pretty words that you're passing around. I'm sure that you mean them, but it's what you do that's more important. Don't hurt my princess. She deserves all things good and I'm not sure that you're the best for her. But time will tell and I'm going to be around to make sure things work out."

"Stick around," J.D. offered in a confident tone. "You're Shae's father and I don't want her to be torn between us. With time you'll see that I want the same thing you do—her happiness."

"Now that we've heard you talk the talk, the real question is can you walk the walk?" Albert leaned forward, holding J.D.'s gaze. "Are you able to back up your declarations with the proper actions?"

"I plan to," J.D. shot back.

"Here's the deal. My daughter wants to save the world. Help stamp out injustice and make this planet we're destroying a better place. Can you support her and back her up in the things she wants to do? Are you the man that can provide for my baby? These are the questions you need to ask yourself. Let me say one more thing and then we'll get back to our meal. I'll be watching and hoping that I won't have to pick up the broken pieces after you," he warned, picking up his fork and stabbing a cherry tomato.

# Chapter 26

From the Bose CD player on J.D.'s nightstand, the mellow saxophone of Marion Meadows wafted through the air. J.D. picked up his glass of Vernor's ginger ale and tipped the glass to catch the crushed ice cubes on his tongue.

Humming softly to the music, he slipped his arms into the sleeves of his white, front pleated shirt, pushing the black buttons through the holes. His thoughts turned to Shae and the evening ahead. J.D. felt honored to be the man at her side when she received the mayor's recognition award. Shae had done an exceptional job of helping the residents on the South Side and this dinner was a direct result of all of her hard work.

Grimacing, his thoughts turned to Shae's father and his less than subtle warning. Mr. and Mrs. Weitherspoon were worried over the relationship between Shae and him. After all, he and Shae had dived into a relationship within weeks of meeting. They were suspicious of his motives and J.D. understood. The Weitherspoons were wealthy and from the details he'd learned from Shae they were overprotective of their only child.

J.D. needed to convince the Weitherspoons that his feelings were sincere. The soft hum from his cell phone drew his attention as he shoved his shirttails inside his black trousers. For a moment he ignored the incessant buzz, debating whether he should answer it. He didn't recognize the number. Curiosity got the better of him, he picked up the cell, and answered the call. "Hello?"

"Mr. Daniels, it's Susan Jonson," she identified herself in an agitated tone.

*Damn!* he thought, sorry he hadn't let voice mail take the call. Mrs. Jonson never called with good news. "What can I do for you, Mrs. Jonson?"

"Amir's gone."

J.D. shut his eyes, fighting the sinking feeling of despair. At that moment his deepest regret involved taking Amir on as a client. He wished that she would go away. No, that wasn't true. He really liked Mrs. Jonson. Maybe he needed to get rid of the son.

"What do you mean gone?" He dropped onto the mattress with the phone attached to his ear.

"His friends, if you want to call them that, have been teasing him about going to prison. They scared him and he ran away."

"Which friends?"

"A couple from high school and that loud mouth kid that seems to be in the middle of things every time Amir gets in trouble. I can't stand that boy." She paused, catching her breath. "All of his clothes are gone and his room is empty of his personal stuff."

Unbuttoning his shirt, J.D. asked, "Have you checked with any of his friends?"

"Yeah. They claim that they haven't seen him."

"What do you mean claim? Do you think they're lying?"

"Yeah, I do. I think I know where he's staying," she confided.

He sat up straight on the mattress. "Where?"

"Amir's with that little thug friend of his on the East Side."

"How do you know?"

"I checked our caller ID and that's the last number that came up."

A wave of acceptance surged through his veins. It looked as if he didn't have another choice. "Do you have the address?"

"I was able to track the telephone number back to his address."

"Good. I'll drop by to get it."

"Please bring him home. Amir has to be here for his trial and finish school."

"I know. We'll get him back here. I'll see you in a short while."

He couldn't let Mrs. Jonson lose her house. Amir was an idiot, but that lady had always tried to do the right thing for her son. Besides, David would kill him if he found out that J.D. knew where Amir was hiding out and didn't do something to convince the young man to return home.

J.D. studied the digital clock on the nightstand next to his bed, calculating the amount of time it would take him to drive across town, drop Amir at his house, then make it to Shae's apartment in time for the banquet. If he moved quickly he had just enough time.

He took an additional moment, debating whether he should call Shae and offer her an abbreviated explanation about Amir situation. J.D. shook his head as he rose from the mattress. No. Why worry her on her big day?

J.D. rose from the bed and stripped the garments from his body. He replaced them with a T-shirt and a pair of denims before slipping his feet inside a pair of white sneakers. He buttoned the pleated shirt on a hanger, then added the black jacket and trousers and placed the tux inside a dark brown garment bag. Hunting for his keys and wallet, J.D. tossed the bag over his shoulder. Once he got the kid home, he could take five minutes to finish dressing at Shae's house.

*I'm going to kill Amir when I find him,* J.D. promised, pulling his cell phone from his pocket. His eyes flicked across the car's dashboard and settled on the clock. It was close to eight and he needed to call Shae and let her know that he wouldn't be able to drive her to the banquet. His stomach tightened into a thousand knots. *Damn!* He rubbed a hand back and forth across the back of his neck, massaging the tense muscles.

J.D. had to find Amir. David had been quite specific about what would happen if the young man skipped his court date. The bail bondsman would seize Amir's mother's home and put her on the street. Shaking his head, J.D. blew out a hot, frustrated puff of air. After taking a quick trip by David's house to switch cars and talk about what might happen if he didn't find Amir, J.D. drove by Mrs. Jonson's for the address of her son's friend.

That address hadn't worked out. But the kid did give him a couple of addresses to check. The second had been another dead end. When he went up to the third house, he heard voices coming from the back of the house and one of those voices had been Amir's. He was wrong. He'd asked the home owners if he could speak with their son. The kid had come to the door with the same sullen expression that seemed to be perpetually painted on Amir's face. Yes, indeed. This was one of his friends.

At the fourth address, J.D. walked around to the back porch, then took the steps two at a time and landed at the back door with a loud thump. He rapped on the door. He believed Amir had taken up residence at this place while he planned his next move.

"Just a minute," called a woman from the house's interior. The door opened a crack, and a fraction of a brown female face with one thick eyebrow gazed curiously back at him. "Yes?"

"Hi," J.D. began, removing a business card from his wallet and slipping it through the slit in the door. "I'm James Daniels. Amir Jonson is a client of mine. His mother asked me to check with you to see if her son has stopped by? Mrs. Jonson needs him to return home as soon as possible."

"I'm sorry. Who?"

"Amir Jonson. He's one of your son Albert's friends."

Shaking her head, she answered, "No. He's not here."

A small noise beyond the woman drew J.D.'s attention. His glanced down the hallway and caught a glimpse of a young man sitting on the floor in a bedroom. The leg of a second person was visible for a few seconds before the door closed with a soft click. J.D.'s eyes narrowed. He felt certain that he had just seen Amir's size-fourteen foot and skinny leg with the tattoo of medieval crossed swords above his ankle. "If you see

him, please let him know that I'm looking for him. His
mother is very worried."

She glanced at the card, then nodded. "I'll give you
a call if he comes this way."

."Thank you, ma'am." J.D. turned away and bounced
down the stairs. He marched down the street and out of
the visual range of the house before climbing into the
driver's seat of his brother's sedan. Minutes later he
coasted down the block and parked a few houses away.

He was certain Amir planned to flee. If J.D.'s luck
held out, he would catch Amir sneaking out of the
house. Sliding lower in the car seat, he waited as
thoughts of Shae filled his head. How was he going to
make this better for her? He ran a hand across the tight
cords of his neck. What he'd done was unacceptable no
matter the reason. At this moment he didn't know what
he could do to make things better. In his heart J.D.
knew that he'd blown any chance of a long term relationship with her.

For the next thirty minutes J.D. debated and discarded numerous ideas to gain Shae's forgiveness as he
waited for Amir to leave the house. Sure enough the
front door opened and Amir poked his head out of the
door before stepping onto the porch. He moved down
the stairs while slipping the straps of his red backpack
over his shoulders. When he started down the walk,
J.D. leapt from the car and confronted the younger man.

"Hi, Amir," J.D. said, stepping into the younger
man's path.

Wide eyed, Amir took a step away from J.D. "What
you doin' here?"

"Waiting for you." J.D. folded his arms across his
chest. "Your mother is worried about you."

"I'm straight. She don't need to think about me."

Shrugging, Amir ignored J.D. and tried to push past the older man. Refusing to give an inch, J.D. stood his ground and gave Amir a little shove backwards. "But she does. If you don't show up for your hearing tomorrow, she'll have to forfeit her home. Are you going to leave her without a place to live because you screwed up?"

"Hey, it's not my fault she decided to put up the house."

"But it was your mistake that caused her to do it," J.D. reminded. Moving closer, he added, "Maybe I'm being too subtle. You messed up. So it's up to you to fix things."

"She'll be okay."

"You're wrong. Your mother won't be okay. Mrs. Jonson has been a good mother to you and the only parent you've ever had. Don't do this to her—she doesn't deserve it."

Amir glared at J.D. with such hatred in his eyes, that the force of it stunned him. "It's none of your business. What goes on in our home has nothing to do with you."

"It does when you act so irresponsibly."

"Get out of my way," Amir demanded, using both hands to push J.D.

J.D. took his arm and started toward the car. "You're coming with me."

Amir tried to drag his arm from J.D. but failed. "I ain't going nowhere with you. So move."

J.D. shook his head and squeezed a bit tighter on Amir's arm. His voice took on a deep menacing tone. "I'm sick of you. It's time for you to grow up. You want everything, but you aren't willing to give anything in return. Let me tell you this. Today is the day that you take responsibility for the things that you've done. You're going back to jail."

"No," Amir screamed, fighting with all of his might. "Stop. I'm not."

"Why shouldn't you? A moment ago you were willing to run off and leave your mother with nothing. My brother has been working on your case free of charge and you didn't care that you wasted his time." J.D. didn't add his loss. That he'd probably destroyed his relationship with Shae with this stunt. He shook his head, removing thoughts of her from his mind. He'd worry over Shae and their relationship and a way to get her back once he got Amir where he belonged. "The place for you is jail."

Amir clawed at J.D.'s hand, trying to break his grip as J.D. marched him to the car and shoved him inside the passenger seat. J.D. pointed a warning finger in Amir's face and advised, "Don't move."

Hurrying around the hood of the car, he slid into the driver's seat and immediately started the engine, pulled away from the curb with a shriek of tires.

J.D. paced the precinct floor as he waited for news about Amir. He checked his watch for the fifth time and realized that he couldn't forestall the inevitable any longer. Speed dialing Shae's number, he drew in a deep breath, waiting for someone to pick up the phone.

"Hello?" Mr. Weitherspoon asked.

*This was already off to a bad start,* J.D. thought. He'd been hoping Shae would answer the phone. "Mr. Weitherspoon, can I speak to Shae?"

"You're late," Mr. Weitherspoon said, stating the obvious.

"I know." He didn't plan to give Mr. Weitherspoon any additional information. "Can I speak to your daughter?"

"I hope you're on your way. We're going to be late if you don't get here soon. Hold on."

"J.D., where are you? We're waiting for you and we're ready to go!"

"Honey, I've got a problem."

"Problem?"

"Yeah. I don't know how long I'm going to be. You guys need to go on without me."

A silence thick with questions followed. "Are you telling me that you're not going to make the banquet, after all?"

"I don't know. I'm going to make every effort to get there."

"When?" Shae asked.

"As soon as I can."

He could hear Mr. Weitherspoon in the background, talking to his wife. "This is completely unacceptable. I knew this joker wasn't right for my princess."

The quiet on the other end was deafening. J.D. felt ready to explode from the tension. Why couldn't things work out for him?

"Is there a problem with one of your clients?"

J.D. knew Shae would figure it out. "Yeah," he admitted, tensing as he waited for the explosion.

"I see," she stated stiffly. "As you said, I need to get on the road. We'll talk later about this."

"Honey, I'm so sorry. Please forgive me. I'll try to get there. I'm on my way as soon as I finish here."

"I'm sure you are." After that statement the line went dead.

# Chapter 27

Shae was stunned. Her quick intake of breath drew her parents' attention. They waited impatiently at her side while she finished her telephone call and hung up. "It's time to go," Shae said in a quiet, emotionless tone.

Her father spoke first. "Is J.D. on his way? That boy needs to work on his time-management skills."

Vivian gave her husband a quick jab in the side, then asked, "Is J.D. going to meet us at the dinner?"

"No." Her voice broke miserably. She stopped, cleared her throat, before continuing, "We're going to the dinner without him." Somewhat dazed by this turn of events and fighting tears, Shae had moved her hand to her temple, then dropped it to her side.

Albert Weitherspoon shook his fist in his daughter's direction. "What!" he roared. His chest puffed out and his eyes practically popped from their sockets.

She needed to be alone with her thoughts. "Let me get

my purse and keys, then we can go," Shae said in a tense, clipped voice that forbade any further discussion as she moved stiffly down the hall toward her bedroom. It took all of her energy to put one foot in front of the other.

"Who does James Daniels think he is, reneging at the last minute?"

Shae brushed her tongue across her dry lips and answered, "Pop, I don't want to go into the wheres and whys right now. As you just reminded me, we're going to be late if we don't start moving. I'll be right back."

Her father's voice trailed her as she made her way down the hallway. "What possessed her to think she could make a life with a complete stranger? All she did was pick up a strange man that she met on a plane. They've only known each other for a few months. Hell, look at her, she thinks she in love with that idiot."

Her mother's soft murmurings were too low for Shae to hear. She didn't care what her parents thought or said. At this moment, she felt too tired to fight them. All she wanted to do was get through the evening.

J.D. had truly let her down. Until she found time to be alone and think the situation through, she had no other choice but to go to the dinner and put on her best face for herself and the clinic.

"I don't care if Shae hears me. She needs to accept the truth," her father bellowed. "Look at what he's done to my princess. Let her down on the most important night of her life. He needs to burn in hell."

Her father's ranting and raving would be comical, if it hadn't hit so close to the truth. Obviously, he had a selective memory regarding the countless times he'd disappointed her and let her down.

Yes, indeed. She knew how to pick them. Maybe she needed to chuck the whole love and relationship scenario and concentrate exclusively on her career. Her luck ran better when she put her personal life on the back burner and focused on her work.

Weary, Shae closed her bedroom door behind her, moved across the room, collapsed onto the edge of the bed and covered her face with her hands. *How could J.D. let me down this way?* She desperately wanted to cry, but she didn't have time for such a luxury. They needed to be at the dinner within the hour and she still had her father's rant to listen to.

Determined to make the best of the evening, Shae picked up her handbag and left her room. She cleared her throat as she made her way to the front door. "I'm ready. Let's get on the road."

The trio left the apartment, took the elevator, then crossed the lobby in silence. The quiet helped Shae focus on the night ahead while avoiding the need to make small talk with her parents.

As she pulled out of the parking lot, her father began his second rant of the evening. "No good son of a bi—"

"Albert!" Vivian Weitherspoon warned. Her tone cracked like the snap of a whip. "This is not the time."

Shae switched on the radio in an effort to drown out her father. It didn't work. The sexy saxophone jazz ballad seemed inappropriate for all the emotions swirling around them. Her father raised his voice above the music as he reached for the dial, turning off the radio with a flick of his wrist. He glared at her with a hard, warning gleam in his gray eyes.

"When is it the right time?" he challenged, shifting on the front seat to study his wife. "At the altar when he decides to skip out because he's realized that marriage isn't for him? Why should we give this jerk any consideration?" He thrust a finger in his daughter's direction. "This is a perfect example of why you shouldn't let yourself get too wrapped up with someone you've just met. They'll let you down every time. If you'd listened to me, you might have avoided all of this drama and met someone nice from the company."

Shae rolled her eyes toward the heavens, remembering the missed school plays, music concerts and birthday parties that he'd forgotten. Yes, he was correct. The men in her life had made a habit of making her feel as if she were less important than their careers. Tonight J.D. had capped the situation and hurt her more than she thought possible because she loved him.

"Hush, Albert," her mother commanded, turning to her daughter and probing in a gentle voice, "Shae-Shae, did J.D. say why he's not available?"

Shae shook her head, focusing all of her energy on getting them to the dinner in one piece.

"Do you want to tell me about it?" Vivian said and leaned toward, stroking her daughter's shoulder.

"There's not much to say, Mommie. He let me down." As hard as she tried, she couldn't disguise the slight quiver in her voice.

"I don't think J.D. did it intentionally. But there are a lot of feelings churning inside you. Am I right?"

Shae nodded.

Vivian Weitherspoon continued, "I don't want you to go into the dinner with this burden weighing you down. Care to share?"

Nodding, Shae began to speak. "I think this is about one of his clients. Amir is a kid that seems to stay in trouble and J.D. is always getting him out of one scrape or another." She chuckled unpleasantly. "Actually, J.D. admitted once that Amir is his client from hell."

"Then why does he keep him?" Vivian asked. "Couldn't he get out of the contract?"

"He's a poor businessman. That's why," Albert answered with contempt. "If J.D. knew his business he'd dump this joker at the first opportunity. When you're working for yourself, you have to cut your losses as soon as possible. You don't let deadbeat clients bring you down."

"Albert, please." Vivian turned to her daughter and prompted, "Shae?"

"I think J.D. wanted to help Amir. He hasn't had the easiest life and J.D. wanted to make things better for him. Give the young man some direction and assistance so that the he can obtain his dreams."

"That's noble," her father mumbled sarcastically.

"Albert," her mother admonished a second time.

"Yeah. There's a situation brewing—that might be why J.D. found it difficult for him to remove himself."

"Is it a legitimate reason?" her father questioned.

"Possibly."

"Well, Shae, you have to give your friend a little credit. J.D.'s trying to do the right thing," her mother stated. "Sometimes people can't or won't let you help them. Is Amir one of those people?"

"I don't know. It could be." Shae shrugged. "Maybe."

"We can't fix Amir's or J.D.'s problems tonight. You are going to leave them in this car when we get out. Put everything behind you and forget it until tomorrow. This is the night that you've worked years for. What J.D. has to do is his business and we're not going to worry about it," Mommie ordered. "You, your father and I are going to have a wonderful evening and celebrate your accomplishments. Agreed?"

Shae opened her mouth, but shut it instantly when

she felt hot wetness burn a path to her cheeks. She brushed away the moisture with the back of her hand.

Her mother leaned closer, noting the tears dotting her daughter's cheeks. She produced a tissue and handed it over the back of the seat. "Oh, Shae-Shae. This is supposed to be a happy time for you. Don't let your evening be ruined by a misguided fella."

Grabbing the tissue, Shae mopped away her tears. This was not the way she wanted her parents to see her. It was time for her to pull herself together and get on with the evening. She drew in a deep calming breath and dried her remaining tears. "You're right, Mommie. This is what I've worked for. What I've wanted all my life. I'm going to enjoy it."

As they had promised, Kenyatta, Paula and several members of the nursing staff were among the guests sitting at the table with Shae and her parents. At the beginning Paula inquired about J.D. Once the explanations had been made, everyone made an effort to help Shae get past her disappointment and enjoy the evening.

For the first time since they arrived, Shae relaxed, enjoying her friends and colleagues. A glass of wine, baked rubber chicken, rice pilaf and limp green beans represented the hotel's culinary fare.

As soon as dinner ended, the servers had silently but quickly whisked away their used dishes while filling their cups with fresh coffee. The banquet room lights dimmed and a spotlight focused on Mayor Richard Daley as he strolled purposefully toward the podium. He welcomed the audience, then began with an overview of how this program began.

Mayor Daley went on to discuss the merits and good deeds of the other five recipients before turning his attention to Shae. "Our last recipient is a transplant from California," Mayor Daley began his introduction. "Shae Weitherspoon moved into our city with the specific plan to make a difference in our community. In a few short months, this nurse practitioner has helped families with limited resources make their dollars stretch just a bit further while maintaining optimum health.

"We wanted to do something a little different this year. So we sent a crew to the clinic to help us get some insights into Ms. Weitherspoon and her role at Urban Health Clinic. Ms. Weitherspoon was away, but the staff at the clinic provided wonderful information about this award recipient. While we were at the facility we taped several patients' candid remarks about Ms. Weither- spoon. We thought you might enjoy hearing and seeing what they had to say. Roll it."

The lights dimmed and a projection screen lowered before the audience. The waiting room from the clinic appeared on the screen and Shae watched as the members of the area went about their day at the clinic. Mrs. Walls, Desmond and Sterling were pictured in the waiting room. The boys looked so cute in matching shirts and denims. Mrs. Walls had makeup on and a dress with a mixture of green and rose floral pattern covering the front.

Mrs. Walls talked about the home repairs she needed and how the clinic employees canvassed the local builders in the area for donations. Not only had the building company responded favorably by providing new windows, but they had made several additional repairs to the house to bring it up to code. The mother of three went on to talk about how Shae had provided her family with fresh fruit. And finally, Desmond's mother gave details about the time Shae treated Mrs. Walls's nephew after he'd been hit by a ball.

So much praise embarrassed Shae. After all, she was doing her job. Nothing more. Heat ran up her neck and settled in her cheeks as she squirmed in her seat. A warm, masculine hand covered hers, quieting her fidgeting, and she stared at her father, seeing pride in his gaze. He winked, giving her hand a second squeeze.

As the video ended, Desmond's happy, brown face appeared on the screen. "Miss Shae can fix anything!" he promised enthusiastically. The audience broke into a rumble of laughter, then applauded.

Mayor Daley returned to the podium and said, "Ladies and gentlemen, I'd like you to meet Shae Weitherspoon."

Amid the applause, Shae rose and moved between the tables toward the podium. When she reached the stage, Mayor Daley offered a hand to help her. She stood next to him, waiting patiently for the applause to die down.

Mayor Daley displayed her award and they held it between them as the flashes from cameras lit up the room. After shaking her hand, the mayor stepped away from the podium, offering Shae the microphone.

For a minute, Shae caressed the gold award with her name inscribed on it. A sense of pride overcame her as she fought back tears. "Thank you." Shae scanned the crowd for the few familiar faces, gathering strength from their presence. "I'm going to let you in on a secret. I'm a bit overwhelmed by this event. There's a part of me that questions why I'm being given this award. I feel as if I was doing my job and nothing more. I came to Chicago with one plan, to help those who needed it with the skills that I have." She smiled gently as she thought of Desmond and the place he occupied in her life. "I'm not the only hero here tonight. Everyone in this room owns a piece of this award. We're all heroes in one way or another. We give of ourselves unconditionally and that's where it all starts. When you open your heart and show a little compassion, you're well on your way to claiming the title of hero."

Shae paused, gathering her thoughts before continuing, "You don't have to be a nurse or doctor. I don't think you need any special skills. Sometimes it's as simple as giving an extra minute to a person who needs a sympathetic ear. How about offering a meal to a homeless person? Or here's a switch, go through your closet and give away the clothes that you don't wear to a shelter. Being compassionate should be the norm, not the exception, and I believe that we all have those emotions in us.

"I want to leave you with this thought. Let's all be heroes by giving a little of ourselves. Thank you for this wonderful award." Shae held her award in one hand and followed the gentleman waiting at the edge of the stage to lead her down the stairs and off the stage. As she took the last step she gazed beyond the crowd, noticing a lone figure standing at the back of the room. Their eyes held across the length of the room and everything disappeared as she focused on the one person she'd needed to be here with her tonight.

Dressed in a black tux, J.D. leaned against the door frame watching her descend from the stage. With a slight nod of his head, he acknowledged her, mouthing the words "I love you," before turning away and heading for the hallway.

His dark, tortured expression begged for forgiveness. A wave of longing hit her. It broke her heart and it took all of her strength to turn away before continuing toward her table.

# Chapter 28

She's apartment seemed far too quiet now that her parents were back in Malibu. It was funny. She'd worried over their visit and now that they had left, she longed to see them again. As she wandered through the vacant rooms, her thoughts revisited the lecture that she endured from her mother at the airport.

Purposefully, Vivian had linked their arms, steered Shae away from the boarding area crowd and her father before whispering, "Honey, I know you don't want to hear this, but I'm going to say it anyway. Your young man has let you down in a painful and embarrassing way, but that's not the end of things. Before you can move on, you must talk with him. Listen to his explanation, then tell him how you feel. Say your piece and get the hurt out of your system as quickly as possible."

"Mommie—" Shae protested, shaking her head. Those feelings were far too raw for her to discuss rationally at this point and she didn't believe that talking with J.D. would magically soothe her soul. Shae envisioned a shouting match where everything came out wrong and embarrassed them both.

Vivian listened to her daughter while navigating them to a quiet spot near a ceiling-to-floor window. She cupped her daughter's cheek before saying, "Shae-Shae, pay attention to me. Whatever you decide about J.D., that's your business and I'll support you. But you've got to talk to him. Soon. I don't want your sorrow to turn into bitterness. Promise me you'll call him and clear the air."

Frustrated, Shae stood in front of her mother like a child who'd just gotten caught swiping a chocolate from the candy dish. Vivian Weitherspoon rarely backed down or allowed herself to be sidetracked when she had made up her mind. Shae chuckled without humor; she felt certain that having her mother leave Chicago wouldn't change a thing. Vivian would hound her about the situation long distance until Shae relented. Sighing, she steered her mother back to the boarding area where her father waited impatiently. "Okay. I will."

Mrs. Weitherspoon hugged her daughter close. "Good. I love you, babe. I know it hurts now. And I understand that it's not the thing that you want to do. You'll see that I'm right. Believe me, it'll be just fine and you'll feel better once you've got everything out in the open."

From the patio doorway, Shae watched downtown Chicago shut down for the evening. "Get everything out of her system"—that's exactly what she planned to do. Shae wished that she hadn't agreed to her mother's suggestion and had given herself additional time to think this situation through before confronting J.D.

A tentative knock on her door had Shae's throat close

up. She remained where she stood for a minute, plotting out what she planned to say to J.D. When the second knock came, Shae realized that she couldn't delay any longer. Her time was up. J.D. had arrived.

She roused herself from the numbness that weighed her down and started down the hall. At the door, she shut her eyes and prayed for the strength to get through the next few minutes before unlocking the door and removing the chain. J.D. stood in the corridor, tall and handsome, and her heart fluttered uncontrollably in her chest. Not for the first time she wondered how things had turned out so badly. She loved J.D. and she didn't want to let him go. Where had all the trust and love gone?

The uncertainty in his eyes told her that J.D. questioned what kind of reception he might receive. He held her gaze, examining her features, then reached for her hand, smiling tentatively at her.

She pushed her hand behind her back, flattening it against her pants as she shook her head.

"Hi," he said in a subdued tone while at the same time shoving his hands into the pockets of his denim slacks.

"Hey." Shae pivoted on the heels of her shoes and started back down the hallway. In the apartment, she plopped onto the sofa and intertwined her fingers in her lap.

J.D. shut the door, followed her to the living room. Unsure what to do next, he stood in the center of the room.

"Have a seat." Nervously, Shae ran a hand through her curly hair, then waved a hand at the chair across from where she sat.

"Thanks."

Shae sat quietly watching J.D. sink into the chair

opposite her and fidget, trying to get comfortable. Tension swelled as the silence lengthened.

"Shae—" J.D. began.

At the same time she said, "J.D.—"

Smiling apologetically, he dipped his head slightly forward and said, "I'm sorry. You go first."

"Thanks," Shae answered. Clearing her throat, she studied the designs in the sofa pattern. "J.D., you disappointed and embarrassed me in front of my parents when you skipped out on the dinner."

"Shae, honey. I planned to be there." He started talking fast and furious while he made sweeping gestures with his hands. "I was ready to leave the house when Mrs. Jonson called. Believe me, I debated long and hard before answering the phone. I picked it up because I thought it might be you needing something. I wouldn't have missed your evening for anything but an unavoidable emergency."

"I know," she answered wearily.

"Amir intended to skip town. His mother would have lost her house if that idiot had gotten away. I couldn't let that happen. She's too nice a lady."

"I understand."

"I did make the dinner at the end. You saw me? Right? I made it in time to see you receive your award and I heard your speech," J.D. assured. "You were awesome, sweetheart. Just awesome. And I felt so proud."

"I saw you," she said, drawing her bottom lip between her teeth. "But it's not enough."

Frowning, he scooted to the end of the chair, facing Shae. "What do you mean?"

She spoke in a soft tone. The undeniable and dreadful facts were that he'd hurt her and deeply. "J.D., we talked about this after your brother's housewarming party. I told you then that I refused to continue in a relationship where I came in second."

"I understand that. But, honey, this was different. Mrs. Jonson would have lost everything she's worked for."

Ignoring his outburst, she began a second time, "All of my life I've been let down and disappointed by my father. The occasions and situations began to blend together because it happened so often. He'd arrive late with some lame excuse or not at all." She held his gaze with her own. "Just like you. I've always come second in his life. My father pushed Prestige Computers ahead of his family and friends. You made your clients more important than our relationship. I thought you were different and believed that I held the first place in your life."

"You are. You do."

She smiled sadly back at the man that she'd come to love so dearly. "No. I don't. I know you believe what you're saying, but you've already proved it when you went after Amir while my parents and I sat here waiting for you."

Embarrassed, J.D. looked away. She felt no satisfaction at seeing the red stain on his cheeks. "I was trying to get things done ASAP so that I could get to you."

Silently, Shae focused on J.D., waiting until he looked at her. "I'm sure you were. But it doesn't matter. It's too little, too late. We talked about my feelings weeks ago. I told you what I expected. If you think back, I told you that I wouldn't take second place in your life. The bottom line remains, you chose Amir and his problems over me and my family."

"No," he denied. "That's not true."

"Yes. It is." Shae's voice quivered. She stopped, gained control, then started a second time. "J.D., this isn't working for me."

He shot to his feet and hurried around the coffee table to take her hands in his. "Shae, don't give up on us. Give me a little time to put everything in its proper place and I'm sure we can work things out. This is what I'll do. I'm going to drop Amir as a client. That should put an end to a lot of our problems. Then we can concentrate on us and getting back on track."

Her hands lay limply within his. "You think I don't understand Amir and his issues? I do. But I also believe that you don't realize how important your career is to you. Getting rid of Amir won't change anything. You'll get another client that will cause as many problems as Amir, and you'll be off and running with him. That's where we have our problem. When do you tell your client that my family needs me? Or I'm sorry, we'll work on this tomorrow—I have plans now."

"Tell me what you want me to do," he whispered. "I'll do it."

"You can't do anything. It's over between us."

He shook her hand, demanding, "Look at me."

Shae refused. She examined the carpeting.

"Sweetheart, I know I screwed up. And I can't take that back. What I can do is promise you that I won't let anything like this happen again. I am and will continue to be completely devoted to you."

"You can't make a promise like that. You may believe that you can. But it's not going to happen. Whether you admit it or not, you love your work and it's the most important thing in your life."

"No. It's not. You're more important than the job. I know I messed up and I'm sorry for that. Think. We have something special. You and I love each other. Are you willing to end our relationship because I screwed up?"

Tears pooled in her eyes. "I do love you. But I want more than you can give me. I'm not blaming you. We have different priorities. Your business comes first. My career plays a major part in my life, I don't deny that. But it's only a part of the life. You and my family are more important. Can you say the same?"

Shocked, J.D. dropped her hand.

Shae got up from the sofa and went through to the dining room. Seconds later she returned with a box in her hands. "This is your stuff. I want you to take it with you today."

"Shae," he stammered, shaking his head and taking a step back. "I'm not doing this."

"You have no choice."

Desperately, J.D. cried, "Honey, stop and think about what you're doing. I understand that you're upset with me, but we can get past this and move on."

"We could. I don't doubt you at all, until the next time. J.D., you're trying to do the right thing for everyone, but you can't have it all. It's time you set priorities. Make up your mind what's the most important thing to you and then go for it."

J.D. stood in the center of the room with his arms folded.

She sighed, tired of the argument. "If you don't take it, I'll just drop your stuff at your mother's," she warned, shoving the box into his hands, and starting down the hallway to the door. "Bye."

Stunned, J.D. trailed behind her. On the opposite side of the door, he halted. "Are you sure about this?"

"Yes. I'm not going to spend the rest of my life

playing second fiddle to a job. I'm not living my life that way." She leaned forward and gently kissed J.D. on the lips. "I wish you every success. And I hope you find what you're looking for."

He took a step toward her. Before he could move closer Shae shut the door. She leaned against the wood surface, fighting the hot tears that demanded release.

## Chapter 29

Five weeks later, a limousine pulled into the Weitherspoon circular drive and stopped. The chauffeur shifted the transmission into park and turned to Shae. "Your total comes to $55."

She handed the bills and a hefty tip to the driver. Before she closed her purse the driver had hopped out of the car, opened her door and offered her a helping hand. Taking his hand, Shae swung her feet onto the ground and stood. After adjusting her hip-hugging jeans and spaghetti strap silk top, she casually strolled up the walk in a pair of high heels, and rang the doorbell while the man followed with her luggage.

Sighing contentedly, Shae waited, feeling the pain and tension that had gripped her for the past month ebb away. Since her breakup with J.D. Shae had focused all of her energy on getting her life back on track and putting everything aside, except her work. Unfortunately, it hadn't been easy. Her home and the clinic were filled with wonderful memories of the man she'd broken up with, but continued to love.

Concerned that his nurse practitioner might need a break, Kenyatta had generously given her a week's vacation. At first, she'd turned down the medical director's offer, certain that he felt that she couldn't do her job effectively. Once he had assured her that he was only trying to help, Shae had decided that a short trip to Malibu for a few days seemed the perfect way to bring her life into balance.

Now that she'd arrived, anticipation filled her. Her mother would be thrilled to have her daughter at home for a little while. And if Shae was honest with herself, she was looking forward to being pampered and spoiled during her visit. Shopping and lunches with her friends could be the answer to the breakup blues.

The door opened and Mia, her parents' housekeeper, stood in the entrance. "Ms. Shae!"

"Mia!" Shae stepped into the foyer and gave the housekeeper a quick hug. "How are you?"

The older woman beamed, running a warm hand up and down Shae's arm. "Fine. You look gorgeous!"

"Thank you," she said, offering Mia a second hug of greeting. "I thought I'd come and surprise my folks with a short visit. Are they home?"

Nodding, Mia pointed toward the bedrooms.

Surprised, Shae frowned back at the housekeeper. It was after two o'clock. Her parents never stayed in bed this late. During their visit to Chicago, they had both wandered into her kitchen before 9 a.m. looking for a cup of coffee. A twinge of uneasiness settled under her skin. This didn't feel right.

Her father never slept in when there was work to be

done. And he always found something that needed his attention at Prestige Computers.

She lifted an inquiring eyebrow at Mia. The house-keeper shrugged and shut the front door before heading toward the kitchen. "Mr. and Mrs. Weitherspoon will be so happy to see you."

Determined to find out what was going on Shae took the steps two at a time. As she crested the second floor she darted down the hall to her parents' bedroom. A soft moan of pain followed by the unpleasant and harsh retching sound of someone emptying their stomach filled her with worry. Was her mother sick? Maybe that was why her father had stayed home.

Shae burst into her parents' bedroom in time to see her father flop against the pillows, pale and weak. Her mother stood over him, patting his sweaty face dry with a washcloth. Albert raised a shaking hand and picked up the glass of water waiting on the nightstand, slowly sipping the water.

He looked as if death had paid him a visit. Was it the flu? No, this was something more. But what?

Her parents glanced her way and her father's pallor grew more striking. Suddenly, her mind switched from daughter to nurse mode and she did a quick survey of the things she noticed while they were in Chicago. Loss of weight, lack of appetite, weakness and extreme fatigue were just a few of the symptoms her father had displayed during his visit.

"Shae," her mother began, pulling the covers around her husband. "We weren't expecting you."

"Obviously," she explained, keeping a close eye on her father. "I thought I'd come home for a few days to recharge my battery. I really missed you guys after you left and wanted to spend a bit more time with you."

"Well, honey, we're happy to have you." Mrs. Weitherspoon removed the glass from her husband's trembling hands. "Why don't you let me get your father
settled and then you and I can chat."

Feeling dismissed, Shae left their bedroom and
headed down the hall to her room. What had she just
witnessed? Her father looked pale and weak. If possible,
he had lost additional weight in the weeks since she had
last seen him. When they had been in Chicago, she'd
stopped questioning her mother about her father when
it seemed to make her mother feel uncomfortable.
Whatever the problem, she planned to drill her mother
until Vivian admitted the truth.

Shae pushed opened the door to her bedroom and
was surprised to see the room in order with fresh sheets.
Also, her luggage had been placed in her room. She
perched on the edge of the mattress, hugging the
Cabbage Patch doll her father had bought her when she
turned ten.

Scanning the room where she'd grown up, Shae
chuckled over memories of her adolescent years and the
times her mother had sat on the edge of this bed, disci-
plining or listening to the maddening problems of
Shae's youth. Her smile faded as she thought of what
she'd just witnessed. The voice in her head whispered
that whatever the issue, there wouldn't be a quick fix
for what ailed her father.

Within minutes her mother arrived and shut the door
behind her. She crossed the floor, sat next to her
daughter and took her hand. "Your father is asleep."

"What's wrong with him, Mommie?"

"Your father has cancer."

Shae gasped, shutting her eyes as her throat squeezed
shut against what this meant. Mental pictures of the

patients ravaged by the horror of cancer flipped through her mind. She shook her head, trying to deny what her mother was telling her. But she knew better. Her training as a nurse recognized the symptoms even when her conscious mind refused to put a name to them. Instantly, she offered up a silent prayer to God. *Please don't let my father die,* she thought. *Let him be all right.* Her voice quivered as she asked, "Where?"

"Prostate."

"What stage?" Shae shot back, aware of how important the stage of his illness would be in terms of his chances of survival. The stage could determine whether he had months or years to live.

"Three. Some lymph nodes."

This news wasn't good, but not completely bad. Turning to face her mother, Shae questioned, "Metastasis?"

"Not so far."

"Treatment?"

"Surgery. Radiation."

Almost afraid to ask her next question, Shae quizzed in a soft voice filled with fear. "Did they get it all?"

"The doctor believes so."

"When did he have surgery?"

"Right after we got home from seeing you." Vivian refused to look at her daughter.

"You knew about this before you came to Chicago, didn't you?" Shae accused.

"Yes."

"Why did you wait? Pop should have had his surgery as soon as he was diagnosed. Cancer is not something you put on hold."

"Believe me, his doctor and I tried to tell your father that. But Albert refused to listen to anything we had to say. Come hell or high water, he planned to fly to Chicago and be there when you received your award."

"Why?"

"He told me that he knew how much he'd disappointed you over the years and this was one time he wanted to be part of your cheering section. So Doctor Miller sent your father off with a boatload of pain pills and a promise that he'd agree to surgery the minute we returned home," her mother explained.

"Why didn't you tell me? I knew something was wrong when you guys were visiting. But I didn't put things together," Shae wailed. Her hands clenched into fists in her lap. "Some nurse I am. I didn't see this."

"Your father didn't want to upset your life." Vivian covered Shae's hand with her own. "He wanted your award dinner to be perfect and free of our problems."

"Newsflash. Your problems are mine and vice versa. You're my parents. What affects you, affects me."

"I know, honey. I'm sorry. This was your father's decision. Albert made me promise not to tell you. You don't know how difficult it was to talk to you without blurting out the whole situation."

Hurt, she turned on her mother, demanding in a sarcastic tone, "When were you going to tell me? After the funeral?"

"That's unfair. You know I'd never do that to you. Your father knew you would come straight home if you found out and he wanted you to have the life you've chosen without worrying about us. He understands how much your career means to you. The last thing he wanted to do was interfere in any way. We didn't want to disturb you. Remember, you had found a new job and new man."

"My career means nothing compared to how I feel about you and Pop. Nothing is more important."

"We know that, honey. But your father and I didn't want you to have to make that choice. You seemed so happy in your new life."

Dismissing the issue, Shae shook her head and added, "I'm here now. What can I do to help?" Shae rose from the mattress and started for the door. "Never mind. I'm going in to see him."

Her mother's words stopped her. "Shae, he's not ready to see you. He had his first radiation treatment this morning and he's not fully recovered from that. Give him a little time. Your father needs his rest."

Nodding, Shae returned to the bed, looking at her luggage. "I'll unpack and take a short nap. Maybe by that time Pop will feel up to a little company."

"Shae-Shae, that's a wonderful idea." Her mother rose and cupped her daughter's cheek. "Your father will be thrilled to have you here for a little while and so am I. I'm so glad that you came."

Shae gazed into her mother's eyes and said, "Where else would I be if you need me? You're all the family I have."

Vivian Weitherspoon leaned down and kissed her daughter on the forehead. "We always need you, Shae-Shae. Get some rest and we'll talk later." Her mother crossed the carpeted floor and shut the door after her.

Shae stretched out on the bed, thinking about what her mother had told her. Fear like nothing she'd ever felt before surged through her veins. She didn't want to lose her father, but that was an awful reality that she might have to face.

# Chapter 30

Swallowing loudly, J.D. knocked on the door to his brother's home. He wasn't looking forward to this visit. David and Cynthia were astute people who would question him about Shae. J.D. didn't want to get into a discussion about the relationship.

His older brother opened the door. Dressed in a torn pair of jeans and a paint splattered T-shirt, David hugged his younger brother, then led him into the house. "Hey, man, thanks for coming. I really need the help."

J.D. slapped his brother on the back. "No problem. It's the least I can do considering all the help you gave Amir. I know that kid messed up, but you still stayed on his case. That was beyond the call of duty."

"Not at all." David waved away J.D.'s concerns. "Don't worry about it. Amir needed good representation. The public defenders office would do their best, but eventually they'd suggest that he plead guilty. This way he has a shot at a reduced sentence or probation with some community service."

"I'm glad. In a lot of ways he's not a bad kid, just misguided."

The brothers strolled through the house and ended in the kitchen where Cynthia stood at the island, mixing lemonade. A platter of turkey and Swiss cheese sandwiches on onion rolls sat on the island. "Hey, baby brother. How are you?"

"Good."

Frowning, Cynthia glanced beyond him and then gave J.D. a stern look. "What's the deal with Shae? We received a letter from her with the balance of the rent for the year. When I called the clinic, the office manager said that she'd resigned. Did she go back to Malibu? Is she coming back?"

This was what J.D. wanted to avoid. The time when he had to tell his family what happened between him and Shae. Eventually everyone would learn the truth. He might as well start with his older brother and Cynthia. "No. She's not coming back. Shae and I split up."

"What!" David turned to his wife, looking for additional information. She shrugged.

Cynthia skirted the edge of the island and moved to her brother-in-law's side. Touching his arm, she asked, "How did that happen?"

"That Amir situation took her over the edge," J.D. explained in a dead tone.

"I don't understand. How did Amir cause your breakup?" David asked.

J.D. sighed. "Remember the night Amir decided to skip town?"

His brother and his wife nodded.

"That was the night that Shae received her award from the mayor. I chased him down, but that made me really late for the dinner."

Pouring glasses of lemonade, David asked, "How late is late?"

"I walked in on the tail end of the program. I missed everything except her receiving her award and her speech. She was pretty pissed off."

"I don't blame her. J.D., how could you do that to her? We always want our men at our side. You spoiled her shining moment."

Shutting his eyes against the memories and pain, he growled, "I screwed up big time. You don't have to keep reminding me."

Planting her hands on her hips, Cynthia shot back, "Somebody should. There has to be a time when the woman you love comes first. You let your job and your friends interfere on more than one occasion. That wasn't fair to her. How do you think that made her feel?"

"I thought Shae understood," J.D. said defensively. "Amir's mess needed to be dealt with swiftly. I had to find him that night so that his mother wouldn't lose her house."

"I understand what you're saying," Cynthia admitted. "But you were still wrong. Maybe if you hadn't screwed up so many times before this, she would have understood. That was the day Shae should have come before anything else, short of someone in the family dying. David and I would have helped you find that kid another day. Actually, we would have helped you that night. I'm sure my husband would have found a way to help Amir's mother. There are always loopholes."

Head bowed, J.D. sighed dejectedly. "I know that now."

"Too little, too late, if you ask me," Cynthia retorted sharply.

David wrapped an arm around J.D.'s shoulders and steered him away from the wrath of Cynthia and toward the patio doors. "Honey, give the man a break. I'm sure he's suffering enough. We're going to get started on the deck."

The glass patio door slid back and the two men stepped onto the wooden deck. For the next thirty minutes, the brothers worked in silence. J.D. added a coating of varnish to the wood surface while David built the steps.

Cynthia appeared from around the side of the house with a tray of lemonade for the Daniels men. She placed the tall glasses, sandwiches and potato chips on a small table at the foot of the deck, then returned to the house without any comment. David offered him a glass. They sat on the grass, enjoying the late afternoon sun while eating their snack.

"You know, Cynthia and I messed up pretty bad at the beginning," David began. He munched on his sandwich for a few silent moments. "I kept letting my job get in the way."

Surprised, J.D. turned to his brother and stared. "When? I always thought you and Cynthia had everything together."

"Nobody has everything together. Just before we got married things fell apart. Cynthia decided that she wanted to know about her biological parents and I didn't support her. I had my reasons and I thought they were pretty good. But I didn't let her in on them."

J.D. nodded.

"Well, up to that point I kept screwing up, making really bad decisions about our relationship, taking her for granted. I believed my job came before everything else and that Cynthia should understand until I had time for her." David slapped his younger brother on the back. "Let me tell you, I was wrong."

"What are you saying to me?" J.D. asked.

"I'm saying if you want this woman back in your life, you better get your sorry butt in gear and go get her. Get on your knees if necessary and apologize until she agrees to take your back."

J.D. groaned. "David, I don't think she'll forgive me."

David shook his head and speared his brother with a stern expression. "If you want Shae bad enough you'll find a way to make her forgive you."

"I don't know."

David chuckled. "That's pride talking. Let me tell you, pride won't love you in the middle of the night."

J.D. nodded, thinking about how he continued to reach for Shae at night and how much he missed her. Her warm spirit and gentle laughter had filled his loft and heart; now it was like visiting an empty, quiet tomb.

"Being Cynthia's husband and having the life that we have comes before anything else. The woman in that house is my wife, my partner and one day she'll be the mother of my children. She's the one who listens to me when my days turn crappy. She sympathizes with me when the cases I'm working on go sour. She sustains me and gives me the strength to go out and fight another day. So how can I tell her to wait until I'm done playing attorney? It doesn't work that way. Whatever happens, whatever the day brings, Cynthia Williams Daniels comes first."

"How does it work? Tell me, because I don't understand this particular game," J.D. shot back. He was so tired of trying to figure everything out.

"Ask yourself a couple of simple questions. How important is Shae to you? Is she worth any sacrifice?

Can you in good conscience walk away from her and feel that you've made the right decision? The bottom line is, how much do you miss her?"

"What are you saying? I should swallow my pride and go crawling back to her?"

"If that's what it takes, yes. Look at you. Don't deny it, you're lost without her. Shae Weitherspoon is the other half of you. Are you willing to go through life this way?"

*God, no,* J.D. thought. He was barely able to function. His thoughts turned to the next problem. "Damn, I hate flying."

"And?" David prompted.

"Thanks for all your sympathy," J.D. mumbled sarcastically.

"You haven't earned my sympathy."

J.D. admitted, "I'm afraid of those sardine cans masquerading as flying machines."

Shrugging, David switched to his most formidable attorney voice and reminded, "You've flown across the country for fame, glory and money. Why can't you do the same for love?"

David had him there. As much as he hated flying, if a client needed him or he needed to be present at some contract business, J.D. always found a way. Shae was certainly worth more than money.

His decision made, J.D. handed his glass to his brother, rose from the ground and brushed off his denims. "You're right. I've got to go."

"Where to?"

"Go home and pack. I'm headed to Malibu," J.D. said, fishing in his pocket for his keys.

"All right! That's my baby bro. Don't come back without that woman."

"I won't," J.D. promised, heading for his car.

* * *

Shae entered her parents' room and found her father asleep. She tiptoed across the carpet and placed the tray of medication on the nightstand next to her father's side of the bed. Slowly awakening, he opened his eyes. "Hey, princess."

"Hi, Pop."

He stretched. Shae was at his side immediately, lending a helping hand as he pulled himself into a sitting position. Frowning, Albert glanced around the room and asked, "Where's the nurse?"

"You're looking at her," Shae responded, waiting patiently for the explosion that she expected. It didn't take long.

"No!" he yelled, setting off a coughing fit.

"Yes," she countered, sitting on the edge of the mattress and holding a tissue to his nose and rubbing his back. Once the coughing ceased, she presented a bottle of Gatorade for him to drink. She balled up the tissue and tossed it in the wastepaper basket, then went into the bathroom to wash her hands.

After taking a few sips to help clear his throat, he folded his arms across his chest, "I can't have you bathing me and changing my bandages. I'm sorry. My daughter will not be doing that."

"Well, I don't want to see anything that I shouldn't, so Mommie and I have talked this through. She'll do the bathing and the bandages with Mia's help and I'll do medication and any other essentials as they crop up." Shae grinned down at her father and shrugged. "That should appease your sensitivities. Although the rest is out of your hands, old man."

Shaking his head, her father stated, "Shae, I won't let you stay here. You have a life to get back to."

Laughing softly, Shae asked, "How are you going to stop me? I'm sorry, Pop. I will be here until I'm ready to leave, not before."

"This isn't right," her father said. "All your life you've wanted nothing more than to follow your dreams. Now that you've got everything where you want it, are you truly willing to give it up to nurse your old man?"

"In a heartbeat. Actually, in your heartbeat." His daughter stated with complete conviction. She gently stroked his hand.

"Well, I'm not willing to let you do this. You've got your career and your boyfriend to think about. I don't want you leaving either unattended while you waste your time here with me."

"First, it's not a waste of time being here with you. And, you're a little late about the other stuff. I've already quit my job and the boyfriend and I broke up weeks ago."

"Oh, princess, I'm sorry. Are things beyond repair?"

"Yeah. Besides, when have you ever cared for any of my boyfriends? Especially J.D?"

"I may not like that man, but I could tell that you cared for him. Are you saying that I'm wrong? You didn't love him?"

"No. You're right. I do love him," Shae admitted, studying her hands as she spoke. "But we've hit a point in our relationship where neither of us is willing to bend. So, here I am."

"I think you should go back to Chicago. That's where your life is."

"What!" Shae placed a hand on her chest and answered in mock surprise. "Are you trying to get rid of me? Your only daughter? That's just shameful."

"Stop playing. Go home."

"This is my home. The only way you're going to get rid of me is when I see you get out of that bed and get back to work. Once I know you're a hundred percent, then I'm off to my next adventure. Until that happens, you're stuck with me."

The light banter ended with his next comment. "I may never be one hundred percent again. There's a possibility that I won't beat this."

Stunned, Shae swallowed past the lump in her throat. She couldn't let him see how much his words affected her. It would add ammunition to his plans to send her back to Chicago. "I know," she admitted softly. "That's even more reason for me to be here now."

Frowning up at her, he threatened, "I'll talk to your mother. That'll solve everything."

"Actually, it won't. Mommie and I have already worked everything out. My apartment is being packed up as we speak. Everything will be shipped to Malibu and will be stored in one of the garages. By the way, one of your precious cars is going to be parked in the driveway."

"Shae Weitherspoon," her father warned. "You better not."

"Sorry. I'm in charge until you're back on your feet. Maybe I'll take your Jag out for a spin. That will keep it in tip-top shape. What do you think?"

Albert puffed up like a balloon full of helium. "Young lady, if you touch my car, I'll get out of this bed and tan your hide."

Flippantly, Shae taunted, "Promises, promises. When you get out of that bed, then you can threaten me."

"Don't dictate to me."

Giggling, Shae removed the glass of water from the

nightstand and refilled it in the bathroom. She returned to the bedroom and handed the glass to her father accompanied by a pain pill. With a shaky hand he accepted the medication and swallowed it with a sip of water.

"Get used to having me around. Until you're better, you'll be seeing a lot of me." She kissed her father on the cheek and started across the room to the door. "It's time for a nap. You have to build up your strength for the next round of radiation treatment. That's scheduled for the end of the week."

Shae shut the door after her and braced herself against the opposite wall. Weariness and fatigue assaulted her. Although she tried to fight it, tears sprang to her eyes and wet her cheeks. How was she going to keep this up? This was her father and she hated the idea of him getting sicker, weaker and possibly dying. Lord, she didn't know how she would cope with that turn of events.

She had to pull herself together. There was her mother to consider, as well as her father. They needed her. Although she was putting on a brave face, Vivian Weitherspoon was showing the effects of the situation.

No. Shae wasn't leaving, not anytime soon. Her parents needed her. Her father, because of his illness, and her mother, for emotional support.

# Chapter 31

*Tissues,* Shae thought, snatching one from the personal-size pack, then returning the pack to her pocket. It seemed as if she needed tissues at every turn to mop away the tears that fell whenever she took a close look at the future. Here she stood outside the front door of her parents' home, crying like a high school senior who'd been stood up by her prom date.

Since returning from Chicago, she had kept a tight rein on her emotions whenever she entered the house. There were times when Shae thought she would explode from the tension. Unfortunately, there were only two places that she felt comfortable enough to let go of her emotions: her bedroom or outside the house.

Shae refused to let her father see her this way. He deserved the best that she could give him and bursting into tears wouldn't help the situation. Taking several deep breaths, Shae blew her nose and pulled her compact from her purse, checking to see if her eyes were still red.

Today had been especially difficult. It took everything in her for Shae to control her emotions until they got her father into bed after his latest radiation treatment. Mia had been a godsend when she informed Shae that the moving company had arrived with her belongings. Thanking Mia, Shae headed through the house, slipped out the patio door, and hurried across the deck. She had a few minutes for a good cry before facing the movers.

A sting of sadness shot through Shae as she watched the men unload her furniture. She'd chosen those items with such anticipation in her heart and hope for her future. When she thought of Chicago, J.D.'s image filled her head. Her rational mind had already processed the end of the relationship, yet her heart and body still ached for the man that she loved. Alone in her bedroom at night, Shae remembered everything they shared and wished that she could go back and change the outcome of their relationship. She missed J.D. terribly and truthfully needed his support right now. But she'd made her decision and she had to live with it.

Returning to the present, Shae leaned against the patio railing and watched the team place protective covers over her furniture and store the items in the garage. Sighing heavily, she turned away. For the present, her future belonged with her parents while she helped her father recover.

Shae returned to the house once all of her furniture was stored. She asked the movers to place several boxes in her bedroom so that she could sort through them and determine what and where she'd like the remaining items to be stored. Cardboard containers covered her bedroom floor. Shae glanced at the clock, measuring the amount of time she had before her father awoke from his nap. There was about an hour before he needed his medicine. Enough time to go through a few boxes.

There were so many things Shae needed, like her own comb and brush and her toiletries. First and foremost, she needed access to her *Physician's Desk Reference.*

Lifting a box off the floor, Shae placed it on the bed, and tore into it. The box contained framed photos from Chicago. The clinic's opening day and the afternoon she bought her car were captured in color prints. Shae sifted through the shots, wondering how such a promising relationship had fallen apart. Two short months ago, she'd been happy. Now, she was alone again.

Shaking herself out of this melancholy mood, Shae stormed across the room and dumped all of the photos into the trash. She wanted all reminders of her relationship with J.D. out of her life. Looking down into the trash, she reached down and plucked them from the basket. She couldn't do it, not yet. Placing the frame on her nightstand, Shae continued her hunt through the box.

"Finally," she muttered, lifting the red tome from a box and placing it on the bed. Curiosity got the best of her and she decided to finish unpacking the box. Her hand latched onto a small item. When she removed it she realized that she had J.D.'s lucky cards. Surprised, she turned the box over and over. She could have sworn that she gave them back to J.D. She knew how much they mean to him; as soon as possible, she'd return them. Searching the room for an envelope, she glanced at the clock and realized that her time was up. She needed to check on her father.

Dismissing the whole mess, she stuck the cards in the

pocket of her jeans and headed down the hall to her parents' room. Quietly opening the door, she peeked inside. Her father was struggling with the covers. She hurried across the room and straightened the blanket.

"Hey," she greeted him softly, brushing a hand across his forehead. He felt a bit warm. "How are you feeling?"

"I'm okay," Albert answered in a tired voice. "I could use something for pain."

"How about some Gatorade or a glass of milk?"

"No milk," he said and slapped a hand across his mouth. Shae raced into the adjacent bathroom and returned with a basin. She positioned the tub just in time, holding her father's head as he emptied his stomach. Exhausted, Albert Weitherspoon flopped against the pillows.

"Let me get you some water," Shae offered, removing the basin from the room returning minutes later with a clear basin and a glass of water. Her father rinsed out his mouth and placed the glass on the nightstand.

"This isn't one of my good days," he moaned.

There wasn't much Shae could do other than comfort him. The side effects from the chemotherapy and radiation treatments were something he had to ride out. "I can give you something, but it'll put you to sleep."

"No. This is what's left of my life. I don't want to spend it in Never-Neverland."

"Pop, don't talk like that."

"Come here." He patted the spot next to him on the bed. She sat on the edge of the mattress as he took her hands. "Princess, I know it frightens you. Hell, it frightens me. Unfortunately, this is one of those times in life that we have to be real. I don't like it, but it is something we have to face."

Nodding, Shae turned away and pulled a tissue from

her pocket. The deck of cards hit the floor. Hearing the noise, her father peeked over the edge of the bed and asked, "What's that?"

"Cards. They belong to J.D. I found them in my stuff. I'm going to send them back when I get a chance," Shae explained, picking up the deck from the floor.

"After all those etiquette classes and finishing school programs we sent you to, you let that man corrupt you with cards?" Albert shook his head sorrowfully, but a smile lurked beneath his frown. This was the first happy moment they had shared since she returned to Malibu and she didn't want to lose it.

"J.D. and I may have had our problems, but he taught me how to play blackjack, shades and hearts," she said proudly, remembering the first time they had made love.

"Shades! You know how to play shades?"

Shae nodded.

Her father patted the spot that she had recently vacated. "Let me see."

Now it was her turned to be surprised. Her mouth dropped open. "You know how to play shades?"

He chuckled gently. "What do you think your mother and I did when we lived in Compton? Believe me, we didn't have money for much. Our entertainment choices consisted of cards or TV, maybe a new record every once in a while. Pull out that deck, I want to see how well he taught you the game."

Doubtful, her eyebrows rose. "Are you sure?"

Spreading his arms wide, Albert Weitherspoon demanded, "What else do I have to do? Besides, it might just take my mind off this queasy stomach that doesn't go away."

Shrugging, Shae set up the bed tray between them and began to shuffle the deck. "Two-hand shades?"

"Yup."

As they drew cards and began the game, her father spoke about his life in the Compton town house. He added information that she never knew about the lean years as he struggled to build Prestige Computers. After losing her third hand, Shae grinned at her father. "Now I know how you supplemented your income before Prestige took off. You moonlighted at the Las Vegas tables, right?"

"Not at all, but I do like to keep my skills up," he said. He studied his hand. "Your mother and I still play a hand or two," he said and winked at her.

"Oh, we're going to have to get her in here. I want to see how well she plays." Checking the score, Shae suddenly realized that Pop had gone quiet. She looked up and found his eyes on her, shimmering with unshed tears.

"Did I ever tell you that your mother and I cried for days after you went away to school?"

"Pop?"

"No. Let me talk. I may not get another chance."

"Don't," she warned, afraid of what his words implied.

"It was my dream that you would come into the company. You're a smart woman with a lot of drive and determination. You pissed me off when you decided to become a nurse. Besides, you're my only kid. Everything I did, I did for you and Vivian. I never wanted you to have to ask anyone for anything."

Touched by his words, Shae turned away, mopping at the wetness on her cheeks. She stayed that way until her composure returned.

"I don't think I've ever said it, but I'm proud of you. That's something you need to hear from me before I leave this earth." Albert Weitherspoon's voice was strong and firm. He reached out and stroked his daughter's cheek. "You've done good things in your life. You put people before money and that's important."

"I did what I believed was right."

"Yeah, you did. Even when you made your old man mad. My princess did the right thing. You followed your dreams and that's what you were supposed to do." Leaning against the pillows, he added, "I get a kick out of some of our friends. Their kids are either lazy bums or want to get rich quick. Mostly, they are silly people pretending to be something they are not. I can brag about you. You're doing something with your life. My child is special. And that's saying a lot in this day and age."

"Oh, Pop."

He opened his arms to her. "Come here." Shae pushed the tray out of the way and went willing into her father's arms. He held her close and kissed her forehead. "There one more thing we need to talk about."

"What's that?" Shae asked, drawing away from her father's embrace. She examined his face, searching for a clue to what he needed to say.

"Over the years I've missed a lot of special moments in your life and I've disappointed you more times than I want to admit to. Now is a time for truth. You need to know that whatever mistakes I've made, you and your mother were my prime concerns."

"What do you mean?"

"There were times when I've been off on a major project or too busy to take time to watch you grow up. I deeply regret that. I think sometimes that you believed that you didn't come first in my life."

Unsure of the direction this conversation was taking, Shae shifted on the bed. Uneasiness coursed through her veins as she silently admitted that he'd hit a sore spot with her.

"Princess, you and your mother have always been the most important things in my life. Nothing rates above you guys. I didn't always show it, but it's how I feel."

With a shiver of vivid recollection she recalled her feelings of despair when her father missed her dance recitals and award ceremonies, and how he complained when she chose to attend college away from home. Shaking her head, Shae found the words to say what had been in her heart all of her life. "Pop, you missed so many things. How can you say we came first?"

"True. You're right. I've always wanted you to be financially secure. If you didn't want to work, you didn't have to. I did everything in my power to make Prestige Computers the best. That company represents my legacy to you. That's why I wanted you to come into the business. Who better to control the company than the person who owned it? You would have a vested interest in making it successful."

Her father took her hand between both of his and added, "Everything I did, I did for your future. But more than that, I want you to know that you are first in my heart. I love you, princess."

Emotionally moved by his words, Shae smothered a sob and turned away.

Her father squeezed her hand. "Don't turn away. This is something you need to hear and I should have said it a long time ago."

"Oh, Pop."

"Let's start fresh. You're my baby and I want to hear about your life. So, what does a nurse practitioner do in a clinic? Can you write prescriptions?"

Smiling back at her father, she nodded.

"Excellent." He leaned closer to her and asked in a conspiratorial tone, "Can you write one for pain for your old man?"

Laughing, Shae hugged and kissed her father. "No."

"Oh, come on," he whined playfully. "This is like having a doctor in the family. You have to give us free medical advice."

"Advice you can have. But sorry, Charlie, if you want drugs, you've got a doctor and he already prescribed your medication."

Albert pouted, but a smile immediately burst free. "I raised a tyrant."

# Chapter 32

**J.**D. pulled into the circular drive behind a bronze Lexus sedan, shoved the transmission into Park, and switched off the engine. Pocketing his keys, he sat in the rented car for a beat, fighting the urge to march up to the front of the house, bang on the door and demand to see Shae. This was his sixth attempt to see Shae in as many days. Unfortunately, on his previous visits, Mia, the housekeeper, denied him entry.

Today, he refused to be put off. Shae and their relationship were too important for him to leave without at least one face-to-face confrontation. J.D. felt confident that if he gained a few minutes with Shae, he would be able to convince her to listen to him. After all, he was a top sports agent and negotiating was one of the skills that he'd mastered.

*No point in dallying,* he thought, climbing from his rental car and strolling across the driveway. He rang the doorbell and waited. In his head, he ran through a series of scenarios and apologies that he believed would open the door to some honest dialogue between him and Shae.

Absorbed in his internal monologue, it took J.D. several minutes to realize that he was still waiting for someone to answer the door. Although Mia kept him out of the house, she always acknowledged him. J.D. punched the doorbell a second time. Maybe no one was home. *That was silly.* He dismissed the thought silently. The Lexus belonged to someone in that house.

J.D. laid his ear against the wood. He faintly heard movement from inside, then pressed the bell a third time. Suddenly, the door swung open. Her face contorted into an annoyed frown, the housekeeper took her position as guard dog and said with a clipped edge to her tone, "Yes?"

For a second, J.D. was taken aback and felt very much like a teenager on his first date. Pushing away those emotions, he cleared his throat and asked, "Hi. Is Shae available?"

A painful grunt and soft curse drew J.D.'s attention past Mia and to the staircase. Shae and Mrs. Weitherspoon stood on the stairs, trying to get Mr. Weitherspoon to the second floor. From J.D.'s vantage point, it looked as if the man was having a difficult time navigating the stairs. If they weren't careful, the trio would tumble backward and someone would end up with a broken bone or two.

Reacting instinctively, J.D. pushed past the housekeeper and raced into the house. He took the stairs two at a time and reached the Weitherspoons seconds before they toppled backward. J.D. braced a palm on each woman's back, then used his shoulder to add leverage and support to Mr. Weitherspoon while steadying the two women.

Surprised, Shae gave a startled cry, then glanced behind her to see who was helping them. Her eyes grew large like two bright full moons. At the same time Shae's eyebrows shot into her hairline. Concerned for everyone's well-being, J.D. decided against an explanation; if they wanted to get Mr. Weitherspoon on the landing safely, anything else would have to wait. Now that he'd steadied the trio, J.D. slipped to the right of the older man and placed his arm around Shae's father's shoulders, edging Mrs. Weitherspoon out of the way. "I've got him."

Shae's father was heavy. Mother and daughter had absolutely no business trying to lift this man. J.D. took a moment to glance at Mr. Weitherspoon. Pale and shaky, the man looked as if he'd been tossed in the washer and left in the sudsy water far too long.

Hitting the top of the stairs, J.D. addressed Shae for the first time, "Which way are we going?"

"Bedroom," she answered, pointing to the right.

He nodded and carried Shae's father down the hallway. Shae raced ahead, hurried across the room and tossed the bed's comforter to the floor.

J.D. placed Mr. Weitherspoon on the bed, gently helping him to sit on the edge of the mattress. Groaning painfully, Albert flopped across the bedding. J.D. swung the older man's feet off the floor and removed his shoes before placing his feet on the sheets. Mrs. Weitherspoon sat down on the mattress next to her husband.

"Let's get him more comfortable," Shae suggested, gently slipping the jacket off of her father's arm. Taking the other arm, Mrs. Weitherspoon tugged at the garment. The women struggled to get Mr. Weitherspoon into a sitting position.

270 Someone To Love

J.D. held the older man by his shoulders as the two women removed the senior Weitherspoon's jacket. After they were done, J.D. eased the older man down on the mattress and stepped away.

As Shae and her mother fussed around Mr. Weither-spoon, J.D. felt out of place. He stepped out of the bedroom, waiting in the hall for Shae to finish taking care of her father.

From the doorway, he watched the Weitherspoon family. Although he'd been heavy, the older man had certainly lost weight and his pallor indicated some form of illness.

Minutes later, Shae stepped out of the bedroom and led J.D. down the stairs to the living room. She waved a hand at one of the sofas as she took the one across from him. Fidgeting with her fingers, she waited as J.D. got comfortable. "Thank you. We needed some help and you showed up right on time."

"You're welcome."

"Can I get you anything? Coffee or a soda?"

"No. Nothing." As he watched Shae twist the edge of her top, J.D. got the distinct impression that there was more. "Although, I wouldn't say no to an explanation."

She sank back onto the couch. "My father is very ill."

"That much I figured out for myself," J.D. stated, studying her pale face and dead eyes. He realized that whatever the situation, Mr. Weitherspoon had more than a twenty-four-hour bug or flu. J.D. rose from his place, edged around the coffee table and sat next to her, linking her fingers with his. "What's wrong?"

Unable to control the quivering in her voice, Shae answered, "My pop has prostate cancer."

"Oh, sweetheart, I'm so sorry. Is there anything I can do?"

"No. Everything that can be done is being done. My mother and I are trying to get him through the chemo and radiation treatments. Unfortunately, he's pretty sick a lot of the time. After that, we'll have to wait and see."

"Mr. Weitherspoon is a big man. You're not trying to handle everything without some assistance? You have help, correct? Does he have a nurse?"

"Yes, he does. Me. I do most of the nursing stuff, and there are a couple of men who do work around the house who help lift Pop and get him in and out of the car. Today, they were both out on errands. My mother and I thought we could handle it."

J.D. asked gently, "How are you doing?"

He saw tears pool in Shae's eyes before she turned her head. Her tears tore at his heart and J.D. wished that he had a way of absorbing this pain, taking it on himself so that Shae didn't have to hurt like this. With everything in him, he wanted to gather her into his arms and tell her that everything would be fine. But it wouldn't, and he couldn't comfort her with a lie.

Shae pulled a tissue from her pocket and mopped ineffectively at her tears. "It's hard. But I'm coping. I'll be all right." Her face crumbled and she began to sob uncontrollably. Worried, J.D. pulled Shae into his arms and rocked her back and forth, letting her cry. Sobs slowly gave way to whimpers and shudders turned to hiccups.

Embarrassed, Shae straightened and turned away, wiping at her tears with trembling hands. A look of tired sadness passed over her features when she faced him. "I'm sorry."

"You don't have to be. I understand," J.D. whispered soothingly. Glancing over Shae's shoulder, he noticed her mother starting across the room toward them. He lifted his hand and gave a quick, curt shake of his head. Shae's mother halted, unnoticed by her daughter.

"I guess I needed to let it out."

"Probably." He brushed the remaining tears aside with his thumb. "Is there's anything I can do? Anything that will make this easier for you, let me know. I want to help."

A flicker of a smile came and went on her taut face. "Thanks."

"Yes, thank you," Mrs. Weitherspoon stated, entering the room. "We appreciate all that you've done so far. If you hadn't come along I believe we were headed for an accident."

"No problem."

Smiling at the young man, Vivian Weitherspoon asked, "What brings you to Malibu?"

Standing, J.D. answered, "I wanted to see Shae. If she were free I thought we might spend a little time together."

Nodding, Shae's mother asked, "Where are you staying? Have you got a hotel room?"

"Yes, at one of the hotels downtown."

Mrs. Weitherspoon's forehead crinkled into a frown. "Shae doesn't leave the house very often. She's providing most of the care for her father." Shae's mother perched on the edge of one of the sofas and turned a sharp, assessing eye on her daughter. "Since you were looking forward to seeing her, why don't you stay here?"

"Mom!" Shae cried, shaking her head furiously.

Mrs. Weitherspoon chose to ignore her daughter. "There's plenty of room. We really appreciate the help you gave us earlier. It's the least we can do."

J.D.'s insides were churning. If he were this close to Shae, he could help her, make things easier for her. She wouldn't have to do everything alone. "I don't want to put you out."

Shae tossed in her objections. "Mommie, I'm sure J.D. has other things going on. He doesn't want to be stuck with us."

"Actually, it's a very generous offer, Mrs. Weitherspoon," J.D. replied, expecting an explosion. He wanted to stay here, be close to her. He suspected she needed him more than she'd ever admit. But J.D. felt uncertain about how much she would let him help her. *Don't worry about that now,* he thought. *Just be here for her.* "If you're sure it's not too much trouble, I'd like to accept. This is a difficult time for you both. I don't want to intrude or cause additional work for either of you."

"Nonsense." Mrs. Weitherspoon dismissed the idea with a wave of her hand. "I'm sure things will be fine. Besides, Shae refuses to leave her father. There's no way you'll be able to see her without coming here."

"You've got a point. Thank you. I accept."

"You're welcome."

J.D. read pain and worry in Mrs. Weitherspoon's eyes. He felt so much for these women going through this crisis alone. He'd stay and help in any way that they'd let him, try to take some of the burden off their hands and help them cope with this painful and heartbreaking situation.

Shae wouldn't have to do this alone. Whether she believed in him or not, J.D. was here for her and he didn't plan to leave.

# Chapter 33

The Weitherspoon household was silent. Everyone had settled in for the night. J.D. climbed into the bed and tossed a sheet across the lower half of his body before switching off the lamp on the nightstand, and stretching out on the mattress.

Sleep was elusive. It had nothing to do with the mattress and everything to do with what he'd learned about Mr. Weitherspoon.

Shae hadn't been happy with her mother's offer. Throughout dinner she cast reproachful glares at her mother, then snarled at J.D. He didn't care. Now they needed his help and whether they wanted it or not, J.D. planned to support Shae and her mother in every way possible.

Flipping onto his side, J.D. glanced at the crescent moon visible through his bedroom window. A muffled thump invaded the silence of the night, capturing J.D.'s attention. He tossed his legs over the side of the bed and moved into a sitting position, listening more carefully. This didn't feel right. Could it be Shae? Possibly helping her father? Or had the sound come from another part of the house?

Ready to check things out, J.D. set aside the sheet and rose. Instantly, he crossed the room and headed out the door.

Silently making his way down the hall so that he didn't wake anyone, J.D. stopped outside the senior Weitherspoons' bedroom. Listening intently, he cautiously pushed the door open a fraction and peeked inside. He expected to find Shae or her mother somewhere close.

In the darkness, he made out the bed. Sheets were rumpled and tossed on the floor. No one was in the room.

"Shae?" J.D. called, although he didn't expect her to answer. "Mrs. Weitherspoon?" For the second time, silence provided his only response.

A moan of pain came from the connecting bathroom. He entered, swiftly crossing the room. "Mr. Weitherspoon!" he whispered, pushing the door open farther. J.D. found the older man on the bathroom floor. The senior Weitherspoon's skin was cool to the touch. J.D. shook him by the shoulder, "Mr. Weitherspoon?"

Shae's father opened his eyes, focusing on J.D.'s face. "Can't get up."

Checking Shae's father for injuries, J.D. asked, "What happened?"

"Bathroom. Almost made it."

"I understand."

Suddenly, Shae flew into the room. "I'm sorry. I overslept." She halted, examining the empty bed with a confused expression on her face.

Mr. Weitherspoon drew in a shallow, uneven breath and begged, "Don't let her see me like this."

Sympathy shot through J.D. as he glanced at the older man. J.D understood how Mr. Weitherspoon felt. All of his dignity as a man had been stripped away by this illness and its treatments. He had little privacy or pride left intact.

"Don't worry." He pushed the door shut with his foot. J.D. hoisted the man into a standing position. Mr. Weitherspoon swayed unsteadily. It took J.D. a moment to get his balance, then he placed Shae's father on the small chair.

"Pop?" She tapped softly on the door and asked, "Is everything all right?"

"We're fine," J.D. answered.

"Is my father in there with you, J.D.?"

"Yes. He'll be out in a minute."

"I thought I heard something," Shae explained in a tone filled with concern and worry.

Mr. Weitherspoon flinched. J.D. patted the older man's shoulder reassuringly and said, "It was me. I ran into the coffee table when I was moving around in the dark."

J.D. opened the door a fraction. "Your father's fine. Give him a minute."

Shae turned away. "Let me get George."

Waving a dismissing hand at her, J.D. reassured, "I've got it. Mr. Weitherspoon is fine."

"Are you sure?" she asked, trying to see around him.

"Yeah. He's fine."

"I'm ready to get back to bed, J.D.," Mr. Weitherspoon called from the bathroom's interior.

"No problem." J.D. shut the door against Shae's prying eyes before slipping an arm over the older man's shoulder. They moved from the lavatory and opened the door. When the two men stepped out of the bathroom, Shae stood in the doorway.

"Excuse us," J.D. muttered, waiting for her to move.

She stepped aside. J.D. and Mr. Weitherspoon started across the room to the bed. Like a replay of this afternoon's events, they stumbled their way back to the bed. Mr. Weitherspoon collapsed in the middle of the bed.

Her father slowly opened his eyes an inch. "Princess, I'm fine."

Shae hurried to her father, checking his pulse. "I should have been here. It's just that I was tired." She looked at J.D. for the first since entering the room. Guilt and tears filled her eyes. "Thank you for taking care of him."

"He's good," J.D. assured, touching her hand. "Don't trip out. We're all here to help."

"Pop, anything hurt?" Shae asked, examining his legs with a gentle hand. "Are you all right?"

"No." Shae's father grunted.

J.D. propped several pillows against the headboard, then shifted the older man into a sitting position, resting his back against the wood. After straightening the bedding, he started for the door. "Sir, do you need anything else before I leave?"

Albert shook his head. "Thanks."

"You're welcome," J.D. answered. "Get some rest."


"You're pretty good at this," J.D. said in an admiring tone. He pushed a pile of coins across the bed tray in Mr. Weitherspoon's direction.

Stacking his quarters, Mr. Weitherspoon grinned back at the younger man. "I told Shae that when we lived in Compton we didn't have money for much. So playing shades became one of our evening pastimes."

J.D nodded.

They were silent as Mr. Weitherspoon shuffled the deck and dealt the next hand of cards. He swallowed hard, then said, "Thanks for helping me the other night."

"No problem," J.D. shrugged, organizing his new hand of cards. "Shae looked as if she needed the night off."

"She probably did. This hasn't been easy for her." Mr. Weitherspoon studied his cards for a moment before looking at J.D. He held the younger man's gaze. "She's determined to stay here until I'm better."

"Is that a possibility?"

"Maybe. After the chemo and radiation my doctors will start all over again with poking me with needles and MRIs and if I survive it all, then we'll do something called 'watchful waiting.'" The older man brushed a tear from his eye.

"This will work out. Shae won't allow things to go any other way."

"I hope you and my daughter are right," Mr. Weitherspoon muttered softly. "I've missed times with her that I can't get back. I want to get to know her better, be part of her life."

J.D. pointed a finger at Shae's father. "You concentrate on getting better and eventually everything will come your way."

They played a few more hands in comfortable silence.

"You've asked me some personal stuff and I've been pretty forthcoming with the answers," Shae's father said. "Now, I've got a few questions for you."

Surprised, J.D.'s gaze returned to the other man's face. Cautiously, he waved a hand in the older man's direction. "Go right ahead."

"Why are you here?"

"I came to talk with your daughter. Originally I

wanted to ask her to come back to Chicago with me," J.D. explained.

"What's changed?"

"She needs to be here with you."

Nodding, Mr. Weitherspoon probed. "Huh. Shae hasn't mentioned anything about going back to Chicago. You haven't talked to her, have you?"

"No. This isn't the time. Right now the only thing Shae can handle is taking care of you."

"I'm sorry," Mr. Weitherspoon said, tossing out his first card.

J.D. followed with his card and took the book before tossing out an ace. "I'm not. She needs me to be here with her. To help and periodically take the burden off her shoulders. I'm doing whatever I can to help. Shae's strong in a lot of ways, but this is taking its toll on her."

"I'm glad you're watching out for her. I worry. How will she survive if I don't make it? And you're right, she's not as strong as she'd like everyone to believe. She's a bit of a sucker."

"Not a sucker, just very caring. Shae can't help it."

Mr. Weitherspoon stroked his chin, studying J.D. with a shrewd eye. "I think I might have misjudged you."

"Probably not. I've made some dumb moves for what I believed were the right reasons. My decisions hurt the people I love. That's why I'm here. I want to put things right."

"If something happens to me, take care of my princess. She needs a partner. Someone that will be there for her, support her through whatever she chooses to do."

Before J.D. could answer, Shae bounced into the room. "Hey!"

"Hi," J.D. greeted, getting to his feet. He gathered the

loose cards together, shoved them inside the box and placed it on the nightstand.

She glanced at him and quickly turned away. "I need to take his vitals. Can you come back a little later?"

"Sure. No problem." J.D. lifted the tray from Mr. Weitherspoon's lap and snapped the legs under it, then leaned it against the wall. "I'm not going to let you take all of my money. I'll be back."

Waving J.D. off, Shae turned to her father. "You two seem to be getting along."

"He's all right" her father said, watching Shae as she returned her blood pressure monitor to its case.

"Your vitals are good. They're much better than yesterday." She held his wrist while checking his pulse. "No pain after your incident in the bathroom?"

"Nope."

Shae sat on the edge of the bed. "J.D. surprised me. I never saw him as a Florence Nightingale."

Albert hunched his shoulders. "He seems like a decent guy."

"Where did you get that idea from?" Shae asked in surprise.

"I don't know. He helped me when I needed him. He's in here every day, checking on me. I've got to give the guy credit for that."

"Yeah. But let me remind you of a few observations you made when you were staying at my apartment." She tapped a finger against her lips. "Let me see, I remember things like, irresponsible, needs to get his act together. Oh yeah, my personal favorite, he needs better time-management skills. Does any of this sound familiar?"

"Can't a man change his mind?"

"Not if he's my pop," she replied.

"Hey! What are you trying to say?"

"My pop is always right. At least he thinks he is." Shae grinned at her father.

"You could do worse."

Sitting on the edge of the mattress, Shae firmly stated, "I'm not ready for this conversation. So let's talk about something else."

# Chapter 34

As Shae paced outside the front of her parents' home, tears fell from her eyes and burned her cheeks. She searched her pockets for a tissue and pulled one from her pocket.

It had been six weeks since Shae had returned to Malibu and learned of her father's illness. Six long weeks packed with anger, frustration, hope and pain. Through it all, J.D. had stood firmly at her side, offering silent encouragement. His support had been instrumental in getting her family over the rough periods.

Mopping the tears from her face, Shae tried to get control over her emotions. What did J.D. want from her? Was he here to try to convince her to go back to Chicago with him? If that were the case, why hadn't he brought up the subject? Maybe he just wanted to end things in person and got caught up in her family problems. Anyway, returning to Chicago was out.

Her parents needed her and she planned to stay right here with them.

Shae's eyes widened and panic immediately set in when she noticed J.D.'s car cruising up the drive. *Oh man,* she thought, *what was he doing back so soon?* When J.D. had left the house that morning, he'd told Mia that he'd be away most of the day, handling paperwork for some of his clients.

J.D. pulled to a stop in the circular drive, cut the engine and emerged from his car. He glanced at Shae and then back at the house before inquiring in a cautious tone, "Is everything all right?"

Nodding, she moved away from the house and stood near the flower bed.

"Then what are you doing out here?" he queried, strolling up the walkway.

Shrugging, Shae shifted away from his prying eyes, frantically wiping at the tears staining her cheeks. She didn't want anyone to see her this way, least of all J.D. Fighting for control, she took in large gulps of air.

With a gentle hand on her shoulder, J.D. turned her to face him. The concern on his face broke through her barrier of fear and her control completely crumbled. Pain-filled sobs escaped her. Without hesitation, he drew her into his arms. "Oh, sweetheart," he murmured into her hair. "Go ahead. Let it out."

His words opened the flood gates and she cried her heart out. J.D. held her silently within his embrace, rocking her back and forth while cooing soft words of encouragement into her ear. "Let it out. You need to do this. Come on. I've got you."

A feeling of déjà vu came over her and she cried until her tears dried up. Slowly Shae pulled away. Embarrassed, she muttered a soft "thank you."

Smiling down at her, he answered, "No problem.
You haven't answered my question. Why are you out
here?"

Feeling ridiculous, she explained, "This is the only
place where I can cry. I don't want my father to see me
this way. It would upset him too much. So, I find a
quiet spot out here and cry my eyes out. After that I have
the strength to go in the house and take care of him."

"First of all, this is not the only place where you can
cry. Come to me. I'm always here for you. You don't
have to hide out here. Remember, I told you that I'm
here to help. Second, you're not alone. I can't do the
nursing stuff, but I can help with anything you want me
to. Just ask."

Latching onto one part of his pretty speech, Shae
asked, "For how long?"

"What do you mean?" he asked, drawing away from
her and putting a little distance between them. "For as
long as you need me."

"No, J.D. I don't believe you. You've been here for
six weeks. I know you do most of your business on the
phone, but what about contract negotiations? How are
you going to complete those? And your family. Don't
you miss them? What about Sunday dinners?"

Pulling her back into his arms, he laid his cheek
against her hair. "First of all, nothing, and I mean
nothing is more important than you and what you're
going through. Not the business. Not even my family,"
J.D. explained with totally sincerity. "Second, most of
what I need to do can be handled over the telephone,
using my computer or faxing. What I can't finish, my
assistant completes. I'm good. Now, tell me why all the
tears? Your father appeared to be getting stronger. He's
certainly looks better. Healthier."

"I feel sad. Overwhelmed." Silently she added, *I don't want to lose you a second time.* Gnawing on her bottom lip, Shae inhaled the unique fragrance that was J.D. and held him a bit closer.

"Come and talk to me whenever you need to. I'm here to help."

She wrapped her arms around his waist and whispered softly, "Thank you."

Smiling into her hair, he replied, "You're welcome. But I don't know what you're thanking me for."

"For caring and being at my side."

He nudged her with his hips. "Tell me the rest."

"So much is going on. Pop being sick. Us breaking up. And I had to quit my job. Sometimes it all gets to me and I can't control myself."

"That's understandable. I've told you before you don't have to do this alone. I know you're strong and can handle a lot, but I'm here for you for as long as you want."

"One day soon, you're going to go home. What am I going to do then?"

"No. I won't. It's my plan to stay as long as you need me. Just remember two things. I love you and nothing is more important than you are. I know we've had our problems and I've made some pretty stupid choices. That won't happen again. Whatever you need, I'm here to give it to you," he promised. Using his finger, J.D. tilted her head up and captured her lips with his. It was a sweet and tender kiss that created a swirl of longing within her. "I love you," he whispered a final time.

Humming one of Anita Baker's tunes, Shae parked the car in the circular drive and entered the house with shopping bags in each hand. She left her purchases on the bench near the front door and headed down the hall toward the kitchen. She took a quick glance at the grandfather clock on her way. It was almost six. No wonder she felt so hungry. She smiled to herself. She remembered how her mother had insisted that she take the day off and go shopping.

She cut across the living room, stepped into the formal dining room and stopped dead in her tracks. Her parents were sitting at the table, talking quietly together. The table was set for dinner. Her father sat sipping a soft drink with the plastic bottle next to him. Her mother crossed her legs at the knee as she swirled the red wine in her glass.

After weeks of looking frail and ill, her father had taken a turn for the better. His pale face and weak limbs were beginning to show signs of improvement. His cheeks were rosy and he'd even started to sit up for longer periods of time.

"Hi," she greeted with a quick wave of her hand. Moving closer to the pair, she asked, "What's going on?"

"Hey yourself." Her father grinned at her. "Why do you think something is going on?"

This was a surprise. Since his illness had become the focal point in their lives, her parents had made a habit of having dinner in their bedroom. This was a wonderful change.

Always the nurse, Shae moved to the head of the table and touched her palm against her father's forehead. His temperature was fine. Making certain that he was okay, she checked his pulse. Normal. "Are you feeling all right?"

"Never better," he responded, reaching across the table to squeeze his wife's hand. He patted the chair to the right of him. "Sit down with us."

Vivian rose, turned to the breakfast bar behind the

table and removed the bottle of wine from the ice bucket. "Can I pour a glass for you?"

Stupefied, Shae sank into the chair her father had offered. What in the heck was going on here? Her parents just looked so pleased with themselves.

"Shae, where's J.D.?" Shae's mother asked.

"I don't know."

Frowning, her mother questioned, "He didn't go with you?"

"No. When I got in my car this morning, he pulled out right behind me. He probably had stuff to do for his clients."

J.D. marched into the room as if he'd lived in this house all of his life. He winked at Shae, then turned to her parents. "Did I hear someone call my name?"

"Hey, J.D.," Albert said.

"Hi, Al. Are you feeling okay? You look pretty good," J.D. answered.

"Yes, I'm feeling really well. Actually, we're wondering about you," he admitted. "We're getting ready for dinner. Are you ready?"

"Sure. Food always works for me." J.D. slid into the chair next to Shae and settled in.

Everyone sat quietly while Mia brought serving tray after serving tray of appetizing food into the dining room. The rich aroma of grilled beef brisket, garlic mashed potatoes and green beans almandine filled the air. Before leaving the room, Mia whispered to Shae that she had a dessert of strawberry shortcake waiting in the kitchen.

Albert blessed the food, then the dishes circulated around the table. Halfway through the meal, her father cleared his throat. The other occupants of the table focused on him. "Well, Vivian and I have some news for you."

Anticipation flashed through Shae. Something was up. From the moment Shae had walked into the room, she had sensed an undercurrent of excitement.

"First, I want to thank you, J.D., and you, princess, for all the help you've given me. I know it hasn't been easy." He blushed and his eyes darted away. "I'm not the best patient. But you stuck with me and I appreciate that. J.D., we didn't get off to a good start, but I've come to understand who you are."

J.D. bowed his head slightly.

"I bet you're wondering where all of this is leading. Well, here it is. My PSA has stabilized and it look as if the tumor has gotten smaller."

"Pop!" Shae jumped to her feet and sped around the table. She hugged her father, while kissing him on his cheek. J.D. met her on the other side of her father. He patted the older man's shoulder.

"Don't get too excited," her father warned. "The doctors are doing something called 'watchful waiting.' They'll keep a close eye on me and I'll have my PSA tested regularly, but I'm better."

Vivian rose and stood close to her husband. She touched J.D.'s arm, then pulled Shae into an embrace. "Baby, thanks for staying. You made things so much easier for me."

"Where else would I be?" Shae asked. "We're a family."

Sighing heavily, Albert brought the attention back to himself. "Now, Ms. Shae, you can return to Chicago if you'd like and get on with your life."

"I'm not leaving. I'm home to stay. Now that you've mentioned it, I was checking out the pool house and I think I'm going to move out there. That way I can have my space and you can have yours."

Shock registered on her parents' faces. Her mother was the first to recover. "We assumed you would be returning to Chicago."

"No."

Albert studied J.D. "What about you, son? I'm sure you have business you need to complete back home."

"Nope. I'll be staying," J.D. answered.

## Chapter 35

Three weeks later Shae opened the door to the carriage house and stepped inside. Renovations had begun the previous week and she made a habit of checking out the builder's progress each evening. So far, construction in the living and dining room had been completed. A brand-new fireplace and ceiling-to-floor sliding doors that led to a tiny patio were the finished additions. Carpeting would provide the final touch to both rooms, then the furniture Shae purchased while living in Chicago would fit perfectly.

Continuing her examination, Shae moved through the house. After the order of the last two rooms, the chaos in her kitchen shocked her. She scrunched up her nose against the sawdust and male sweat permeating the small space. Nodding approvingly, she opened the new cabinet door and peeked inside. If the workmen kept up their current pace, she'd be moving into the carriage house within the month.

Shae allowed her thoughts to focus on J.D. while looking out the kitchen window at the back of her parents' home. A lump the size of Texas swelled in her throat as J.D.'s handsome image formed in her mind. By the time she moved in here J.D. would be back in Chicago. That knowledge twisted inside her.

He had been away from his home office for more than two months and Shae knew from prior experience that J.D.'s business needed regular attention. In addition, Shae felt certain J.D. missed the Daniels clan as much as they missed him.

Footsteps echoed off the empty walls. "Shae?"

*J.D.! What was he doing here?* Softly moaning, she searched unsuccessfully through her pockets for a tissue to dry her tears. Lately, each time he found her alone, she had been crying. Shae dabbed at her eyes with the edge of her T-shirt, calling, "I'm in the kitchen."

Seconds later, J.D. popped into the room. "Hey!"

Clearing her throat, Shae answered, "Hi. What's up?"

J.D. stood in the doorway with his hands shoved into the pockets of his jeans. "Nothing. I saw you head back here awhile ago. I thought I'd come and check out your new digs." He strolled around the room, nodding approvingly. "Things look like they're really shaping up. It won't be long before you'll have your own place again."

"Yeah," Shae agreed, glancing around her. "But it's smaller than the penthouse."

"True. It's just you, so it should be fine. How many bedrooms?" he asked, shifting nervously.

"Two."

Nodding, the sports agent strolled around the kitchen, rubbing his hand over the cupboard's smooth sanded wood. "If you need any help moving your stuff, let me know."

Fuming, Shae balled her hands into fists at her sides. Talk about your empty promise! Pissed off, Shae wanted J.D. to know that she recognized it for what it was. "Why would I do that? Won't you be in Chicago by that time?"

J.D.'s forehead crinkled up like a prune and his lips pursed out. "Where did you get that idea?"

Regretting her outburst, she shrugged. "You've been here for two months. Don't you need to get back to your business and your family? I'm sure Nick and Helen are missing their son and would like to see you."

"They're fine." He dismissed with a wave of his hand. "I talk to my parents every week. I told you that I plan to stay here as long as you need me. I'm not going anywhere. That hasn't changed."

Confused, Shae approached J.D., muttering, "Pop's better. He's going back to work in a couple of weeks. There's nothing keeping you here."

He grinned down at her. "Yes, there is."

"What?"

"You."

Shae's head jerked back as if J.D. had struck her. "Me? Why?"

"You need me and I plan to be here for as long as it takes."

"Why?"

Now it was J.D.'s turn to look away. He moved across the confined space to the window over the sink and studied the landscape surrounding the main house. "There've been times when I haven't been as support-ive as you needed me to be. I feel like I've let you down and it's never going to happen again."

She strolled to J.D.'s side and placed a comforting hand on his shoulder. "That's all in the past. There's no need for you to feel you have to stay."

Turning to face her, he stroked her cheek, "There's one very important reason."

Without looking away, Shae backed away from his gentle touch, asking, "What's that?"

Sighing, J.D. took Shae's hand and led her from the kitchen. "Look, there's something I want to talk to you about." He halted in the living room and faced her.

Shae felt her muscles tense, sensing that something important was about to happen. It was decision time. They had to decide what to do next, determine exactly where they were headed as a couple.

J.D. held her hands in his and opened with, "I wanted a better time and place to do this, but we keep getting interrupted. So it's now or never."

Remaining silent, Shae let out a shaky breath.

"I know you and I have driven down a bumpy road with a lot of problems. But I've always wanted you to be part of my life. Being here in the same house with you 24/7, sharing meals and helping your family, I realized how much I want you to be with me. So I'm asking you to be my wife. Will you marry me?"

Shae's heart pounded against her ribcage. Marriage! Was he crazy? How were they going to accomplish that with her in Malibu and him in Chicago? No way would she be part of a long-distance marriage. If that's what he envisioned, it was out of the question. "You want to marry me?"

"Yes." A frown of confusion marred his handsome features, although he spoke in a tender, persuasive tone. "This isn't the way I planned to ask you. But I say seize the moment."

Shae shook her head, uncertain what to say. Marriage was too important to take it so frivolously. *How serious was he?* Shae wondered, examining J.D.'s expression.

*I know one way to find out.* "Do you have your cards with you?"

His lips pursed and he looked at her as if she'd sprouted a second head. "Yeah. I always carry them with me."

"Good." Grabbing J.D.'s hand, Shae started toward the doors. "Come on." J.D. allowed Shae to pull him along while he pulled the cards from his pocket. Shae stopped at a spot near the patio, plucked the deck from his hands, and sank into the hardwood floor, then waved a hand at the floor. "Have a sit."

He complied. But the confused expression remained on his face.

"You've always loved this deck of cards. Are you willing to bet your future on a game of shades?"

"What?"

"Let's play a hand or two. If you win, I'll marry you," Shae explained in the same tone she used when talking to patients. "If I win, then you'll have to start all over and do the proposal thing in the proper way. That includes a romantic evening capped by a second marriage proposal."

Stunned, J.D. ran a hand over his shaved head. "You're kidding, right?"

"Not at all," Shae denied, shuffling the deck. "We've allowed clients, friends and games to rule our lives for the past few months. A client kept you from the mayor's dinner. You left me at your brother's for a friend. It seems appropriate to let a game determine our future."

Bewildered, J.D. shook his head and muttered, "This is different."

Studying J.D. innocently, Shae asked, "In what way?"

"We're talking marriage here." J.D. dropped his hands on Shae's shoulders and spoke to her as if she were a small child who needed specific instruction. "This is about spending the rest of our lives together. Loving and living together. Are you willing to trust our future to a game of chance?"

"That's my point." Shae dealt the cards, tossing them back and forth between them. "Until you came to Malibu, games dominated your life. Games put food on the table. Clients and friends controlled our private moments." She leaned her back against the wall and folded her arms across her chest. "Why not now?"

"Shae, I know I made some bad decisions in the past, but you are my life. The *love* of my life." J.D. picked up his hand and arranged his cards before tossing out the first.

"And I love you," she answered in a husky whisper. "But if you want me to say yes, I need to feel that I can trust you. No more coming second to whatever craziness interferes in our lives."

"That's not going to happen. Believe me, I've learned my lesson." J.D. won the book, then led with another card.

"Right! I need a bit more reassurance than 'You will always come first in my life, Shae.' Remember, we went through this after your brother's housewarming?"

Embarrassed, J.D. studied the floor. "I understand what you're saying. And you're right. I have said one thing and done another. But I only know of one way to prove it to you. Shae, I'm moving to California."

Shocked, Shae gasped. Had J.D. lost his mind? Did he realize that he would be giving up his family and friends for her? After all, the Danielses were a close-knit clan that worked and played together. "What do you mean, move here?"

Dropping the cards, J.D. crawled across the space separating them. Leaning close, he whispered softly,

"This isn't the time to leave your parents. They need you and you need to be close to them. I've already listed my loft with a real estate agent and I'm working with an agent here to find a place. My business can be managed from anywhere. I've chosen California."

"Are you…" She stopped, swallowed hard. "Are you sure?"

"Absolutely!" J.D. answered enthusiastically with a wide sweep of his hand. "If I've learned anything from our situation, it's to stop getting personally involved in my clients' lives. Whatever decisions they make, it's their problem. Not mine. I want to be here for you. You've had a rough few months with your dad and me. You deserve a chance to lean on someone. It's going to be me."

Uncertainty crept into Shae's voice. "I don't know. You've broken so many promises."

"Sweetheart, I'm asking you to trust me one more time." J.D. lifted one finger. "Give me an opportunity to prove it. You don't have to believe anything I say. Let me show you. And I promise that I'll never let anything come between us again."

Shae studied his earnest expression and felt herself begin to melt. She loved J.D. There wasn't a doubt in her mind. Could she believe him? Granted, there had been problems with clients and their jobs, but since his plane landed in California, he'd been as caring and patient and dependable as any person could want.

"No matter how stupid I acted, my feelings for you never changed." J.D. swung into the place next to her. He lifted her hand to his lips and kissed the palm, continuing to hold her hand as he spoke. "I loved you when you were in Chicago. And I love you more now. You are the most important person in my life. Without you, I'm lost and empty. But I guess the real question is, do you love me enough to try one more time? Are you willing to give us another chance?"

Sitting on the floor next to J.D., she glanced at their linked hands and wondered, *What do I really want? Do I have enough love in my heart to forgive him and move on?*

Memories of how J.D had helped her father to and from the bed without embarrassing him flooded her thoughts. She felt the warmth of J.D.'s soothing touch when he held her during a good cry of frustration. There were so many times when he'd tenderly wrapped his arms around her when she needed a hug to make it through a particularly painful day.

J.D. had stayed within reach, quietly offering support and love whenever she needed him. No pressure. No concern for his needs. He was only interested in making sure that she felt okay.

A tiny voice in her head clinched the deal for Shae when it reminded her that J.D. had made preparations to move permanently to California to be with her. He chose to leave his family and friends to keep her close to her parents. J.D. had made a commitment to their future and the life that he wanted to live with her.

Yes, she loved him and the truth of the matter was she didn't want to lose him. Turning to face J.D., she answered, "Yes. I love you, too, and I want to marry you."

Happiness filled J.D.'s face. He reached for her, pulled her into his arms and held her close, whispering into her ear, "Shae, I love you. I promise to always be at your side. If I start acting like a knucklehead, just smack me and bring me back to the real world because I don't want to lose what we have ever again."

Held securely in J.D.'s arms, Shae tossed the cards

aside and took J.D.'s face between her hands. They didn't need the cards to determine their life together. Their love would provide all the guidance they would ever need.

Leila Owens didn't know
how to love herself let alone
an abandoned baby
but Garret Grayson knew
how to love them both.

# She's My Baby

## Adrianne Byrd

**(Kimani Romance #10)**

**AVAILABLE SEPTEMBER 2006**

FROM KIMANI™ ROMANCE

*Love's Ultimate Destination*

---

**Available at your favorite retail outlet.**

Single mom Haley Sanders's
heart was DOA.

Only the gorgeous
Dr. Pierce Masterson could
bring it back to life.

# *Sweet Surrender*

## Michelle Monkou

**(Kimani Romance #11)**

*AVAILABLE SEPTEMBER 2006*
FROM KIMANI™ ROMANCE

*Love's Ultimate Destination*

**Available at your favorite retail outlet.**

Visit Kimani Romance at www.kimanipress.com.

KRMMSS

## Silhouette® Desire®

**Introducing an exciting appearance
by legendary
*New York Times* bestselling author**

# DIANA PALMER
## HEARTBREAKER

He's the ultimate bachelor...
but he may have just met
the one woman to change his ways!

Join the drama in the story of a confirmed
bachelor, an amnesiac beauty and their
unexpected passionate romance.

---

"Diana Palmer is a mesmerizing storyteller
who captures the essence of what
a romance should be."—*Affaire de Coeur*

---

**Heartbreaker** *is available from Silhouette Desire
in September 2006.*

Introducing...

# nocturne

### a spine-tingling new line
### from Silhouette Books.

These paranormal romances will
seduce you with dark, passionate tales
that stretch the boundaries of conflict,
desire, and life and death, weaving
a tapestry of sensual thrills and chills!

Don't miss the first book...

# UNFORGIVEN

by *USA TODAY* bestselling author

# LINDSAY
# M<sup>c</sup>KENNA

*Launching October 2006,*
*wherever books are sold.*